P9-CQS-446

"A haunting story about dislocation and its effect on children and women, *Deep Singh Blue* exposes the brutal side of life in suburban America. A counter narrative—the uprising of the Sikhs in the Indian Punjab and the massacre by the Indian Army of Sikh fighters—mirrors the struggle and survival of Deep's family in suburban California. A master story-teller, Sidhu has weaved an original and refreshing multi-layered narrative."

— MOAZZAM SHEIKH,
AUTHOR OF *CAFÉ LE WHORE AND OTHER STORIES*

"*Deep Singh Blue* is a brutal and darkly comic story of a young man's journey into adulthood. An extraordinary novel, and a thrilling ride into the future of American letters."

— JAKOB HOLDER
AUTHOR OF *HOUSEBREAKING* AND *BEDTIME SOLOS*

"In flawless, terse prose, Sidhu gives us the tale of a suffocating and often unhinged family, and leads us to the kind of authentic sympathy that only tragedy provides."

—TITI NGUYEN
ESSAYIST, *THE NEW YORK TIMES, NINTH LETTER*
AND *THE THREEPENNY REVIEW*

"I don't know which virtue of *Deep Singh Blue* to recommend: the love-hate letter to northern California, the rich portraiture of Deep Singh, his family, and his tempestuous girlfriend, or the oh-no-did-he-just-do-that storytelling. Enjoy them all, weeping and laughing and gasping."

—MATTHEW SHARPE,
AUTHOR OF *JAMESTOWN* AND *THE SLEEPING FATHER*

The Unnamed Press
P.O. Box 411272
Los Angeles, CA 90041

Published in North America by The Unnamed Press.

1 3 5 7 9 10 8 6 4 2

Copyright © 2016 by Ranbir Singh Sidhu

ISBN: 978-1-939419-68-2
EBook ISBN: 978-1-939419-86-6
Library of Congress Control Number: 2016930995

This book is distributed by Publishers Group West

Designed & typeset by Jaya Nicely
Cover design by Scott Arany

This book is a work of fiction. Names, characters, places, and incidents
are wholly fictional or are used fictitiously. Any resemblance to actual
events or persons, living or dead, is entirely coincidental.

All rights reserved, including the right to reproduce this book or
portions thereof in any form whatsoever. Permissions inquiries
may be directed to info@unnamedpress.com.

DEEP SINGH BLUE

A NOVEL

RANBIR SINGH SIDHU

The Unnamed Press
Los Angeles, CA

FOR RAPHAEL ROTHSTEIN
1936-2015
FRIEND AND MENTOR

CAIN SAID TO HIS BROTHER ABEL,
"LET US GO INTO THE OPEN COUNTRY."

GENESIS 4

ONE

A WINDING DRIVE TOOK ME ALONG BLANK BOULEVARDS
with their cross-eyed strip malls and condos screaming in a pastel-colored language all their own. I punched the lighter, waited
for it to pop, and lit a cigarette. The road stammered in the heat
and dust blew in streaks along the gravel sidewalks. The neon
sign for a discount foam store fluctuated on and off and smoke
curled across the windshield. I rolled the window down. Warm
afternoon air gusted against my face. The sharp exhalation of a
truck's air brakes coming to a halt crowded out the closing bars
of a song on the radio.

I took a left into the mall and found a spot outside the diner. I turned the ignition off and the engine stuttered to a stop.
The metal snapped and creaked as it cooled in the hot sun.
The lunchtime crowd had thinned and several spots sat open
at the counter. I didn't see anyone I recognized. Lily's shift
didn't start till four on Wednesdays, but I hadn't come here
to see her, just to leave her a note. I took a seat and pulled
the menu out from where it stood filed vertically between the
ketchup bottle and milk jug. My hands shook as I spread it
open across the counter.

The year was 1984, the state was California, Ronald Reagan was president, and I was a kid, sixteen, the son of immi-
grants, who'd told himself he was in love. More than that,
I was in love with a married woman a full decade older. I
couldn't guess what she'd packed into those ten years. None

of that mattered to me—what mattered was that she love me back. And right then, as I wrote her a letter in my head, one I probably should have written long before I walked into the diner, it was a task I was failing miserably at.

My folks traveled here from India; not from the city but from the village. That journey must have been more unsettling than moving in the 1920s from a lonely farm in Idaho to the bright lights of Manhattan, with its flapper dens and speakeasies. When they arrived, they knew less about America than I had ever known about India, which meant they knew practically nothing. They weren't doctors or engineers, neither had much of an education; they were the other Indians, the ones who don't get talked about and whose stories don't get written—the children of farmers, not even farmers themselves when they left. It was history with a small *h*—the kind that happens to ordinary people, not to countries—that tossed them like a handful of pebbles across a map of the world. Dad came to look for work, Mom came to marry him. They had no handholds to keep them secure, and the world they encountered was as mystifying as it was terrifying.

Out of that, I was born.

I'm not proud of the person I was that year, my sixteenth on this rock, but given the chance, I doubt I would have done a thing differently. Maybe I was throwing rocks into the well of my soul, listening for an echo to try to learn a little of what lay hidden deep within me. Or maybe that's who I was that year, a regular messed-up kid who for all his smarts couldn't see himself for the trees.

What I tell myself is this: You're who you are, people do things, sometimes really stupid things.

And there I was, another American, just one of the people, doing things.

Behind the counter, a middle-aged woman bustled back and forth. She had arms like a stevedore. I could see the flesh of her

body alive under her uniform, the muscles contracting and releasing, I could almost smell the film of perspiration sticking to
the tiny hairs growing out of her skin, feel the pulse of blood
shooting through her veins.

When she passed I called out, "I'll have a coffee, black's fine."

I'd eat and leave the letter for Lily—something honest and to
the point, that got to the heart of the matter. The waitress found
a mug and filled it and carried it toward me, but instead of stop-
ping where I sat, she deposited it at the seat of a young woman
sitting at the far end. I'd add a little extra to her tip, I decided, to
make sure my note made it to Lily. The goal, I told myself, was to
pick the words carefully.

Not *love*, but *passion*, not *desire*, but *thirst*, not *need*, but *necessity*.

Several minutes passed before I called out again as she hurried by.

"A coffee over here, but no hurry, take your time."

I realized I'd left the menu open. Of course, she must think I'm
still deciding. I shut it and started tapping it against the counter
when a guy in overalls sat down a couple seats away. The waitress with the thick arms walked up to him without a pause and
set out a knife and fork wrapped in a napkin and asked if he'd
like to start with coffee.

"Sure," he said, and added that he knew what he wanted.

She wrote his order down and shouted through the opening to
the kitchen. Very efficient. Here was a waitress who took her job
seriously, for which I had nothing but admiration. This left one
problem. Had she not heard me? Maybe I'd pulled the menu out
without waiting for her to offer it, committing an unforced error
in the tightly run game of her afternoon shift.

I returned the menu to where I found it, standing tall between
the ketchup and milk, an unequivocal sign that I was now ready
to place my order.

"Miss?" I tried next time she crossed my line of sight. "I've
been sitting here awhile and—"

But she was gone without so much as turning her head. Her
obliviousness left me with a feeling of rising irritation. I wondered if I was sitting in some sort of blind spot, or maybe she

was confused, maybe I'd taken the seat so soon after whoever was sitting here before that she didn't realize she had a whole new customer to serve.

I tapped my knuckles against the counter and half muttered: "I know, I pulled the menu out without asking, but that doesn't mean I don't want a coffee."

The guy in overalls turned and stared at me, so did several others. At last, some attention. The kitchen bell rang and my neighbor's plate appeared on the ledge. It sat for no longer than thirty seconds before the waitress pulled it from the shelf and turned to serve it to the gentleman sitting but two stools away.

"Here, hon," she said. I heard a distinct note of tension in her voice. "Anything else for you?"

A warmth flooded my limbs. I understood the reason for her distraction. I heard it in her voice. A dark and private anguish was troubling her. I felt like a fool for not seeing this before. I turned and looked around the diner. Maybe half the tables were occupied. Single men eating quietly, a few women, some couples, a group of middle-aged guys in overalls, a family in the corner. There it was, in everyone's face, the unspoken sorrow of daily life. My own small troubles deserted me and I was filled with an odd sorta love for these strangers and the daily hardships of their lives.

I knew what I had to write in my note to Lily. It came to me in a flash. I had been staring at it this whole time and I had been blind.

I pulled a sheet of paper from my pocket, unfolded it across the counter, and started writing. *Dear Lily,* I wrote, *I am sorry, I am sorry, I am sorry, I am sorry, I am sorry, I am sorry, I am sorry, I am sorry, I am sorry...*

I was halfway down the page when I looked up. I thought I caught the waitress looking at me with scorn, but she turned her face too quickly away for me to be sure. My heart sank, and I began to doubt myself: Why was I here? What was I doing? Did anyone actually see me?

"Hey," I called out. "Over here."

Nothing. The room began to grow warm as I watched the waitress talk to the woman at the far end of the counter.

I tried louder. Maybe she was deaf. "Miss, I've been waiting twenty minutes!"

She didn't move, and I was filled with a feeling of sudden shame, which quickly spilled into anger. It had become a familiar emotion in recent weeks. My face hot, I turned to the guy in overalls.

"What's going on here? Am I invisible? All I want is coffee?"

His eyes glided across me for a second. It was too brief to judge whether he even registered my existence, and immediately he returned to his lunch.

I struck the counter with my palm. The resulting thwack was louder than I expected while the sting in my hand assured me that most likely I wasn't dead. Heads turned on all sides and silence descended on the diner. A couple of familiar faces appeared in the doorway to the kitchen. I was alarmed to see them glancing at me anxiously and whispering to each other. Finally, the waitress turned her head, acknowledged me with a cold, hard gaze, and walked slowly over, arms crossed over her chest.

She leaned forward, her face contorted, looked down at the letter, twisted her face into an expression of violence, and spat directly onto it. Her faint reflection shone in the distorted light around the edges of the bead of spit and I looked at her in numb surprise.

"I know who you are," she said. Her voice rang with hatred. "We all do. Lily's told us everything we need to know. You're a slimy little lizard, aren't you? You're a rat chewing on a turd. I've met your type before, and if I was you, I'd do the intelligent thing and slide off that stool and crawl out of here. I'll tell you right now, no way, not ever, are you getting service in this place."

The world spun as I slid off that stool. I walked out through the diner's resounding silence, all eyes on me, shame stiffening my face. I knew I had done something unforgivable. Lily had every right to poison people against me. The sharp gray sunlight battered my eyes, and despite a rising anger, I felt small and defeated.

What I didn't know then, what I couldn't know, was that within weeks I'd be lost, as lost as I'd ever been, on my way to lying abandoned on an old army cot in a small room in a forgotten town far north of here. My family would be gone, so would my few friends, and I'd spend my nights learning how to become a drunk.

This is the story of how I got there, and like any story of a lost boy, it contains the seeds of how I found my way back.

TWO

BLAME SPINOZA.

He was a philosopher, and a dead one, but a lot of people were dead so I didn't see why I should hold it against him. The week before I'd bought a book he wrote. It was a paperback with a dull blue cover and its spine cracked. The bookstore was the only used one in town, the only one this side of the county. A pair of white-haired ladies with goofy smiles ran the place and stocked mostly romances and Bibles. They grinned whenever I walked in, showing all their teeth. I figured they were slow. Most of the remaining shelves were devoted to guns and hunting. I went straight for the back. This was where a lone shelf stood, against the left wall, with a handwritten sign tacked to the top reading OTHER. I could find anything here, from the memoirs of Lawrence of Arabia to books by crazy psychedelic gurus.

The book by Spinoza was called *Ethics* and it had been sitting on that shelf for a long time. Most books on the Other shelf did. If there was anything I wanted, it was a safe bet I could leave it there for months without any disturbance. I didn't know who Spinoza was and the title didn't exactly grab me either, but I had pulled it out a couple times to page through and stare. If I didn't, no one else would. I felt sorry for books on the Other shelf. If someone ever filed me, that's exactly where I'd go. The word might as well have been branded onto my forehead.

I had been born in a no-name Central Valley town, somewhere east of Fresno, one of those dots on the map of California locked

in a stranglehold of small-time highways that'd never graduate beyond single lanes. When the air wasn't thick with smog
it was thick with chemicals from crop dusters. The pair tag-
teamed throughout the year, one-upping each other on who
could ruin our lungs the fastest.

My family moved from town to town, each one held fast in
its own Valley noose. As far back as I can remember, a sense-
less urge compelled my father, who made all the decisions,
onward, until one day we found ourselves at the eastern extreme of the Bay Area, so close to the ocean we could smell it.
The spires of San Francisco were visible if you climbed high
enough. We had spent our lives inching toward civilization,
and now, on its doorstep, we lacked the courage to take the
final leap.

The city shimmered in my dreams, a thin, insubstantial and
shifting light that danced in the corner of my eye, in equal measure mocking and enticing. All I had to do was get into my
beater and drive west across the bridge and there I'd be, in the
heart of the heart of things, with people all around, all alive, all
important and busy, with a thousand girls to choose from. Yet
that spring I stayed put, glowering under the warm days and
hot nights that held the town of Todos Santos as its prisoner,
and this story happened at the edge of things, in the gloaming
between Valley and coast, in a land that in those days was still
not one thing or the other, its back turned on the city while, to
the east, a wall of hills kept the Valley at a distance.

I dropped out of school the year before, as much from boredom as fear. Half the kids in class claimed to have fathers in
the local Klan, and for those who cared, the only question was
whether I was a sand nigger or an uppity wetback. It wasn't
what I'd call the catch-all definition of a positive environ-
ment. I took a test, got a certificate, signed up for the local JC.

"What are you going to do?" Mom said.

"Go to college," I explained. It wasn't that I *didn't* want to learn. I'd have stayed in high school if I wanted that, but these were fine distinctions my parents couldn't easily comprehend.

"College?" Dad guffawed. "At his age?" By this he meant that I should already have put such lofty thoughts aside and be look-ing for work.

Dad was working by the time he was fifteen and had worked ever since. My older brother, Jag, had done the intelligent thing and swore off college and got himself a job. Every three months his paystub displayed a modest raise. Each time this happened Dad clapped him on the back and said at least one of his sons might actually amount to something. Jag glowered, indifferent to the praise, and walked into his room, where he shut and locked the door.

Mom made me a cup of tea and said she didn't understand these things, this college business and whatnot, but this was America, she conceded, and in America things happened dif-ferently. After that, she never mentioned it again, looking on my decision with a certain terror, as she did with anything she didn't understand, which was almost everything in this strange new country that was definitely not the India she was born in.

Anyhow, the world was about to end, so what was there to say? Any minute now, Ronald Reagan was sure to press the button and everything would go kaboom. The town was home to one of the largest ICBM bases in North America. We were first strike territory and retaliatory Soviet missiles would rain down on us more or less instantly. When the end of the world happened, we would be the first to know.

The second I opened the book by Spinoza, I realized that some-one else had taken an interest since the last time I'd examined it. Across the title page a swastika had been scrawled in blue felt tip. Below it, crudely written, were the words DIE JEW. The van-dal got the swastika backward, so it wasn't the hate symbol of the Third Reich but the ancient Hindu symbol, which as far as

I knew had nothing to do with hating anyone. The penmanship was casual—the way someone might write their name or a dedication for a present.

I stared at it for a couple minutes, not knowing what to do. I wasn't particularly shocked. I'd had my own run-ins with local racist shits. I doubted most could spell the word Jew, let alone recognize a bookstore when they saw one to go inside. This almost felt like progress. Perhaps I was dealing with one of the intellectual giants of the local Klan. However it got here, I couldn't let the insult go and pulled a pen from my back pocket to scratch out the swastika when I heard footsteps and a voice.

"Good book?" the voice said.

The pen slipped from my grasp and plinked on the wooden floor. I looked up to discover a cow-faced man in greasy jeans and an oil-stained T-shirt with a builder's belt strapped to his hips. He had a fat gut, and the gut moved before he did as he took a step toward me. He looked from the book to the pen on the floor and back to the book.

"Good book?" he asked again.

I made a face and turned away, not bothering to answer, but could hear him shuffling, walking closer. "Hey," he said. "Is that a good book? I'm only asking 'cos I'm searching here for something new." He was just a few feet from me now.

"It sucks," I said, surprised at my own boldness. "I'd go find a real bookstore if I was you." Maybe a little of Lily's wildness was truly rubbing off on me.

He made a sound of disapproval. "Gee, fella, I was only asking."

His feet scraped the floor and moved away, and he mumbled something further under his breath. I felt bad for being a jerk, but I also felt Lily's voice inside me, goading me forward, and that felt better than anything I'd felt in a long time.

There was nothing else to do, I had to buy the book. If I replaced it, Cow Face would be sure to pull it out and find the swastika and think I did it. He'd show the white-haired ladies and I'd be banned from the only cheap bookstore for miles around. Tearing the page out wasn't an option either. He'd hear that for sure, and there I'd be, either pegged for a vandal or the neo-Nazi who wrote this crap.

I was always getting myself into some kind of fix. Only the month before I had walked home from college because my car was in the shop. Passing a vacant lot, I spotted an old lady stumbling through the middle of it in a nightgown with blood on it. The lot was choked with weeds and walled in by a broken-down cyclone fence. The scene looked every inch the outtake from a 1960s avant-garde horror flick, with the woman tripping over bricks and bumping into oil drums.

A hole in the fence allowed me to crawl through and jump down. Her arms were bony and fragile, and when I spoke, her eyes shot around but failed to land on me, the only other person perhaps for miles, because as far as she was concerned the world might well have ended and the two of us, the last of humanity, were lost and panting in its ruins. When I saw a yellow plastic hospital bracelet on her wrist, I felt an instant kinship. I always did for runaways. With my arm supporting her waist, we climbed to the street, where she took up equally oblivious residence on the curb and I telephoned for an ambulance from a pay phone.

The whole time, not one word did she say nor a gesture make, until the first sirens pierced the sky and, far down the road, I spotted lights flaming on the racing vehicle. Her pair of ancient, rheumy eyes turned and settled on me, and she belched uncomfortably and leaned forward, raising her hand to her mouth. She opened wide, and out popped her teeth. Both sets, uppers and lowers, as if this was all a person needed. These she offered, hand held out and trembling, her last possessions in this life. I was gone before the ambulance stopped.

My white shirt was covered in her blood: blood on the sleeves, the front, everywhere. All the way, rubberneckers in their way-too-large-for-anything-vaguely-practical trucks cruised alongside and honked like I'd been in some fight.

Halfway home, a cop car's lights flashed on out of nowhere and pulled over right where I was walking. Two cops jumped out and started talking fast like they were auditioning for a pointless new television pilot: Who was I? What was going on? Why was my shirt covered in blood?

The blood wasn't mine, I explained, it belonged to some crazy old lady who couldn't keep her teeth in her mouth, but not to worry, because the ambulance had already taken her away.

This admission caused a lot of shouting. The truth often does. The cops grabbed my arms and called me a couple of choice names. "A-rab," "Mo-hammed." One threw me against the warm hood of the cruiser while the other one started screaming into his walkie-talkie. The shouting went on for a good deal longer than seemed necessary; all they really needed to do was handcuff me and kick me into the backseat. I didn't try to explain. I knew no one would listen. They read me my rights and took me to the station, where I got fingerprinted for the first time in my life. I even had my mug shot taken.

I sat around for a couple hours looking at the wanted posters and wondering what my face would look like on one of them. I'd do fine if I could get my eyes screwed up tight and a good scowl going. I overheard on some cop's radio about an old woman found bleeding on the road, but I never did find out what it was all about. No one seemed particularly bothered about putting two and two together and letting me go.

When my parents arrived, my mom immediately started crying. Dad apologized repeatedly for my behavior and promised that his good-for-nothing son would get the belt liberally applied the moment I arrived home. Back inside the car, his tune changed. The cops were racist bastards and lazy blacks, he spat, even though the only black person we met at the precinct was the receptionist, who shot me a secret smile as I walked out. It all turned out okay, if not going to prison is the catch-all definition of what is okay.

Standing at the bookstore counter, I pulled a dollar from my pocket and handed it to the white-haired lady.

"Do you know anything about this guy?" I said.

She picked up the book and turned it over. Nothing was written on the back. She opened it to the contents page, skipping the swastika without seeming to notice it, and stopped, edged her reading glasses down a notch with a finger. "Philosophy, huh?" she said, struggling with the word. "This what the kids are reading today?"

If I said yes, I wondered if she'd search out a dozen copies, hoping to corner the local youth market on medieval philosophers.

"No one reads," I responded flatly. I leaned forward and whispered one thing I was certain of. "He was a Jew," I said.

The short bio on the inside flap told me so. Baruch Spinoza, a.k.a. Benedictus. 1632–1677. Jew. Born in Amsterdam. Expelled from his synagogue in 1656 for apostasy. Converted to Christianity. Committed rationalist and philosopher of the emotions. Died of lung disease. That was all.

The scandalized reaction I was hoping for didn't materialize. It didn't matter, because once again I'd heard Lily's bold voice inside me. It was like she was standing next to me, whispering in my ear. The elderly clerk looked at me with bemused concentration, her eyes screwing up. I felt certain she was on the verge of saying something unexpected. What that might have been I had no idea. But all she did was tuck the receipt neatly between the pages and shrug.

"Enjoy!" she chirped.

THREE

I WALKED OUT THROUGH THE STORE'S GLASS DOOR, SETTING off an irritating string of bells attached to the handle—it was like they were scolding me—and headed in the direction of my car. A semi was pulled into a nearby loading dock and a dump truck roved noisily across the faded yellow lines marking the empty spots. It was still morning and the air was cool and I had nowhere to be for a couple hours. A familiar sense of desperation sank into my bones. The town sat at the easternmost extreme of the Bay Area, flat and dusty and ever drifting, like some colossal sand dune, into the levee-divided fields of the Valley. We'd lived here barely two years and already I felt the dull suffocation of its pointless streets and boulevards and all the hours that had to be filled every day as a person who lived among them.

I stared out into its monotone facade and wondered what to do with myself. I juggled the possibilities. A second-run dollar cinema at the far end of the mall where my shoes stuck to the floor and creatures scurried across the seatbacks in front. The small park next to the Kmart where the winos would now be stirring and preparing for a fight. The campus quad at the JC with its row of tables staffed by the Young Republicans, the John Birch Society and, in a nod to political balance, the Future Fascists of America.

I thought better of all three. Walking through a short tunnel dividing the back lot from the main section of the mall, I went into a diner where I picked up a coffee and a glazed donut. Back in the car, and before I'd started on the donut, I opened the dead philosopher's book. What happened next surprised me. I read, and I kept on reading.

The coffee was cold and untouched when I looked up. The back parking lot had half filled with cars and the sun angled down onto the dash from on high. I shut the book and opened it again to the front with the swastika and the hate slogan. I didn't even have to ask myself whose side Lily would be on. It was the vandal's. Like her, I was on his side too.

Before I saw him, I knew it was Chuck, and knew he was carrying his guitar case. His breathing was always labored, announcing his presence before he appeared, and it was always that little more labored when he carried his guitar. He lifted it with a deep sigh and deposited it on the counter of the AV Lab, where I worked most afternoons, and took a step back and performed a somber little bow, seemingly proud of his exertions.

He said nothing for a minute while he caught his breath, then reached forward as if to actually unlatch and open the case, but his hands paused just short of it. He screwed up his face and pulled his arms back and folded them across his chest and said, "It ain't happening."

"What ain't happening?"

He looked at me like that was the dumbest question he'd ever heard.

"It," he said finally. "The *it* that ain't happening is it."

With Chuck more than most people, a certain degree of telepathy was assumed if you wanted to call yourself his friend.

"And it ain't happening?" I attempted.

"Uh huh," he nodded, and repeated evenly, "It ain't."

I took a stab. "Your new song?"

"I guess Einstein remembered to switch his brain on this morning."

Ever since I'd known him first, Chuck claimed to be a songwriter, yet he'd hardly ever played me a single composition. Occasionally, when he did threaten to play one, he almost always backed out at the last moment, usually with some vague and incomprehensible excuse. I was glad that day was no different. I had my own concerns and wanted to hear Chuck's thoughts about them.

"I'm reading this book," I said finally.

"Yeah?" Chuck said. "The kind with words or with pictures?"

"Words."

"Well, ain't that clever of you. When did you graduate?" I ignored the sarcasm and he fell back into a swivel chair and started spinning in circles, the chair making a high-pitched grinding noise under Chuck's weight. He stopped himself when his face turned green and it looked like he was going to puke.

"Spinoza," I said when I guessed he might actually be listening. "He wrote a book called *Ethics*. He was a philosopher."

I placed the copy on the counter. He ignored it and spun some more, but this time more slowly. He pushed his legs out and made small whee-whee sounds. I stared at him until he stopped.

"Does he have something interesting to say?" Chuck asked finally.

"Like what?"

"Like how to score pussy?"

"I haven't finished."

"Why don't you tell me when you do."

"I want to read you one line," I said. "If you listen, I'll go with you to Bill's tonight."

"Bill's?" He eyed me with suspicion.

"I'll buy you ten minutes in a booth all by yourself."

"I don't need ten minutes."

"Okay, I'll buy you five."

He shrugged. "Okay."

The line I wanted Chuck to hear was the one that had set my hair on fire when I sat reading in the car.

"It comes early on," I said, searching for the quote.

Chuck grunted in response, produced a stick of gum, unwrapped it, popped it into his mouth, and lowered his head onto the lab's counter, where he instantly closed his eyes.

"Go ahead," he yawned. His head rose and fell with the chewing motion of his jaw.

I found the page and the line. "Here it is," I said, and read slowly to give weight to the words: "'Reality and perfection I use as synonymous terms.'"

The lab was a large room with no windows. I worked behind the counter, checking out tapes and videos and 16 mm movies for classes. A maze of carrels snaked through the room where students listened to cassette tapes or watched filmstrips or videos. A screening room sat to one side, and a couple of smaller rooms housed recording equipment and record players.

Chuck used to come in late, just before we closed, and stand around not saying anything to anybody, looking vaguely ironic and wheezing so loud he drowned out the noise from the projectors. No doubt that's how we became friends. It was the middle of the 1980s and everything anyone might ever have done or said had long since been done or said; what else was there to do except stand around, like we had all the time in the world, looking pissed off and ironic.

One of the first things Chuck ever shared with me was that he was a virgin, still, at the age of twenty-six. In his rare moments of optimism, Chuck said God was saving him for a single grand, orgiastic mission where he'd lose his virginity to not one but a host of sixteen-year-olds while simultaneously saving the world through the power of his thrusts.

I wasn't holding my breath.

In the interim there was Bill's, the local low-grade porno store. It sat in a dingy back lot, the door hidden by a pair of rusted dumpsters. You took your life in your hands walking into Bill's. Chuck believed hanging out at porno stores would get him laid. His logic involved sympathetic magic and the ease of leading a conversation toward sex if a woman ever dared navigate the dumpsters to walk through the grime-covered doors at Bill's. But most important was the fact that beyond those doors existed proof that thousands and thousands of men, admittedly all of them on video, were somehow, somewhere, getting laid. This gave Chuck hope.

I closed the book and stepped back and watched Chuck. I was sure it would affect him just the way it had affected me, because Chuck was my friend, and what did friends do if not see with each other's eyes. "'Reality and perfection are synonymous terms,'" I repeated, but louder this time, almost shouting.

Chuck remained unmoved. It took me a minute to realize he was asleep.

Conversation at home was seldom any better. Dad was usually crouched in front of the television, while Mom angrily chopped things into smaller things in the kitchen. I'd sometimes think about Dad as I sat there watching him. He left India at the tail end of the fifties, when there was considerably less happening in that country than there is now. He was from Punjab, so was Mom, though they didn't know each other over there. According to Mom, Punjab was like the Valley, only no one spoke English and even less happened. Dad once wanted to become a rancher, but how he was going to do this, I never had any idea. Actual animals terrified him.

I brought home a kitten once from the local ASPCA and let it loose into the living room. Dad reacted as if I'd released a wild and dangerous animal. He jumped onto the couch and held up one of his shoes and refused to come down until "that creature" was removed from the house. I let the kitten play for an hour or so. Every few minutes, it leapt valiantly onto the couch and let out tiny, terrified meows, and Dad performed a delicate operation of shooing and shoving with the tip of his shoe to get it down. I didn't know whom I felt more sorry for, the kitten or Dad. When Mom showed up, she clipped me around the head and told me I had no right tormenting my father like that. She ordered me to return the kitten as if it were nothing more than a pair of ill-fitting shoes.

At the animal shelter, the woman behind the counter stared at me with disgust. As I walked out she hissed, "Cat murderer." I felt bad about it, but what else could I do. I really did want to keep that kitten.

Mom and Dad were married in a field in the middle of a rainstorm, outside one of those towns along old Highway 99 that neither one says they can remember. In photographs, they are both holding umbrellas. Everyone is holding umbrellas and their feet are lost in the mud. They were supposed to be married in the living room, but the night before Dad decided to carry out prenuptial improvements on the plumbing. This resulted in several pipes bursting and most of the house finding itself inches deep in water.

The wedding party moved out back. As soon as the ceremony started, the rain did too, and one of Mom's cousins drove to the nearest hardware store, purchased fourteen umbrellas, and distributed them among the guests. They didn't have a honeymoon. Dad spent a week pretending to fix the pipes, but instead managed to cause one leak after another before admitting he had no clue. When the plumbers showed up, half the pipes had to be replaced.

Mom claimed it wasn't so bad. She got a lot of knitting done and got to know my father.

Their wedding day was the first time they met. Mom had seen a photograph of Dad, and Dad had seen one of Mom. It was all arranged by their parents, none of whom knew each other either.

Before the wedding, Mom was in India, then she was on a plane to California, then she was standing in the rain getting married to Dad. And then, for one week straight, she was knitting thick woolen pullovers no one would ever wear. Someone told her it got cold in California. It did in the mountains. But she lived in the Valley, where if it wasn't warm, it was either hot or really hot. When it was really hot, all the pricks walked around saying, "Hot enuf fer ya—?" Mom hated that phrase. She knew what real heat was, Punjab heat she called it, it was much worse than this. I asked her once what it was she learned about my father during the week she watched him pretend to fix the pipes he had bust. She said she learned that Dad was not a born plumber.

Was this Spinoza's perfect world? I wondered that night as I sat watching Dad grunt at the television. For that's what the dead philosopher meant: that the world is perfect, exactly as it is. There was only one response, Spinoza wrote, to such perfection: moderation, plain and simple, a passive regulation of emotion in the face of life's upheavals. In a perfect world, all a man could do was resign himself to fate. Change his emotions, not the world.

That afternoon, I cut classes and took the road east. I sometimes did that when I wanted to think, and after Chuck's decided lack of help, it was what I needed most. A single-lane highway wound between hills and horse farms and into the foothills of a state park. I pulled over in a turnout and hiked a half hour through tall grass to an outcrop of rock and sat on it, meditating on Spinoza and the world.

From my mountainside perch, I looked down on streets laid out in a grid that broke apart at the edges, at hills rising and freeways twisting like artificial rivers. Beyond, amid the islands stretching across the Delta, wiry channels snaked through the warm afternoon and the sun gave the water a look of rusted iron. A riot of grass was turning a crisp yellow while insects buzzed in the air. Roadways threaded through towns and fields, and canals, man-made and natural, cut fingers into the landscape, forming a single vast, interlacing pattern, all of it hugged by an epidermis of smog.

Here was a different vision of the world, penetrating itself, maddening, a clenched glove suffocating all who lived here, a painting of cryptic disorder in search of interpreters. It was a vision I was sure that Lily shared. Finding that book had brought me closer to her. I could feel her reading over my shoulder. Where Spinoza saw perfection, I saw confusion and turmoil, anger and mayhem, and looking back at the vandal's swastika, I found not just the evidence of a bigot's mind, but also something of myself staring back at me. It wasn't the vandal's rage, it certainly wasn't against Jews or anyone specific, but at the world itself—a teenager's unbidden anger erupting deep inside me.

FOUR

THE FIRST TIME I SAW LILY, SHE WAS WALKING LATE INTO DAY one of Psych class and nervously shot out her name at the prof, who was doubly annoyed, not just because she was late but because she was smoking a cigarette. I couldn't take my eyes off her. Her mixture of awkwardness and self-confidence, her total lack of any deference toward the professor, the panicky shuffle of her hands as she found a desk, all mesmerized me.

During break, she walked outside the same time I did and turned sharply on the balcony and muttered, "What a creep." I'd been staring at her all through class and was sure she was talking about me. She must've guessed because she quickly added, "The guy up front I mean, Mister Loves The Sound Of His Own Voice."

She lit a cigarette and asked if I wanted one. I had never smoked before and when I took my inaugural lungful I doubled over coughing. This made her laugh. If it wasn't for that cough I don't know if I would've had anything more to say, but now I could admit I was smoking my first cigarette. She tapped out another and handed it to me.

"For later," she said.

"Thanks."

"What are you anyhow? Paki?"

"What are *you*?" I shot back.

She laughed. "A fucking half Chink, half cracker, that's what I am."

The way she laughed, the way she answered, it swallowed my anger and I laughed too, laughed in a way I'd never laughed with a girl before—but she wasn't a girl, she was a woman, with dramatic brown eyes and a body that sang of a kind of sex and sexuality I'd only ever read about. Here was an adult, or at least an adult's body—I could almost smell the sweat beading her breasts in the warm California afternoon. I was already jealous of the air because it touched her and I didn't. She seemed to read my thoughts.

"I'm married," she said casually, proudly flashing her wedding ring. "Eddie's all American. He's biceps and blue sky and engine oil, that's Eddie."

He sounded like one of the oversized trucks that roared through town, horn blaring, barreling heedlessly forward. I asked her why she was telling me this, and she grinned. "I don't want you to get ideas. I know how boys can be."

I thought of lying about my age, telling her I was nearly eighteen, but decided against it as I watched her walk back into the classroom. Her dark hair fell to the middle of her back and she moved in a way that said she didn't give a fuck, not about anything or anybody. She was wholly her own person and wanted everyone to know this. Why would she care how old I was? I stuck Lily's cigarette behind my ear and followed her. As she crossed the threshold, the prof was already talking, and I'd forgotten about Eddie and watched her move along the row of chairs and find her seat. During the remainder of the lecture, I felt Lily's cigarette sitting behind my ear. It had touched her hand and now it was touching me.

"Later" wasn't anywhere near as long as I had feared it might be, because after class she said she had a couple free hours and wondered if I did too. I didn't, I had my own classes to figure out, but pretended none of that mattered. We wandered off campus and out along the concrete sidewalk while cars murdered the air, tires scraping their rubber knuckles along the blacktop. The sun was high and beat against my forehead, but I felt none of it, because Lily was walking by my side and talking, just like we were friends and had been for years. I smoked the cigarette and she bought a fifth of gin, and we sat in the shade of a tree on a patch of grass in the Kmart parking lot, passing the bottle between us. Cars circled us like predators on the African savannah.

"Why you here?" she said. "You look young. You special or something? A savant?" She pronounced that last word *say-want*, as if someone had told her that and only that was the way to say it. That made me like her all the more.

"I'm sixteen."

"Going on seventeen?" she mocked.

"Going on twenty-seven."

She shook her head seriously from side to side. "You're a boy," she said. "You'd be a boy even if you were twenty-seven. I *know* men." With that last phrase, I could almost see a row of all the men she'd ever known spread out behind her, fading into the distance. "Besides," she added, "that's how old I am."

I nodded as if I knew that already, though of course I didn't. Far as I could tell, she could have been twenty-five or thirty-five, but I didn't say that. I had read somewhere it was rude to discuss a woman's age.

It was the first time I'd drunk gin and it burned the back of my throat. After a few sips I was already tipsy.

"Eddie and I married when I was nineteen. It was a good idea then."

"And now?"

She ignored the question and took a drink and lit a cigarette. There was no breeze and the smoke played over her face like a veil.

"I wanted to get away from Mom," she said. "And there he was, good ol' Eddie. He had a sweet set of wheels back then, a Camaro, but souped up, so the backside jumped at the press of a button like it was getting fucked in the ass. I laughed so hard the first time I saw that. You ever see cars like that?"

I had, but only on TV, which I knew would sound lame so I

said a friend of mine had a car just like that, but added that he totaled it a month ago in case she asked me if she could see it.

"Eddie sold his, for a bundle too, some jackass out of Gilroy, drove all the way up here when he heard what that car could do." She shook her head in dismay, "Men."

"Sure," I said, missing the connection.

"I wish to fuck Eddie hadn't'a sold that car. I loved that car."

I was getting tired of listening to stories about Eddie, so I asked why she wanted to get away from her mom.

She lay back on the grass and closed her eyes and smoked a cigarette and said nothing. Twenty minutes passed like this. I watched her most of the time, taking sips from the gin and smoking another cigarette, and decided, first, that she was beautiful, like truly beautiful, and second, that this was the closest I'd ever been to a beautiful woman.

She opened her eyes and sat up.

"What time is it?"

"Almost four."

"Shit!" She jumped to her feet and grabbed her bag. "Gotta go, Paki boy, it was fun."

She was already striding away, but stopped and turned to flash a smile and call out, "See you in class."

When she was gone, I stretched out on the patch of grass where she'd been resting. The sun had moved and its rays cut across my face. Clouds drifted lazily by. The branches of the tree shivered momentarily in the pulse of a breeze, which seemed to start but then didn't, and the world became still and hot and sticky and my skin shriveled under the heat, and there I was, lying at the very heart of things where nothing moved.

Class was twice a week, a T/Th schedule, but come Thursday afternoon she was nowhere to be seen, nor did I see her again the following Tuesday. The prof's words glazed over my mind, and after, I stood on the balcony searching in all directions for Lily, with no idea what the lecture had been about. I expected Lily to run up the steps and appear, and as the minutes knocked shoulders with one another and nothing happened, I wished I hadn't smoked the cigarette. She had given it to me, and now it was gone. She had left me the gin too. A few mouthfuls remained. I stored it under my pillow and in the mornings unscrewed the top and inhaled, telling myself it still held her scent.

On Thursday, she appeared ten minutes into class, wearing big-framed sunglasses that covered half her face, almost tripping over herself as she apologized to the prof for being late and missing two sessions. She took the free seat next to mine and whispered, "What page we on?" I showed her my book, and she searched for the page and found a notebook and held a pen over the blank sheet and started moving it rapidly across as if she were taking notes, except that she had left the top still on the pen. She looked like a toddler, playacting at writing. At the end of class, that page remained as blank as when she arrived. She hadn't even taken the sunglasses off, and I sat there, fascinated, feeling the extraordinary tug of her presence, having again lost all interest in the prof's words or the subject of the day's lecture.

She took it for granted that after class we'd spend the afternoon together, and this time, instead of walking out into the suburban ruins where the sun blasted down on what looked at times like a single pastel-colored wall stretching all the way to Livermore, she led me to her car, a small red sports car with a bashed-in fender and a broken taillight.

"You drive stick, right?" she said, tossing me the keys.

"Sure," I said.

The hand-me-down beater I drove had once been my brother's. He bought it used, and buying a stick shift was cheaper. Dad couldn't drive stick, wasn't much of a driver in general, and the first time he saw that car, he told Jag there was no way he was parking it in the garage, not ever.

"What if I want to move it, what am I supposed to do?" Dad argued. Jag said nothing, as usual, and parked it on the sidewalk and went inside.

Dad's objections to the car persisted, however, and he refused to ever ride in it, claiming the stick might crack at any moment and plunge driver and passenger off the road, and should they be driving along a cliff, over the edge and into a ravine. The result would be everyone's fiery death. There weren't a lot of cliffs in town, nor did stick shifts, as far as I knew, have a habit of spontaneously cracking, but it was a theory and Dad refused to be disabused of it, claiming it happened all the time in India, and so he never once rode in that old beater.

I started the engine of Lily's car and put it into reverse and pulled out of the spot.

"Where we going?" I said.

Lily said nothing and I drove around the lot and onto the main road and finally she said, "Just drive."

"Anywhere?"

"Anywhere's fine. So long as it's not nowhere."

I wondered then if this was some kind of test—a love test— and if it was, whether I'd passed or not. A wild thrill ran up my body as I nosed the car through the afternoon traffic, then out onto increasingly deserted boulevards heading east. People had money on this side of town, the houses were bigger, a few with large double doors, and the lawns unrolled to the curb like great green tongues. If you took one wrong step around here, you were liable to be swallowed up and eaten.

After twenty minutes we found ourselves on narrow roads with horse farms and orchards crowding their branches over the cracked tarmac. Sunlight dappled the highway as it twisted ahead and neither of us said a word. The radio was on, a college station. An old Romeo Void number started playing, then Echo and the Bunnymen. I felt nervous, a man on a first date, and gripped the wheel so tight my knuckles turned white.

"Pull over," Lily ordered. We'd left the hills behind and before us stretched the wide, flat fields of the Valley. There were two colors out here and only two colors. A sort of gray gray with flecks of brown and a sort of gray brown with flecks of gray. If you squinted and concentrated, the effect was like looking through a poor man's kaleidoscope. Shapes formed, twisted, did somersaults right before your eyes. A fella with some imagination could conjure up a whole mythology just by sitting here and watching the landscape shift over a single afternoon.

I parked the car on a gravel shoulder abutting a levee ditch and switched off the engine. The radio died and the day's heat, which had been kept at bay by wind blowing through the windows, descended on us, exaggerating the sudden silence.

Lily sat upright, her back so straight she was almost perfectly vertical. Those great brown sunglasses covered her eyes like shields and she stared directly ahead, offering me nothing else apart from her crisp profile. She lit a cigarette and smoked it down to the filter and crushed it in the small metal ashtray, her fingers trembling. Something in her pose, in the almost absolute stillness of her posture, in the tension of her silence, kept me from talking. To speak felt like a violation, though of what I had no idea, and for a moment, as I watched her, I thought it was not Lily I was looking at, not a woman in her twenties sitting beside me in a car at the edge of a hot California highway, but someone else, someone stranger, even more unknowable. It was as if she grew larger before my eyes, posed suddenly on a movie screen.

The spell broke in a flash when she turned to me and said, without any explanation, "We need to get back."

A beam of sunlight hit her face and pierced the sunglasses like an X-ray, and I caught a glimpse of what I hadn't seen before: her left eye, blackened, swollen, bruised.

"Sure," I said.

I started the engine and put the car into gear and headed west. We drove in silence and I said nothing about the eye. The wind whipped in through the open windows and took the place of any conversation and I felt small and idiotic for not asking myself earlier why she'd worn those sunglasses and why she'd said so little.

FIVE

TWO WEEKS LATER, LILY STOOD ON THE BALCONY AFTER class, smoking, looking down at her feet. I hadn't seen her since we'd taken our drive. Her absence left me suffering, as if some invisible but vital organ of mine had remained attached to her, while time and distance pulled the rest of me away. I worried she'd been beaten up again by Eddie and wondered what I'd do, how I'd take my revenge. I played out all sorts of scenarios. In most I was the hero, but seeing her then, unharmed and smiling, they all died and I marveled at my own vanity.

"I quit," she said, indicating the college buildings with a tip of her head.

"I figured."

She gave me a cigarette and lit it, leaning in close and cupping her hands around the flame. I could still see the trace of a bruise in an airbrushed halo ringing that side of her face. She wore perfume and it made my head spin to smell her and feel her so close.

She fell back against the railing. "School's not for me. Not this at least."

"Why not?"

"You know, guy's talking, ideas, words on blackboards, shit people said a hundred years ago? I know it makes sense somehow, but I don't see it."

"Don't see what?"

"One thing connected to another. It's just bits and pieces, like someone took the textbook and ripped it up and threw all the crap on the floor and we're supposed to pick it up and do what exactly?"

"I could help," I offered. "This shit's easy for me."

She said nothing, appraising me, then turning away and letting the smoke drift out across the balcony and over the heads of the students sitting on concrete benches below, talking about the coming weekend and crushes and all the bullshit that didn't matter yet mattered so much it made their stomachs burn and their throats scrabble for air in sudden need.

"Thanks," she said. "But I don't think you could." She smiled. "I'm not exactly a brainiac."

"You don't need to be a brainiac," I said, suddenly pedantic. "That's what college is for. *They* teach you, all you gotta do is *apply* yourself."

"Thank you, professor, I'll remember that one for my next life, but this one I think is set in stone."

She took my arm and started walking and we navigated the rush of students on the stairs who were all about to be late for the next period.

"By the way, the reason I stepped a foot back in this hellhole was to thank you."

"Thank me?"

"Yeah you," she said. "I thought you were the one with the brains here."

"What did I do?"

"Couple weeks ago. The drive."

"Oh, that. Sure."

"You didn't say a word. I liked that. Gave a girl room to breathe. Most guys they don't give a girl so much as a mouthful of air, and half the time they think that's theirs too."

It only struck me then that she was talking about the black eye. Somehow I'd done the right thing by not asking about it. The realization made me feel all the more helpless, a child tottering among the legs of adults.

"Oh," I said. "That."

In the quad, someone had let the John Birchers out and one of them was manning a table. He was a clean-cut blond guy wearing a bow tie and shouted something about the Trilateral Commission while he waved a flyer in the air.

"So, you gonna ask me or what?" Lily said.

"About what?"

She rolled her eyes. "What happened."

"Oh, yeah. The eye, right."

"Yeah."

"Well, what happened?"

"Eddie," she said.

"Yeah." I tried to sound sympathetic.

"It wasn't his fault, well not entirely."

"What? Your face accidentally got in the way of his fist?"

"Maybe."

"Right."

"I was goading him."

"And?"

"And what? I was goading him. I know Eddie, I knew what he'd do, give or take. I may not be a genius *but I ain't stoopid.*" She dropped that last phrase in a high-pitched girlie voice like a moll from a thirties' gangster movie. We both laughed, which seemed both strange and natural.

The John Bircher had moved on and was now generously lathering the nonexistent crowd with stories of commie infiltrators in Congress. A guy in a crew cut walked by and started heckling him. The heckler obviously hadn't been listening either, because he called the speaker the kind of America-hating pinko scum who needed to get on the next boat back to Mother Russia. This caused the John Bircher to call the heckler a commie-lovin' Mondale voter whose mommy no doubt spent her nights sucking on ol' Guv Moonbeam's cock. They were about to come to blows when in stepped a lanky, pimpled kid in an ROTC uniform a couple sizes too big for him and called them both a pair of clueless camel-fuckers. This seemed to break the ice, and soon they were clapping each other on the back and shaking each other's hand. So it was with college, forever introducing intellectual peers to one another in a spirit of conviviality and bonhomie.

Lily plastered a hand over her mouth to keep herself from bursting out in peals. I did the same, clenching my belly tighter than my teeth. Once the excitement died down, I looked at her and felt a rush of feeling and wondered why it was she'd picked me out of a classroom to be her friend. I was too afraid to ask directly. Her presence seemed too good, too unexpected, I was sure at any moment she would vanish and I'd be left alone with nothing but my longing.

Soft green light filtered through the leaves and for the first time I noticed in her features an Asian appearance, an echo of her mother haunting her face.

"You never told me," I said, finally thinking of something to ask.

"What?"

"Why it was you wanted to get away from your mom."

She lit a cigarette and let the smoke obscure her eyes. "And maybe I never will," she said.

That same day, I made the mistake of telling Chuck about Lily. To no one's surprise, he didn't believe me.

"She's a woman?" he said. "Meaning of the female persuasion?"

"That would be her."

He was dressed in pajamas and bathroom slippers and a blue and white striped terry-cloth robe cinched loosely around his waist. This would have been fine had we been at his house, but we weren't, we were standing in the AV Lab on campus and it was the middle of my evening shift.

"And she's married?"

"Uh huh."

"To a guy named Eddie?"

"You want to meet her?"

He shook his head in dismay. Obviously I was missing the point.

"We haven't yet established if she's real and you're asking me if I want to meet her?"

Chuck was nothing if not logical. A week before, he had started wearing pajamas day and night. His goal was to break down the barrier between sleep and waking hours, to have the dream world and the real world meld. What exactly would result remained vague, and nor did it matter, for according to him he was conducting the kind of pure, unfettered research that formed the bedrock of all great scientific discoveries. What he learned would be a surprise to everyone. So far, all that had happened was that by refusing to change out of his pajamas he couldn't shower either, and as a result, he was beginning to smell.

"Besides," he said, "we're talking Married Pussy." When he spoke, the capital letters were in place.

"So?"

"Fails on a cost-benefit analysis."

"Huh?"

"You know, the Schlep Effect." He said it like it was obvious what he was talking about.

I stared, uncomprehending.

"Duh. Anthropology, maybe not 101, but close enough. A measure of how much energy is required to harvest and or scavenge or kill food resources and carry them back to the village to share. If there's more energy required compared to the potential energy stored in the food, then it fails the Schlep test. Married Pussy almost always fails the Schlep test."

"Too much work?"

"Not enough protein. I've done the math."

I told him how funny she was, how beautiful, how odd, the kind of things she laughed at. None of this impressed Chuck. His voice intoned through the empty AV room: "Married Pussy is not a she, it's Married Pussy. The moment you humanize Married Pussy, you've lost the battle. Only the most ruthless score Married Pussy, and that ain't you. We're talking top dog players with a schlong they could slap down on the deck of the Golden Gate Bridge and it'd reach halfway across. There's not much harder than Married Pussy, though there is Model Pussy and Sweet Sixteen Pussy. Both of those are way out of your league. If I was you, I'd go for Emotionally Insecure Pussy, or Self-Loathing Pussy, that's some low-hanging fruit. Even you might just score one of those hos. Of course, your so-called Married Pussy might be one already."

Before I knew what I was doing, I'd lunged across the counter and grabbed him by the collar of his PJs. I raised a fist and aimed it at his head. The soft fabric of his top tore as I pulled him across the wooden surface. He flailed his arms in protest. "Shit, man, take it easy, I'm just saying."

I could smell Chuck's unwashed body and feel his breath on mine.

"Say she's real," I insisted. I was surprised at the desperation in my own voice. "Go on, say it!"

"Okay, okay," Chuck wheezed. "I believe you. She's real, you love her, she loves you, the world's fucking nirvana, man. Now let me go."

I released him and he flopped back and let out a nervous grunt. He took a moment to compose himself.

"You tore my pajamas, man," he whined.

"I'm sorry, I didn't mean to. You should wear regular clothes. They don't tear so easy."

Chuck said nothing and stood in his torn pajamas and stared at me oddly, and finally he turned and unlatched his guitar case and produced his guitar and started strumming. Soon he was singing one of his songs—who knows why, maybe to break the tension.

I was still mad and turned to find a student standing at the counter staring at me with wide eyes, as if she expected something magical to happen.

"What do you want?" I barked, as surprised at the violence in my voice as the young woman, who took a step back, looking shocked.

This was probably her first semester, because she smelled

sweet and looked bright and excited, because here she was, in college, where maybe they might teach her something fascinating, show her the world with new eyes or simply break her heart with something she couldn't imagine.

Instead, she met me, if only for a couple seconds.

She burst into tears and ran out. Chuck briefly raised his head and looked at me with his *what's your damage, man?* expression, then went back to strumming his guitar and singing his song.

SIX

THAT SAME WEEK MY BROTHER JAG SAID A WORD. I ARRIVED home to find him sitting on the couch in his usual spot watching MTV with the remote held in his open palm and a glossy magazine spread out at his elbow.

"Hey," I said. The fact that I continued to say anything to him was pure gesture on my part, a one-sided theater of the absurd in which I continued not to acknowledge that which everyone around me had decided wasn't worth acknowledging, which was a strange and simple fact: Jag didn't talk.

Jag never was much of a talker, so none of us knew exactly when he stopped talking altogether. We had different ideas. I thought a year had passed more or less, and the times when Mom admitted he wasn't talking she agreed. Other times she said maybe he'd stopped for a few weeks over Christmas. "Who wants to talk then?" she said. "All the good movies come on TV then."

Dad wouldn't be drawn into the subject, except to say that if Jag had stopped talking, he was showing sense. "What is there to talk about?" he asked rhetorically, and scoffed in answer, "The weather? Politics? Traffic? Much better he doesn't talk. A man who doesn't talk is a man who's never bored." He went on about it for quite some time. Mom finally cut him off by saying that by his own reckoning he must be the most bored man on the planet.

The family room couch was red velvet, a hand-me-down from Uncle Gur, Dad's brother who lived a six-hour drive south in another no-name town east of Bakersfield. The light was off and the room was lit by the glow from the set.

I dropped onto the other couch, a tattered gray one, which sat at a right angle to the one Jag sat on, and threw my feet onto the coffee table. My sneakers thudded softly against the faux wood. I glanced across at the magazine. An old issue of *Time* from the fifties open to a story about the Suez Canal crisis. A picture of a steel-hulled tanker dominated the page, and the headline said something about war being imminent.

When Jag noticed my eyes falling on the article he reached across and slapped it shut.

An upbeat Cure video was playing, filmed in a garden with a piano with floppy keys and with the band's costumes flipping instantaneously from black to white and back again.

"Good song," I said. "The new album, right?" I waited a few bars and said, "That's what I thought. Didn't know it was the first single off it though." I let Robert Smith shake his shaggy mane a few more times and said, "Yeah, guess they *are* softening. Like you said, it happens with success." With Jag there, I just pretended, filling in his part of the conversation in my head.

I reported these conversations to Mom as if they happened. She'd ask what Jag said and I'd make something halfway interesting up and she'd say, "That boy has a lively mind. He has a lot of interests. He said the same thing to me last week." It was one of the games we played that helped us pretend that we weren't pretending that nothing was wrong.

The song ended and the gorgeous Martha Quinn appeared behind the VJ desk. I could tell she'd been joking with the crew before the cameras went live, which always made me jealous. In what world would someone like Martha Quinn joke with me before cameras went live? None that I could imagine. I watched as she took a couple seconds to compose herself, said a few apt words about Robert Smith's changing makeup styles over the years, and promised another Cure video in the next hour. "A real oldie this time," she said slyly. "From all the way back in 1982." She started to laugh, and I wondered if she was drunk, but the camera cut away too quickly to make any kind of judgment.

"Which one do you think it'll be?" I said, continuing my phantom conversation with my brother. "'Hanging Garden' or 'Killing an Arab'?" I hummed the tune to "Killing an Arab," still watching the television, and tried thinking up a pithy response on Jag's part. In our imaginary conversations, he always got the best lines.

I turned to him and was about to give him his line in my head but stopped. He was staring directly at me. His face was rigid, his jaw set, and he was shaking all over.

"Jag?" I said. I couldn't remember the last time he'd actually looked at me.

He rose to his feet and covered the few paces separating us, stopped, crouched and bent forward, brought his face up to mine, and whispered, "Die."

"What?" I wasn't sure I heard him right.

He repeated it more forcefully for my benefit: *"Die."* This time he left me with no doubt. He continued to hold his face close to mine, then straightened and walked around the couch, the whole time refusing to release his gaze. I watched him walk through the kitchen and disappear into the hall and finally heard his door open and close with a thud.

The heavy bass beat of a Frankie Goes to Hollywood number started up and I was left trembling in the frenetic cathode ray half-light of the video. An indentation on the sofa remained where Jag had sat, as if a ghost Jag were still there, staring at me, whispering that word.

Over the years, I had known many different versions of my brother. This newest, Silent Jag, was the least burdensome and most worrying of them all. By retreating into himself, he left me with far more questions than answers, but he also made it easier to ignore him and pretend he wasn't even there, which was what I'd begun to do.

There had never been a Brotherly Jag, or a Convivial Jag, or a plain Whatever Jag, someone who might shrug his shoulders at the world and decide to take things easy. Jag was always sharp edges of one sort or another, as if he had been chiseled out of our mother's womb and not born. There was a time, however, in the shadow world of my earliest memories, that I knew him as a sort of glowing, almost protective presence. I followed him everywhere, grabbing at his jeans, and instead of pushing me away, he tolerated me, treating me, I'd think later, with a sort of curious disdain. It was as if he didn't know exactly what I was, or what I was supposed to do, but that as yet I was no real threat to him.

I was ripe for any sort of experiment. Once, at the local swimming pool, he urged me to walk into the girls' locker rooms to see what would happen. What happened was someone shrieking and my arm being violently yanked by an overweight matron who looked at me scornfully and returned me to my brother, who was told to take better care of his charge. She said something about "your type" and "your country," and I remember wondering if she was a foreigner here. Only later did I realize she meant that we were the foreigners, some rare and threatening species of brown.

The incident left Jag unmoved, and the next time we were at the pool, he tried to get me to do the same thing again. I'd learned my lesson and refused. He walked in instead, and this was followed by a lot more shrieking than my intrusion had met. Soon he was being shoved bodily out, and he shouted, "What's the problem? We're all people! What's the difference between us?" My much younger self thought it was a valid argument. The pool's management didn't see it that way. We were locked in the nurse's office while someone telephoned our parents. Every now and again, a stranger's face peered in through the window and stared at us. As we waited, Jag talked on and on, about things I didn't understand. He said something about what was real and what was not real, about the fakers, who were everywhere, and how one person was secretly every other person.

When Dad showed his face, Jag fell silent. There was a scene, between Dad and a sour-faced woman, and another between Dad and Jag, and then I was sitting in the back of the car while the small downtown disappeared and we found ourselves again on the dusty outskirts of the known world.

One day, when I was four, Jag took me by the hand and started walking out along one of the old highways. The blacktop was all bent and weeds thrust out of the cracks. We were going to see something very special, he said, but he wouldn't tell me what. After a mile I grew tired and hungry and started complaining. I wanted to go home, but he pulled me along, heedless of my whining. Soon enough, we reached our destination, which to my child's eye looked fabulous. It was a gathering of tents, a real circus sitting here in the middle of nowhere, with a jumble of cars parked in a dirt lot. How Jag had heard about it, I had no idea, and though it looked marvelous to me then, later I realized it must have been a shabby, almost pitiful sideshow—the dying embers of something that had once astonished and marveled. There was a shooting gallery and a strong man and a wheezing Ferris wheel and a tent where the real shows happened, but when we tried to walk inside, we were stopped. Neither of us had tickets, or money for tickets, so we roamed, staring, unable to take part in any of the attractions, until an old gypsy, who huddled in front of her threadbare tent smoking a cigarette, took pity on us.

She looked to be a hundred years old but was probably only thirty. I was afraid until she offered me an icy can of Coca-Cola, and thirst instantly triumphed over fear. After I drank, she studied my palm. "You're a lucky one," she smiled. She traced one line after another with her finger. "You'll have everything handed to you. You won't have to work for anything."

She looked at Jag's palm next and said nothing for several minutes. Her brow furrowed and her great dangling earrings clinked in the silent tent. I'd liked what she said about me and all my child's concentration now focused on her. Finally, she raised her eyes and looked at Jag and shook her head. "I can't see anything," she said. "Your lines don't make sense to me," and added, "I'm sorry." She retreated into the back of the tent and disappeared. Jag said nothing, and we trudged the long way home in silence. I was even more tired and hungry, but something in my brother's mood cautioned me against whining. When we reached home, there was a lot of shouting—where had we been? why hadn't Jag told anyone?—and Jag was forced to stay in his room for two days as punishment. I thought my parents were being unfair. I had enjoyed the trip, meeting the gypsy, drinking the cola, and learning a valuable lesson: next time, I would steal a couple dollars first before we took off.

The first time I ran away from home I was nine and something of that four year-old's journey along the old highway shadowed my steps. I wasn't actually running away, I told myself, I was just taking a very long walk. My goal was to reach the ocean, which I'd never seen. I'd heard great things about the coast of California, the sheer cliff edges, the waves beating against the rocks, the glorious sandy beaches. I wanted to see it all. On the maps it was at least a hundred miles away and I knew Dad would never drive us there.

After a half day's march, when I was already getting bored, I was picked up by a state trooper, which was lucky, because I was heading in the wrong direction. The way I was going, I'd have had to cross three thousand miles and at least a couple mountain ranges before I saw any ocean, and then it'd be the wrong one.

I was thirteen the second time I tried and we were living in the south, in one of those Mojave Desert outposts where borax was mined and the air was often thickly white with it, the kind of place B-movie crews picked to shoot post-apocalyptic epics and cheap westerns. This time I was more organized, with a map and compass and a bedroll and a few days' supply of food and some water, and again I told myself I was just taking a walk, that all I wanted was to see the ocean.

Maybe that was partly true, but who knows why a person does what he does. What I remember was that life at home was particularly unpleasant that summer. Jag had disappeared almost entirely into his own world, and because Dad had been conned into making some disastrous investment, in a defunct gas station that never saw its pumps flowing again, we were as broke as we had ever been.

All summer long, Mom and Dad staked out separate sides of the house, a bungalow with timeworn siding and a rusty child's swing set sitting out front. Mom accused Dad of wasting what little money we had, and Dad said she was a know nothing, just another ignorant village girl. Some nights, she sat on my bed, in tears, complaining about the horrible things Dad did and said, and if she was in a particularly bad mood, she blamed it on me. I was no better than Dad—worse, I never helped her, said no to everything, never smiled. It was because I never smiled, she said, that no one in the house smiled. I thought this might be true, but I didn't see much of a reason to smile, unless someone told a joke, and no one I knew told jokes. By fall, Mom was making regular trips to Goodwill to replace all the plates she had thrown against the floor.

That was the summer I started reading and tried to stay locked in my room so I could get out of the firing line. At the school library I checked out a book by James Joyce and another by Dylan Thomas, because they had almost the same title, which I thought was funny. When I carried the books to the checkout desk, the librarian looked at me with suspicion. These weren't the kind of books a boy my age should read, she said. I didn't know what she meant, except that it made them sound dirty. I felt ashamed even walking out with them. I liked the one by Dylan Thomas better, it was easier to read and made more sense. I especially liked when he wrote about his first hangover and how he'd never drink again after it, but the next Friday, there he was, at the pub, pouring pints down his throat. I told myself that one day I'd grow up to be a drunk just like him.

Before I left on my second long stroll west, I stole a twenty for food money from Dad's wallet, thinking I'd have enough left over to get a soda and hot dog when I got to the beach but not thinking how I'd get back. The first night, two kids, maybe a couple years older than me, dressed in flannels and shorts, appeared out of nowhere and spun a story about a girl they wanted to talk to but couldn't because her father wouldn't let them anywhere near. They wanted me to take a message. "Sure," I said, glad for the company, and we started walking toward some distant lights.

We didn't get fifty feet before one of them pulled out a knife and held it to my throat and started calling me all sorts of names, dumbass wetback, sand nigger, that sort of thing.

They took the money and food, and sliced up the bedroll with the knife, but left the water. I sat down and cried, then after half an hour told myself I was being stupid. This was the kind of thing that happened out here and I should've guessed the first moment I saw those kids walk up. It was a cold night and I curled against a sand bank. When I woke the crisp dawn air reinvigorated me. A low mist hung over the valley floor, and distantly, I heard the scrape of truck tires on blacktop. I decided to avoid highways. For three days, I followed the line of the setting sun, tramping through arroyo and dune, and found myself in the blank, litter-covered scrublands, ever more the target of hostile stares, barking dogs, and, in rare instances, a friendly nod from a stranger.

One night, a woman took me in and let me sleep in her son's bedroom. She said I should shower, but I refused. I told her I planned to bathe in the ocean, and she nodded and thought that was a romantic idea. Her son was away, in the army someplace, she didn't know where, he wasn't allowed to tell. There were photos of him in the room. A baby, a kid, some when he was my age, school buddies, and one in his uniform looking steely and proud and suddenly grown up. I liked her because she asked no questions. In the morning when I said I was moving on, she simply wished me well and let me go.

The other nights I slept out and the sky exploded with stars and the cold left me half frozen and starving. I lay curled yet determined, waiting for the sun to break the horizon. The terror I'd expected to feel, lying out in the open, exposed to the elements, prey to any animal or criminal, didn't materialize. Something different happened. A feeling of security wrapped around me. There I was, at the mercy of the universe. Never before in all my life had I felt more protected.

I was picked up at a truck stop trying to steal a couple of stale rolls. When the woman behind the counter called the police, she said, "I've got a kid here looks like a rabid dog." That was a surprise, for never had I felt more calm, and I wondered what it was she saw.

Dad drove two hours to pick me up, and on the drive back he didn't ask why I'd gone or even where I was going. Those sorts of questions suggested worlds outside the enclosed circle of our family, and whatever the answers were, they held no meaning for him. Instead, he talked about how worried Mom was, how she'd been crying, sometimes all night. He'd had to take her to the doctor, who gave her pills to calm her nerves.

When I got home, I saw in her eyes, if only for a moment, something I'd never seen before, a visceral terror at losing her youngest son that seemed to make every atom of her being visibly quake. She grabbed hold of me and pressed me to her chest, so hard I couldn't breathe, then released me and stood back, her lips quivering. She stood there, for a whole minute, staring at me, shivering from head to toe in unspoken anguish, and then suddenly her expression changed to one of scorn. She raised a hand in the air, as if to slap me, dropped it and walked angrily to the stove where she banged a pan and started making tea. "Look at you," she said. "I've raised an *American* boy! Next time, don't bother to come back, stay out there with the other Americans!"

The Frankie Goes to Hollywood video ended and the front door opened and Dad appeared in the kitchen. He deposited his briefcase, which only carried his lunch, on the table.

"Jag talked," I said.

"He got a raise?"

"No, Dad, he *talked*."

Dad unzipped the case and pulled out a couple containers, carried them to the sink and started washing them.

"How much they paying him now?"

"He didn't get a raise," I called out.

Dad shut off the faucet and returned to the table and sat down and opened the newspaper. "So what's there to tell?"

"Because he said something."

"He got a promotion?"

"He told me to die."

"If they promote him, they need to pay him more. You tell him that."

"He told me to die!"

"I heard you, don't get excited. Just like that?"

"Yeah, one word. He said it twice."

"So why do you keep telling us he doesn't talk?"

"Until tonight. Tonight's different. He told me to die."

"You will, it happens to everyone, no one told you that before. I thought you're going to college, isn't that what they teach, all the dead people and what they said. How do you think they got like that? Dead people aren't born that way."

"No—" I said. Before I could contribute another absurd breath to the common air we shared, he slapped a palm against the newspaper and crushed it in a fist and thrust it away.

"Bastards!"

"What?"

Dad raised his head. "Go back to your dying, this is none of your concern."

He stood and walked out, leaving the crumpled newspaper on the table. I unfolded it and pressed the sheet flat. A full-page ad promoted a sale this coming weekend at Sears Auto. All tires twenty-five percent off, including installation and balancing.

Dad had changed the tires on his car at Sears Auto last week. I had told him he didn't need to, that there was months' more wear left, especially considering how little he drove, before there was any thought of a blowout.

He ignored me and shouted into the kitchen, where Mom was cooking, "This boy of yours wants to kill me! I'm going to call the police!"

Mom thumped a cleaver. "Everyone wants to kill you—what do you think the police will do about it?"

"They'll lock this bastard up and lock all the other bastards in with him so they can kill each other!"

He jumped into the car and returned four hours later and sat down and started watching an old western on television.

"Where are the tires?" Mom said, walking in from the garage.

"What do you mean? They're right there. I got new tires. They're on the bloody car." He grabbed the yellow invoice and waved it in her face. "Look at that! What's it say? Paid in full!"

"Those are not new tires," Mom said with confidence. "Those are the same tires you left with."

We all walked out to inspect. There they were, completely untouched, four old tires with six months' remaining wear still etched into the tread.

Dad circled the vehicle like an animal cornering its prey, crouching before each tire and inspecting it individually, then rose and stared at us with a clenched-up fury animating his face. He climbed into the car, softly shut the door, and, without a word, drove away.

He returned three hours later with four brand-new tires glistening on the Chevy along with the spoils of victory, as he proudly showed us, which was a complimentary set of wiper blades. The wiper blades never fit his car or mine or Jag's, but he wasn't concerned. They sat prominently on their own shelf in the garage, and once a month Dad dutifully dusted them as if they were a prized trophy lion's head hanging over a fireplace.

SEVEN

A PAPER-THIN WALL DIVIDED OUR BEDROOMS, AND WHEN Jag's radio was on, the rumble of voices battered the flimsy divider.

His dial was usually tuned to talk radio, one of the paranoid right wing jocks who in those days had already begun to screech nightly through the air like banshees on speed. The country was threatened from all sides. There were commies in Soviet Russia and commies in Red China and commies still in Old Europe. There were homosexuals stalking the nation's budding manhood and women who wanted to fight alongside marines and blacks on welfare driving Cadillacs and Mexicans sneaking across the border and behind every bush there was an Iranian agent waiting to pounce. And if you walked onto a college campus, you got the whole lot, usually masquerading as a social science prof: a Mexican commie lesbian with an Iranian lover teaching your kids how to waste their lives on welfare.

Sometimes I heard Jag's soft chuckle as he laughed to himself, but mostly I heard only the radio.

Before he stopped talking altogether, we'd sit in his room, me on the bed, Jag at his desk. With the radio always on in the background, the volume turned down to an insect's buzz infecting the air, Jag would talk at length about things he believed mattered. Things could only get worse, he told me, before they got even more worse. There was the cliff, we were roaring toward it—didn't nobody see it? The collapse would be longer and harder than the climb had been, and maybe the fall would be so long and hard we'd never hit the ground, and we'd begin to think that all life is is falling, down down down, so fast that the wind whips by our ears and pummels our chest, and we would pass our days thinking that having the air sucked out of our mouths is the only way to live.

If you looked at Jag sideways, out of the corner of your eye, there was always the desert prophet visible rattling around inside him, the wild man in the wilderness preaching to tumbleweeds and prairie dogs, speaking in equal measure of doom and salvation. Of the two of us, he was the true American, something of the sandy western soil in him as if the ground itself chose to stick to his skin and not to the rest of us. Mom and Dad were Indian—the way they talked, the way they moved, the way they looked around a room—you could almost see the old country winking at you from over their shoulders. I wasn't one thing or another, not Indian, not American either, and I wondered if such rootlessness of the soul made me truly Californian.

But not Jag, he was almost feral in his capacity to conquer this landscape that was America. In the days that Dad moved us from one flat-lined Valley settlement to another, a part of the place we left behind always traveled with Jag, hanging there somehow on his shoulders, as if he took on a part of the country with him—its burdens and knotty problems and ironies. I wasn't the only one to see it—others did too—and I lived my childhood with another Jag, a spectral brother around whom rumors circled like hawks in summer.

At school, there was always a murmuring crisscross of tale and accusation, whispered stories, admiring questions. Something in Jag's character, which even then was subdued, moved the souls of those around him to a kind of rising frenzy. I saw this only in retrospect, years later, when I wondered at the young man my brother had been. Jag had ideas, and more than that, he had plans, which he talked about freely to any-one but me—often to a small coterie of fellow students locked away in his room.

If he suspected I was listening, he'd dash out of his room, slamming the door behind him and catching me by the neck to pummel me. I gave as good as I got. I was smaller and more agile, and usually bit and spat and clawed my way to a halfway decent draw. His friends stood around, laughing and evaluat-ing my performance, and when it was over, they retreated to his room and tightly shut the door. Very occasionally, he relented and invited me, when no one else was around, into his room. Spread out across his table were huge sheets of drawing paper, each the size of a desktop, and scribbled onto them were plans for what he called the greatest movie camera ever devised.

The first time I saw it, he pushed me against the wall and pressed his face roughly against mine.

"You can't ever tell anyone what you see here, you understand?"

I nodded.

This wasn't enough for him. "You have to say it!"

"Yes," I said. "I'll never tell a soul."

"On pain of death." He squeezed my throat. "Say it."

"On pain of death," I repeated hoarsely.

He squeezed tighter, then released me and jumped back, and spread his arms wide and laughed. "Well, what do you think?"

That first afternoon I spent studying the plans for the cam-era, it struck me as the most fantastic and bold idea I had ever seen. The theory behind it was simple, as Jag told me. Time didn't flow, it started and stopped, was born and died, and each moment of birth and death progressed the universe forward a fraction of a fraction of a second. For example: the two of us, as we had talked, even in those few minutes, had been created and destroyed countless billions upon billions of times. The camera would catch the moments when reality didn't exist, when the world was either destroyed or yet to be born. It would show a world out of time.

It achieved this extraordinary feat by shooting film so fast it caught the moments in between reality itself. Blank spaces existed, Jag said, from one moment to another, as the world was created and destroyed a billion billion times a second. In the plans, a great concrete tripod held aloft a camera, with a tiny man for scale standing next to it. The camera looked more or less like any other movie camera I had seen, except that the lens was pointing directly up, toward the blank sky. What was different were the truly enormous reels to hold the film stock, which towered above the camera's tiny body like two colossal wings.

I marveled at the designs all afternoon, moving from page to page. Across them, Jag had scribbled endless notes and calculations and thoughts and his own speculations as to what would be learned once the fantastic machine was built and set in motion. I was drawn to one scribbled note, and though I had no idea what it meant, it captured me and I remembered it for years after, word for word. "See the world, the world behind the world, the real one no one sees, or no one says they see. Strip the mask away, the mask from the mask from the mask, a million times over, until there are no masks left."

The next time Lily called I told her about Jag telling me to die. She said nothing for what felt like a minute and finally she let out a laugh, "That's cool."

"Cool? What's cool about it?"

"Betcha he cares." She added, "For you."

"Huh?"

"People have their ways, right? Maybe this is his way, coming out of his shell?"

"By killing me?"

"By threatening to. There's a difference. When was the last time he spoke?"

I didn't see what the difference was, but I was glad she didn't think I was lying or that it was all some big joke.

"A year," I said, "maybe more."

Even as I said it, I felt ashamed. What kind of person has

a brother who won't speak to him? Some kind of creep, I figured, the lowest kind. But Lily didn't see it that way. I liked her all the more for that.

"He loves you. You're the one he chose to talk to."

I thought love was a stretch and said as much. I could almost hear her shaking her head on the other side of the line. She muttered something about men and said it didn't matter, wasn't the reason she called.

"What was it?"

"You free Sunday? Want to go for a drive?"

"Your eye didn't accidentally run into Eddie's fist again, did it?"

"Nothing like that."

"Well maybe he doesn't love you enough."

She laughed at that, and we agreed on a time and place to meet. I put the phone down, giddy at thought of meeting her, and looked up to find Jag standing at the end of the hallway staring coldly at me. He didn't move, not a muscle, just stood, his face as closed up as a lump of rock. After a minute, he turned and walked away, leaving the air bruised behind him.

In one town we lived in, a rumor circulated that Jag was indoctrinating fellow students into some sort of New Age cult. This seemed to involve, as far as I could tell, walking into the desert late at night and lying on your back in silence and staring up at the stars. Jag would say a few instructive words about the nature of time and distance and the origins of the stars, and everyone would shut up and look. No doubt they were all stoned and hadn't heard a word my brother said.

I would have loved to have lain there, with Jag by my side, and stare at the infinity of a desert sky at night, but if there was one point my brother was always clear on, it was that his punk kid brother was definitely not invited.

The story, in local legend, took on the coin that he was conducting rituals under the crescent moon, with whispered claims of the influence of Satan. One grand dame of the town, a certain Edith Miller, said she'd spotted the Evil One flying about at night with his great red eyes burning against the stars. Mom and Dad were called into the principal's office to explain their son's behavior, and their religion, which was now viewed with suspicion. They had no idea what the man was talking about and said as much, for Jag was a good kid, like any other kid. Mom believed the principal invented the whole idiotic tale to make Jag look ridiculous. Why would anyone go out to the desert to see the stars? she asked him forcefully. They were perfectly visible from the driveway!

Other tales circulated, none so fantastic as these, but by the time I reached my teens, such a Jag, the brother of wild invention, my truly American brother, had retreated into the one I was confronted with daily, and that was a sullen, mostly silent creature who haunted his room and resented the presence of others.

I missed the old Jag and hated the change. I felt cheated of a better and more interesting brother. When we moved to Todos Santos and found ourselves perched on the edge of the civilized world, of San Francisco and its siren calls, and where Jag found his job, that other phantom Jag seemed never to have existed. With his disappearance the strange and weird America that lurked at the edges of those rumors, of children lying in the unguarded night and impossible cameras that might crack open time itself, vanished too. A part of me was also lost out there, a little-kid spirit me that forever wandered in forlorn circles in the vast stretches of the desert night, trying to catch up with his older brother.

Sometimes, before he stopped talking completely, he would let me sit in his room and listen to records. He was always ahead of me, buying the latest bands, ones that sounded to me like noise on first playing. They would gradually coalesce into something alive after a couple of listens, and after a few more I would be obsessed: they were the greatest bands in the world; how could good music possibly sound any different? He'd post himself squarely across from me at a cramped, untidy desk where, as the record played, he paged through one magazine after another. We didn't say much, even then, and usually one of us would nod if we liked a song, and if the other liked it too, he'd nod in acknowledgment.

He'd found work at a warehouse in one of the refineries suffocating the western Delta, but what he did there he refused to say. One day he brought home a rock sliced perfectly through the center. The polished interior was alive with color. He didn't know what to do with it and gave it to me. I set it on the windowsill in my bedroom. In the morning, I watched the sun bounce off it, sending colors tripping across the ceiling and walls.

Another time, a tarantula arrived in one of the crates. It was quite a surprise. The guys in the warehouse, Jag said, had a high time chasing it around until someone crushed it with a boot heel.

Dad said I should be more like Jag. I should quit this idiotic college business and get a proper job. His ideal for me was a gig in a bank as a teller. That way, I might move up in the world, become a merchant teller or, with luck and years of hard work, a loan agent.

When he was in a good mood, Dad would lay it all out for me: get a job in a bank, go to work in the morning, come home in the evening, have dinner, sit at home all night watching television, go to bed, wake up in the morning, do it all over again. When I was the right age, he and Mom would pick out a perfect can-cook-and-iron-and-sew kind of wife, and she'd move in and help Mom cook and iron and sew, and at the end of the day we would all sit together and watch television. This would go on for years. I'd have kids. They'd do the same thing.

Finally, one day, if I was lucky, I'd join the oh so happy legions of the mercifully dead.

The plan was halfway there for Jag. He had a job after all. One evening Mom appeared with an Indian woman in tow.

The stranger glared at me and nodded in my direction.

"Not this one," Mom said in Punjabi. "The other."

Hearing this, the woman relaxed. I asked who she was and Mom said no one, just someone she'd met on the bus. Maybe Jag would want to meet her.

"She likes magazines," Mom said emphatically. "Just like Jag."

Indeed, she carried with her an armload of Indian film magazines and these she threw down on the dinner table and sat, hunched and nervous, reading and chewing a stick of gum. When Mom wasn't watching, she pulled the gum out and stuck it to the bottom of the table, staring at me as she did this, daring me to tell on her. Instead, I asked who her favorite movie star was, and she turned to Mom and asked, in Punjabi, to repeat what I'd just said.

Jag soon appeared and stopped. He stood stiffly in the hall and looked from the woman at the table to Mom and back to the woman. Mom was biting her lip and started talking rapidly in Punjabi.

The woman nodded and turned to Jag.

My brother didn't say anything. He walked across to her and grabbed the pile of magazines and held these to his chest. He searched through one, then another.

The first he tossed onto the table, and did the same to the second. He paged through the others similarly. The whole time, the strange woman stared at him. She soon pulled out another stick of gum and unwrapped it and popped it into her mouth. After that, she watched and chewed gum at the same time.

When Jag finished paging through the last magazine, he dropped it at his feet and made a dismissive sound and walked out, straight to his bedroom. A minute later, the loud rumble of his radio echoed through the house.

"That boy," Mom crowed nervously. "He loves his magazines."

She made us all a cup of tea. Half an hour later, the strange woman left, taking her magazines with her.

EIGHT

SUNDAY ARRIVED AND LILY DROVE AND WE TOOK THE HIGHWAY west toward San Francisco. I sat uncomfortably, aware of her body and how she smelled and listening to her voice and not knowing what to say. It was morning and the sun had pitched its tent behind us while the shadow of the car weaved forward among the almost empty lanes of the freeway.

Any romantic notions that had crowded themselves into my head and taken up squatter's rights since the phone call were quickly evicted. We were on our way to visit a convent. There was a reason for our visit. Lily was thinking about joining.

"I've always wondered I have a vocation," she said.

"A vocation?"

"That's when God calls you. He reaches down out of the heavens and taps you on the shoulder and says you're one of his, no one else's, your life has been decided and there's no way out of it."

"You believe?"

She waited a few seconds, then she said, "No, I don't."

"I don't understand."

We were swallowed by the Caldecott Tunnel and spat out a minute later on the far side.

"I want to believe," she said. "Always have. Figure if I have a vocation then I have a reason to believe." She added, "Besides, I don't totally hate nuns. I don't like them, but I see their point, if you know what I mean."

I thought it went the other way around, that you believed first and then God called you. I didn't see her point about nuns either but didn't say anything, and soon we were thumping over the Bay Bridge.

The convent was a large stone building, mostly feature-less. There were few windows, and it looked more like a high school that had been built in the forties than a house of God. It stood halfway up a hill and was attached to a church. The doors were locked, despite it being a Sunday, and dull gray spires rose high, the sun hitting them obliquely.

Lily wrapped her fists around the small, rectangular grille set into one of the doors and started shaking it. When she raised a hand to knock, she seemed to shrink there in the long shadow of that high stone edifice and she looked suddenly like a little girl who couldn't find her way home and didn't know if she ever would.

As if on cue, the clatter of shoes on pavement traveled up the hill and we turned to see a cluster of nuns making its dis-ordered progress toward us. Their heels clicked against the pavement and in their habits they seemed piled together in a ball, but this ball had legs and was climbing and was topped by several bobbing wimples like surf on a wave.

"There they are, they'll tell me." She lit a cigarette and waited. I didn't know what she was expecting. Something magical? A light to shine down from the heavens or the nuns to surround her and usher her inside and lock the doors be-hind her? As the nuns approached her face changed. At first it was serious, like a kid waiting for her parent. Then it became almost giddy and the cigarette danced nervously on her lip, and finally it fell, fell as hard and fast as I'd ever seen any-one's face fall.

Because not one of the nuns turned to look or nod in ac-knowledgment, and they passed us as if we weren't even there.

They soon reached the crest of the hill and disappeared over it. Watching them go, Lily did not move, and only when the nuns were gone from view did she turn to me and say, "I hate nuns. I forgot about that. I always hated them."

She blew a great gust of cigarette smoke at the convent doors and turned and walked toward the car.

Her mood lightened on the drive back, and we stopped in Berkeley and ordered a thick slice of pizza each and sat on the curb on Telegraph Avenue with the sun baking our faces and ate greedily.

She couldn't remember the last time she had sex with Eddie, she said. One day it just stopped and didn't start again and she thought that was okay but he didn't. Sex was like washing dishes, but backward. You did the chore, but instead of feeling clean, you felt dirtier. The next day you did it all over again, even though you hated it. The whole thing made her sick. Maybe she didn't understand sex, she said, maybe she was missing the point, but as far as she could tell, it was a lot of noise and sweat for not much reward.

"That why you stopped?" I said.

She turned to me suddenly. "I didn't say I stopped. I just stopped with Eddie."

She crumpled up her paper plate and handed it to me and we stood. The sun shimmered through her long black hair and I felt an erotic thrill travel along my body just from standing next to a woman who could say things like that.

We walked across the campus and into the winding lanes on the north side, and she told me that was one of the reasons she thought she might have a vocation. "I figured if I don't like sex, maybe I like God better, or he likes me. Guess I was wrong." I'd given up trying to follow the logic of her argument and was simply enjoying her body next to mine, when she asked me whether I thought Jag might have a vocation. "Maybe that's his problem," she said, "maybe he's a man of God and just doesn't know it?"

"Him?" I said. "Once, maybe," and it brought back mem-

ories of the old Jag, the desert prophet Jag. It had been a long
time, years already, since I'd seen any sight of that particular
incarnation of my brother.

Even during the height of summer, Jag kept his door shut
tight, the windows up, curtains drawn. Inside he'd roast. I'd
sit at the end of his bed and sort through his records. In minutes, sweat would be pouring down my face. Jag remained
rooted, unconcerned, at his desk.

In bygone days of Jag the conversationalist, he regularly
ordered me to listen to a record he'd just bought. We nodded our heads as it played, and after he raised the needle, he
asked for my thoughts. He rarely liked what I had to say and
clicked his tongue in dismay and rebuke.

"You don't get it," he said. "Open your ears for once like I
said and maybe something will actually get through."

Jag was listening to something else. It wasn't the music that
interested him, it was the sounds under the music. Rhythms,
beats, codes. For a long while, I believed he meant the messages in the song itself, its metaphors and meanings, what
the artist was trying to say. I'd focus my attention, follow the
lyrics, and attempt to get to the heart of the matter. I wanted desperately to be a part of his life. We moved so often I
rarely had anything resembling close friends, and those few I
did make were ephemeral at best. Jag, however mercurial he
might have been, was the only constant.

If I tried to tell him this, he turned away in scorn. Brothers
were accidents of biology, nothing more, so was family. How
that possibly gave us anything resembling a bond he had no
idea. I was delusional even to think it!

My attempts at reading meaning into the songs didn't im-
press him either. He wasn't interested in what other people
heard. He certainly didn't care about the words.

Then one night he said it, point-blank and flat out, like it
was the most normal thing to say. A record had just ended,
and he left the needle skipping and bumping.

"There's voices under the music," he said.

Outside, a chorus of crickets set about its business.

"The backup singers?" I attempted, pretty sure that wasn't what he meant.

He snorted derisively. "You're not even listening!" He wheeled around in his chair and stared at me. "Don't bother with the lyrics. There's some other fucker on there. He's hidden deep inside the grooves. You've gotta dig to find him. Be a real spelunker in the vinyl. This one is a ghost in the machine. And you know what, he's trying to tell me something."

"You?" I said.

"Me," he grinned.

He picked the record up off the turntable and examined it from all angles and tapped the hard vinyl with his knuckles.

"Hello?" he said, his voice rising to a high, comical pitch. "Hey buddy, you in there? Because I think I hear you."

His grin broadened. The grin was not reassuring.

"What's going on?" I said.

"Having a chat with an old friend." He laughed. The laugh was not reassuring either. I told myself he was joking, and who knows, maybe he was that time.

The following night, he played a new record, the Suite from *Lieutenant Kijé*. It was classical, by some Russian named Prokofiev. The airless room smelled thickly of unwashed clothes but the music sang, and in seconds I was someplace else, speeding through a forest in a horse-drawn carriage. I lay back and closed my eyes. I'd never heard anything like it and felt grateful to have a brother who'd share this with me.

The music came to an end and the feeling persisted. I lay with my eyes shut for a minute or more, letting those final lovely bars wash away like water on a beach as the tide went out.

When I opened them, Jag was glaring in fury.

"You *liked* it?" he spat. It wasn't meant for enjoyment, even the composer knew that, all those decades ago. Obviously I had no idea *how* to listen to music. He would have to teach me.

He pulled the record off the turntable and slipped it into its sleeve and advanced on me and wrapped an arm around my neck. His forearm dug into my throat and he pressed his face against mine. Soon it was difficult to breathe.

Something was happening, he whispered into my ear, a burr of threat at the edge of his voice. I could feel his breath on my cheek. He didn't know what it was, but he knew it was dark and ugly and coming straight at all of us. Not just him and me and Mom and Dad, but the whole goddam country. For decades, who knows, maybe centuries, people had been leaving messages, a trail hidden in plain sight, waiting for the right person to come along and decipher it. It was all there in the music. Prokofiev knew it, and I must be blind not to hear it, for he stuck it in there, in that very piece of music, one more clue to the key to unlock the message, the warning telling us of the coming danger and tragedy and horror.

And there I'd lain on my back, Jag said with scorn, *enjoying* it!

He relaxed his arm and dropped onto the bed. I rubbed my neck and staggered.

"Jag... ?" I said. "Jag?"

He lay stretched out on his back, as oblivious as I had been a minute earlier, and I had no idea what it was he heard, what subterranean echoes, what trail of markers left by some unknown past that led us here, toward an unknown horror, and for the first time in my life, I was afraid for him.

That same week, he called me for a second time into his room. Laid out across the desk were two identical copies of *Life* magazine, dating from the 1950s.

He turned both to an identical car advertisement. They were exactly the same: the same issue, the same car, the same advertisement.

Without preliminaries, he pressed a finger down on one, then moved it hurriedly to the other, and said, "Do you see it *now*?" He was already angry, assuming no doubt I'd be as blind to this as I was deaf to the music.

I shook my head. "What?"

His hands trembled and he took hold of my head and thrust it down. His fingers pressed into the sides of my temples and my nose touched the paper.

"There!" he shouted. "In front of your goddamn eyes!"

The image evaporated into a blur and I pulled my head free.

"What is it?" I said, angry myself now. "There's nothing there."

He slapped both magazines shut. If I couldn't bother to open my own eyes, he said, there was no one who could open them for me. He was in a rage after that, swearing and thumping the desk with his fist, but I got no more out of him that night.

Soon after, magazines were piling up in corners of his room. Not just old numbers of *Life*, but others, the *Saturday Evening Post*, *Time*, even women's weeklies and comic books. All dated from the fifties or sixties, many being duplicates or triplicates.

He'd page through them simultaneously, comparing each page to its twin while minutely studying the images. If something caught his eye, he'd press a magnifying glass to his face.

He could stare at a single page for as long as twenty minutes before switching to another copy of that same page and repeating the process, going back and forth all night long and into the morning. Hidden in the magazines was more evidence of the trail. These microscopic differences, changes between different copies of the same issue, were all part of the same pattern he'd heard in the music of Prokofiev.

The changes could be little more than a dot of ink on one page that was missing from another. I couldn't see the difference. I'd press my face closer, hoping to find something there. Jag refused to believe me. He said I should get my eyes tested or better still my eyeballs replaced.

He showed Mom a couple times too. Her eyesight was so bad she couldn't make out the picture, she laughed. How was she possibly going to see those tiny dots?

It didn't matter to Mom. She was proud of him. "That boy has

an imagination!" She boasted of it at a family party, held to celebrate the engagement of a distant cousin. The men sat in chairs
along the wall clutching whiskey glasses and nodding drunkenly. Someone brought up Jag's marriage prospects. How could a
boy who never shows himself land a good woman?

Mom spoke in response and the room fell silent. "He is not
like other boys, and that is a good thing. All our boys today, they
dance, they wear too big silver karas, they drive stupid noisy
cars. Not Jigu. He sits in his room and thinks. And look at all the
magazines he reads. Who here can say he has read as many magazines as Jigu?" She clapped her hands in triumph. "Nobody,
and we are all much older than he is. I don't want to hear any
more of this nonsense about Jigu. He is a good boy and he will
find a good wife!"

Her defense of him was always ferocious, animal, as if being her firstborn, the idea that he might fail was unthinkable.
If failure was impossible, the opposite must be true. But even
that night, as she soundlessly dared anyone to contradict her,
I could see in her eyes a hint of my own worries, and I wondered later if she, who at times seemed to know her son so in-
timately and at others not to know him at all, already sensed
what was coming and was building a wall to defend herself
against it.

One night soon after this, Jag talked to me in an excited whisper.

The conspiracy, he was realizing, was worldwide. Look at
all those magazines! Tall, unwieldy stacks had risen in all corners of his room. The walls displayed their own city skyline,
erected from glossy paper of the 1950s.

Every one of them, he said, was false. History itself must
be corrupt!

Everything we'd learned, everything we had been taught
and told, was not the thing itself, but was instead a mask, a
defense, a false face. Perhaps all art, all science, all music, lit-
erature, history, perhaps all of it was code for something else,
stranger, darker, more mysterious!

He talked on and on that night, and I understood at best

half of what he said. I'd never seen him talk so much, nothing even close, and he grew genuinely excited. If this wasn't madness, I thought, that if my brother was not losing his mind, then someone new and brilliant and wonderful was emerging, and the brother I always dreamed of having, always thought was there, was showing himself to me at last.

One false face hid another, he said, and that hid yet another, and so on and so on. He was trying to get past the false faces, every last one of them, to find the original, the one true face.

"Of what?" I said.

He looked at me surprised, as if he'd forgotten I was there, and smiled. It was a real smile, no scorn or ridicule hiding in the back of it, and I could not remember another time I'd seen him like this.

"It," he said softly after a minute. Then he said it again, "It." And again, "It," each time subtly changing the inflection, as if each time he was referring to something completely different.

His voice was light and breezy. He started clapping his hands together. "It," he said again several times, now to the beat of his hands. I joined in, surprised at this carefree brother I had never seen before. Soon we were clapping in unison, singing a song together, the *It* song, and I was laughing, actually laughing, at Jag's antics.

"It it it!" Jag and I sang as we clapped. "It it it it itit itit itit itit!"

He danced from one side of the room to the other, stamping his feet and crying out, and fell onto the bed exhausted and stared up at the ceiling as if his eyes were seeing something else, all the way through it and through the roof and out into the stars themselves.

The following evening I walked giddily into his room, expecting to see this new brother I had met for the first time the night before. I found him still lying on the bed, staring up at the ceiling, immobile. He was wearing the exact same clothes and I wondered if he had moved at all. I pushed and shoved, clapped my hands, told him to get the hell up. Nothing. He

barely moved a muscle all night, and that other Jag, the clapping, singing brother of that one strange and luminous night,
never again showed his face.

A week later, when I knocked to say dinner was ready, he called
me inside.

"Look at this," he said. His voice was tense with suspicion.
"The goddam shit is right there. In front of my fucking eyes."

He thumped the desk with a fist.

A pair of magazines lay side by side, both open to the same
advertisement.

I looked from one to the other. The slogan read, "Only Brillo
Soap Pads have this Shining Secret!" The illustration showed a
woman holding high a glistening frying pan.

Jag punched his finger at a spot right in the middle of the page.
There was nothing there, just the grain of the paper.

I bent forward, holding a magnifying glass. Didn't I fucking
see it? he said. Didn't I see how the shits had done it?

I handed the magnifying glass back and told him there was
nothing there, that he was making it up, it was in his head. He
needed help, real help, not the kind any of us could offer. Certainly a doctor, maybe a shrink.

His arm flew out and struck me hard in the chest and knocked
me flying. I tumbled against the side of the bed.

In seconds, he was on top of me. His hand took hold of my
throat and he pressed his knee into my belly. His face came right
up to mine.

"You're lying," he sneered. "I see it in your fucking eyes. All
these years. You're one of them, aren't you? You're right there in
it with those shits!"

His knee shot into my belly and sent a wild spasm of pain
shooting through my body.

"Say it! Fucking say it!"

His palm dug deeper into my throat and soon I couldn't breathe.
With all my strength, I head-butted him and sent him flying

and crying out in pain. He jumped to his feet and aimed a kick. If he had landed it, he would have smashed the side of my head open. I was too fast, and with an arm I threw him off balance and onto the bed.

I started pummeling, using my fists. He punched me in the throat and knocked me to the floor. I rose shakily to my feet, pain riddling my limbs. We stared at each other warily.

"You," he said, wheezing. "It's always been you. The snake in the grass. I should've known."

He gathered up a pile of magazines and clutched them to his chest and told me to get the hell out of his room and never come back.

In the kitchen, Mom was rolling out rotis for dinner.

"What was it this time? I heard shouting."

Dad was crouched in front of the television, tapping the screen with his knuckles and complaining about politicians.

I had trouble breathing and collapsed into a chair.

"Those magazines?" Mom persisted.

I nodded. "Uh huh."

"You shouldn't tease him. You know how much he loves them." She added, "A boy needs his interests."

I stared at her with contempt. Had she chosen, decided who the crazy one was, who the sane one? Gone was any doubt in her voice. It would be a long time before I heard it again, and by then, both our worlds would be overturned, and I'd be cast out into the wilderness, nothing more than a murderer in her eyes.

When Jag stopped talking altogether, the only person other than me to be worried by his behavior was Uncle Gur. He arrived in the middle of winter holding a book high and slapped it on the kitchen table in front of Dad. It was a self-help book with a pastel cover and the photograph of a woman's face on it. Her smile was so wide there was more teeth than flesh.

"Your boy needs help," he announced definitively.

Uncle Gur lived in a town six hours south in the Tehachapi

Mountains, where he drove a Ford pickup and owned a rifle that he liked to show off if Mom wasn't around. Upon arrival, he often roared into my bedroom and shouted, "Blam! Blam!" holding it high. One day it went off and blew out the window. He admitted later that was the first time he had ever fired it. The neighbors telephoned the police and Mom never forgave him.

Dad grimaced when he saw the book. Mom walked over and picked it up.

"What's this?" she said.

The book was about raising troubled teens. Dad looked at me. "There's nothing we can do with that one," he said. "He reads too much already. One more book won't help."

"It's not about this one," Uncle Gur said. He grinned across at me. "Whiskey?"

Unlike Dad, he wore a turban, and his long beard was tied back in a net so it hugged his chin.

"For him?" Dad said.

"He has to start sometime."

I wasn't allowed whiskey that night, but that didn't stop Uncle from slipping me a watered-down glass a couple times during the evening. Mom walked in and out of the living room where they sat facing the window in adjoining chairs, debating the state of Jag's mental health.

"There is something wrong with that boy," Uncle Gur insisted. He was drunk and waved his hands idly in the air.

It wasn't his business to know what was wrong, but he'd be blind if he didn't think something wasn't right.

Dad listened, nodded, and said all would be fine once the boy was married.

When Jag arrived home, Uncle Gur jumped to his feet and wrapped an arm around him.

"Speak to us," he shouted. "Go on, talk!" If Uncle Gur was attempting a welcoming tone, it failed to penetrate. Jag shook himself free and walked with violent steps to his bedroom.

"When was the last time he said one word?"

"I talk to him," Mom chimed in.

"You?" Uncle Gur said.

Every single day, she claimed. They talked, small things, little chats about the weather, what was on television, what he did at work.

"He asks me about work. Every day when that boy comes home, he asks me how my day was."

We all looked at one another in surprise. Mom went on.

"He told me he has a girlfriend. He talks to her on the phone. You've seen him, yes?" She looked at me. "At night when he's sitting right there and whispering."

She pointed to a corner of the living room couch. It was a spot where late at night Jag could be found sitting, phone glued to his ear, whispering wildly. I never knew whom he talked to or what he said. If I made any motion to approach, he'd freeze and remain frozen until I retraced my steps and walked away.

Mom had no doubts. "He's talking to his girlfriend." She knew all about it. Jag told her.

The next day, the self-help book was stuffed into the kitchen trash. Mom was furious at Uncle Gur. He knew nothing about her son, and he had no right driving all this way to stick his nose in.

NINE

A COUPLE TIMES LILY AND I CAUGHT THE MATINEE AT THE
dollar theater and I felt, in that closed-up, dark hall, the ferocity of her physical presence, as if I were being sucked down
into the heart of a dark star. All I wanted was to wrap an arm
around her shoulders or rest a hand on her thigh, but Lily's
almost perfect stillness held me back. When the movie was
over, we said little and went our separate ways. I was left
straddling worlds, feeling alive and dead at the same time. I
would have given anything to touch her, to have her look at
me with a sudden smile. But each time I returned to the half-
life of my home, where my brother haunted the rooms like a
mirror to my own ghostly self.

He didn't talk again, but Jag's behavior toward me changed.
At dinner, he sat himself directly opposite, something he usually didn't do, and when not looking at his plate or at a magazine spread out before him, he stared at me with what felt like
an escalating hostility. I thought back to what Lily said, that
maybe he was coming out of his shell, but looking at him, at
the concentrated violence of his gaze, I found that impossible to
believe. There was too much anger in his eyes, and all of it was
directed at me. If Mom or Dad noticed the change, they didn't
say a word, and as the days progressed, it became clear that Jag
and I were locked in our own private battle. I told myself that
no matter what happened, I wouldn't come out the loser.

When Lily called and asked if I wanted to get some food,
I almost charged out of the house right then, the atmosphere

had become so suffocating. Eddie was away till midnight and she had no one else and she hated eating alone. When she said "no one else," I didn't know if she meant no one else that night or no one else period. I told myself it was the latter. As I drove out to meet her, an almost feral pull seemed to draw me toward her, while an equally violent push shoved me away from home. I would have been happy that night never to go back home.

We sat in a booth at a diner with plastic placemats and where each table had its own miniature jukebox. I fed ours a quarter and nothing happened. Lily struck it with her fist and a tinny song from the fifties started playing. We both ordered burgers and Cokes. Waiting, Lily began tearing apart sugar packets and looking over my shoulder with an expression of rising alarm. When I made a motion to turn, she threw out her arm and stopped me.

"We've got to go," she said. We'd been there no longer than ten minutes and barely started on the food. My heart sank. I was sure it was because of me, that she'd already grown tired of my presence.

She jumped to her feet and told me to leave the burgers and snatched the check from the table to pay for both of us at the register.

When I turned to walk out, I saw that a Chinese family had taken up residence in a booth directly behind us.

"They stank of Chink food," she said when we were outside. "They stank the whole place up. Didn't you smell it?" It made her sick, she said. She was on the verge of puking. Dinner was ruined, she couldn't eat now. I felt a kind of sudden joy, one I was immediately ashamed of but didn't care. It wasn't me she was tired of, and without thinking, I took on her anger at the Chinese family as if it were my own.

"I thought I smelled something," I said, lying. "Didn't know it was them."

She found a bottle of schnapps in the back of the car.

"We drink," she offered in consolation. "Get that stink out of our system."

I needed no persuading.

Her hand was trembling when she offered me a slug. We could see the restaurant from where we sat. Families and couples boomeranged in and out, glowing in the light of the overheads, before vaulting into darkness as they searched for their cars. The night was cool and we sat saying nothing with the windows rolled down, passing the bottle back and forth.

After a quarter hour, the Chinese family appeared and Lily snapped to ferocious attention. She watched them searching for their car in the lot, a boat-like Impala, opening the door and piling in one by one. When their taillights came on, she said she had an idea and started the engine. Soon we were following them out of the parking lot.

We pulled up behind their car at a red. Lily inched forward until we were right on their bumper and clicked her brights on with a foot pedal.

"Watch this," she said.

When the light turned green and the Chinese family pulled away, she rode their bumper straight down North Main. They tried to accelerate, but Lily was right there, inches from them, and when they pumped their brakes in excited signals, a wild Morse code of red lights, Lily flashed her brights and remained glued to their tail.

"The guy is shitting his pants," she told me with excitement.

She gripped the wheel with both hands and leaned far back in the seat and grinned with a clenched jaw. Their car switched lanes and Lily did the same. They made a fast left but Lily didn't budge, and remained stuck to his bumper.

The kids in the backseat turned to stare at us, and I caught their eyes in the headlights, full of rising terror. I told Lily she was scaring them. She was scaring me too, but I didn't want to admit that. Her hands were locked on the wheel and her eyes on the car ahead and she didn't answer.

The Impala's massive rear was lit up in the glow of high beams and the driver's head was cut in half, the lower dark and the upper a bright, bald dome lit brilliantly inside the cab. Finally, he twisted his head urgently and waved a hand, as if in surrender. Lily swerved wildly and shot around him and came up on his right. A middle-aged Chinese woman sat in the passenger seat, eyes wide and on the verge of tears, scared for her life. The driver clenched his fist and swore inaudibly at us.

Lily turned to me, laughing. "Don't you love it?"

Without waiting for me to answer, she hit the gas and shot us forward, blasting the horn and continuing for several blocks before screeching into an empty lot and parking wildly across lanes. The car bounced ferociously on the heat-cracked tarmac and the headlights came to rest on a row of dumpsters lined against a fence that looked like weathered tombstones. Beyond stood a field shrouded in mist. She let the engine run and dropped her head onto the steering wheel. I thought I heard what sounded like sobs. I reached out to touch her shoulder. She brushed me away, raised her head and wiped her eyes.

"At least the Chink had balls," she said. "He raised his fist. Usually they shit their pants."

She'd done it before, she admitted, a few times, when she got bored. I asked what she had against Chinks and why she kept calling them that.

She turned sharply. "I am one, remember. What? You don't like it, Paki boy. It hurt your fucking feelings? Guess what, I don't care. Why don't you fuck with your kind and let me fuck with mine."

I didn't give a shit one way or the other, I said, I just wanted to know. Those Chinks could go hang themselves for all I cared. She relaxed and turned the radio on. Music filled the compartment.

"You liked it, right?" she asked. "It was cool?" A hint of desperation entered her voice. I wondered if I was only there to validate what we'd done.

In the days when my family lived in faraway Valley towns, this exact thing had happened to us. Mom and Dad in front, Jag and myself in back, while way-too-drunk shitheads in their trucks roared past and screamed obscenities and racist garbage. Dad had gripped the wheel tighter and tighter until I thought it would crack under the pressure. He never once looked to his side or over his shoulder to acknowledge the pursuers. Such nights had terrified me, a terror that after all these years had stayed, buried deep in my muscles. I felt it again that night, an ancient wound opening up, and when I looked into the kids' eyes in the back of the car, I had seen myself. I couldn't say any of this to Lily. I was sure she knew it all anyhow, sure too that it had happened to her—even as we were in the car, charging forward behind the Chinese family, we were silently telling each other exactly this, as if acting out a drama from our own childhoods.

"So tell me, you liked it or what?" she pressed.

"Yeah," I said. "Loved it."

Thrill and sickness mixed inside me. The truth was I did like it, at least a part of me did, the part that tried to shut itself off from the eyes of those terrified kids sitting in the back. Lily was taking an axe to a deep part of me and crashing it through all the thick ice of that ancient wound, and however much I told myself I should hate what we'd done, I couldn't help but look at her with a new kind of awe and love and also fear. I knew then and I knew later, I wouldn't have done a thing differently.

She handed me the bottle of schnapps. "You're okay."

I took a long drink. "Next time, an Indian family," I said.

"Paki," she insisted seriously. "A Paki family."

"Paki," I agreed, thinking there it was, the cages we both lived in, for her Chink, for me Paki, like she was shining a light on the bars.

She slid a hand between the seats and onto my thigh and over my crotch. I was already hard and didn't know. All she had to do was squeeze my dick under my jeans and I came instantly. My head fell back and I closed my eyes and I felt her suddenly tearing at my zipper with her hands. She pulled my dick out, its tip wet, and took it in her mouth. A whole new sensation filled my body, somewhere between torture and ecstasy, and I sat there as she gorged on it and I drifted on waves of pleasure and pain. I reached out a hand to try to find the damp cave of her clit, but she slapped it away, and I slipped into a waking dream.

TEN

MOM WAS UP WHEN I GOT HOME, SITTING AT THE KITCHEN table, drinking a cup of tea. The fan turned slowly overhead. She asked if I wanted a cup but all I wanted was a shower and to go to sleep. I had early classes tomorrow.

"Sit down," she said.

The room swam. I'd never drunk schnapps before and was tipsy and high from the blow job. The ethereal qualities of Lily's tongue continued to hum through my flesh. The world felt soft and padded and out of focus and I wanted nothing other than to lie on my bed and think about Lily's mouth on my cock.

After Lily finished, we hardly said a word. She drove me back to my car and dropped me off. I tried to kiss her good-bye and she pushed me away.

"That's for sissies," she said.

I wanted to say I didn't care who it was for, I still wanted to do it, but I didn't and stepped away, confused and elated. On the drive back, I felt superior to every other man in every other car. I was sure that if I were to get into a fight right then, I would take anyone down with a single blow of my fist.

Mom sipped her tea and pushed the cup toward me. "Drink. It'll help you sleep."

I shook my head and prepared to stand when she stopped me again.

"What are you doing to Jag?" she said.

"What?"

"I see the way he looks at you. What's going on? What did you do?"

"Nothing," I said, annoyed. "How he looks at me is his problem."

"You did something. I'm going to find out what it is."

"Then why are you asking me—ask him."

Mom said nothing, shook her head, and after a long minute of staring at me rose to her feet. "You did something to him. I'll find out what it was. Then you'll be sorry." She planted her hands on the table and leaned forward, and something in her eyes told me what she was going to say next. "Don't think I've forgotten what you did to your cousin. He was a brother to you, and look how you treated him."

She clicked her tongue in disgust and left and I closed my eyes and felt the brush of air from the fan kissing my face. The cousin she was talking about was Thakurjeet, the only son of Mom's younger brother, who had come to stay with us for a month that winter after I took my second long walk west to see the ocean.

My balls ached and my body thrummed as if every inch of it had been taken into Lily's mouth. I had never felt anything like it before, but the invocation of my cousin's name brought another name to my mind: Tom Whelp, who, years earlier, had towered over me with a tiny swastika tattooed onto his forehead.

I had gone with Mom and Dad to the airport to greet Thakurjeet, and he appeared in a three-piece polyester suit of an indefinable pale green color, the creases still perfect after the long flight, which made him look like a bellboy at a cheap holiday resort. He was my age and height, but fatter, with a boyish, pudgy face, and wore a topknot in his hair, which young men wore before they were old enough to wear turbans. When he spotted me he turned and, with his arms crossed over his chest, told me his name and added, in a mellifluous singsong, "It means 'beloved of the Lord.' What does your name mean?"

I didn't know, I didn't even know if my name had a meaning, except the English one, which sounded lame, so I made something up. "'Prince of light'?" I said.

He looked at me, astonished for a moment, and burst into peals of laughter. He told Mom what I had said, and she started laughing, so did Dad when he heard. The laughter went on for a while, then they all started talking happily in Punjabi, and finally Mom turned to me with dismay, "This one knows nothing about his roots." None of them told me what the joke was or whether my name had a meaning or not.

In the car, Thakurjeet, sitting with his arms still folded in the front passenger seat, decided to instruct me on the proper pronunciation of his name, which led to more rounds of laughter, as I couldn't distinguish between *th* and *tha* and *thá*, or *kh* and *kha* and *khá*, which was somehow critical, nor could I properly roll the *r*, or find the right stress, and kept mixing up which vowel to extend and which one to cut short. His name was a minefield, and I kept stepping on the trigger. I was also useless at pronouncing my own, which no one had told me before. I was glad when we reached home and I could lock myself away and think about Dylan Thomas and my future life as a drunk.

The peace didn't endure. Thakurjeet was getting my room, which no one had told me either, and I was to spend the next two months exiled on the living room sofa.

"Like camping?" Mom said. "You like camping."

My cousin walked in for an inspection and studied my shelf of a dozen or so books. "What are these?" he snorted, but before I could say anything, he was pulling them off and throwing them onto the bed without so much as glancing at the titles. "All this is rubbish, there's only *one* book." From his inside pocket, he produced a small Sikh prayer book bound in blue cloth and stood it where my books had been. "There," he said, satisfied. "You read that every morning and every night and you will always be happy." Then he made a sheepish grin and started giggling, put a finger to his lips, and confessed that actually there was one other book in the world. He unzipped his bag and produced something wrapped in saffron-dyed muslin. It was a paperback called *Carry On, Jeeves* by P. G. Wodehouse, and after reverently displaying it for me to admire, he placed it on the shelf below the Sikh holy book.

The funniest book in all the world, he said, the only *really* funny book, there was no reason to read any other funny book because once you'd read this funny book, you'd read all the jokes you'd ever need!

He wore that green suit almost every day and sat around the house in a state of oblivion to the life going on around him. When I asked if he wanted to visit my school, he shook his head. He said there was nothing in American schools that could possibly interest him. The same was true of the small city we lived in. He'd seen what America looked like on television—what was the point of taking a walk downtown?

Every morning, he appeared in the living room while I lay sleeping and woke me as he recited his prayers and I buried my head deeper in a pillow. Afterward, he performed a daily ritual of plucking his eyebrow hairs, scraping clean his tongue, and gargling loudly for several minutes as he walked from room to room. If he caught me leaving the bathroom, he'd ask how my "motion" was. According to him, the secret to a long life was "a good daily motion."

Jag ignored his presence, the two hardly ever said hello to each other, and it was left to me, as Mom insisted, to "keep him company." She told me I needed to learn from him, that this was how a good Indian boy behaves. But on this, his first visit to America, all he wanted to do was watch fantasy visions of India and passed his days lounging around the living room, glued to an endless stream of Mom's Bollywood movies and the serials she rented from local Indian stores. When Mom was home, he'd pipe up in that singsong Punjabi voice of his and demand a cup of tea. When I asked what he planned to do with his life, he shrugged, "What my father tells me." He made it sound self-evident. His answer was the same when it came to marriage. He looked forward to it, for one day he'd have his own wife to make him hot, buttery rotis whenever he wanted. He groaned happily in anticipation of the event.

I'd felt a rising anger since that first day in the car when he schooled me on his name, and when he moved into my room, it began to feel as if he were erasing me from my own life. Every night, he sat at my regular place at the dinner table, got served before me, and he and Mom spent the evenings chatting in Punjabi, comparing notes on the latest doings in the serials and movies they watched. If I piped up, they'd shut up and carry on only after a couple minutes of silence had passed. Mom was still angry over my walk to the ocean, and Thakurjeet reveled in his position as golden boy in the household. Even Dad got into the act, offering Thakurjeet a sip from his beer sometimes while maintaining I was too young, though we were the same age.

One Sunday, Thakurjeet cajoled us into attending services at the gurdwara, which was an hour's drive north. I'd been a few times, with Mom and Dad and sometimes with Uncle Gur. Kids were usually running in all directions while old men and women, in their kurtas and their saris, were supported up the steps by relatives. Groups gathered to gossip in the outer halls, while from inside the voice of the granthi could be heard on loudspeakers. I covered my head with a handkerchief because I didn't wear a turban, and knelt down when I walked in and slipped a dollar into the collection box and walked back and sat with the men on the floor.

What I liked best were the musicians. Using a tabla and harmonium, they performed whenever the granthi wasn't reciting. I sat with my back against the wall and let my mind drift. With music playing and the voices of men and women and children on all sides, I could almost imagine myself a Sikh, a man in a turban who believed in something sweet and grand and mysterious.

The time I went with Thakurjeet, he waited for me to prostrate myself first, which I did with an off-hand flourish, dropping to my knees, bowing my head, and stepping away to take my seat on the floor among the men, all accomplished in no more than a few seconds. He waited for me to sit down, then made a show of it, laying himself out to his full length on the floor before the holy book and staying there unmoving for almost a minute, before rising and walking with a bowed, thoughtful head. He sat down next to me and wrapped an arm around my neck and pulled me close.

"You're nothing," he whispered. "Not a Sikh, and what's an American? More nothing."

He sat back, pleased with himself, and started softly praying.

Mom was hugely impressed. She kept asking on the ride back why I didn't behave the way my more religious cousin did. Thakurjeet glowed with self-satisfaction. He was enjoying my discomfort. We reached home and he wrapped an arm around my shoulders and we walked into the backyard. It overlooked a dusty field where kids sometimes played ball in the afternoons.

I'd joined a few times, but was banned after I sent a foul ball through the wrong neighbor's window, a certain Tom Whelp, who came charging out and demanded to know who the hitter was. Tom Whelp was rumored to be a member of a local White Power Shithead outfit. His tattoos and skinhead hairdo didn't do much to dispel the story, and kids said that if you looked close enough into his face, you could see a tiny swastika tattooed right there in the center of his forehead.

To my surprise and enormous relief, another kid, older and as tall as Tom, jumped forward and took responsibility. Tom stared at the kid for a minute, genuinely distraught at the turn of events. The kid was white, blond-haired even, not brown like me, and Tom looked as if he had been robbed. He slapped the kid once around the head, cursed the rest of us, then walked back into the general disaster that was his backyard. I was forever grateful to that kid, who said it was nothing, he'd always hated Tom Whelp, said if Tom'd thought it was me, nothing better than a nigger in Tom Whelp's eyes, I would've been skinned alive for sure.

If I was little more than a rotten foreigner in Tom Whelp's eyes, I was nothing but a lousy American in Thakurjeet's. I would never be a real Indian, he told me as he led me around the garden, certainly nothing close to a real Sikh. Where was my top knot? Where was my kara? When would I ever wear a turban? I didn't even speak the language. If someone dropped me in the middle of Punjab, I'd be a stranger, a know nothing who couldn't even buy a cup of tea. "Just another silly American," he spat. Then, pressing his face into mine, he told me his idea: we would switch places for a year, I move to India and he move here. I would learn Punjabi, learn how to be a proper Sikh, while he stayed, showing my parents what a good boy should really be like. "I'll be you," he said. "And when you come back, you'll be just like me!"

He grabbed my hand and squeezed it so tight it hurt. "Who knows? Why would your parents want you back? They don't even like you! I'll get to stay here, you'll stay there!" He let out a laugh, pushed me away, and walked back into the house and called for Mom to make us cups of tea.

Everything I knew of India was wrapped in the body of my cousin. I had a vision of thousands of pompous, patronizing Thakurjeets in their ugly green suits swarming around me, laughing in my face. If being Indian meant becoming like my cousin, I wanted to run as fast as possible in the other direction. I decided to act and act quickly, if I wanted to derail his plan. Once Mom and Dad agreed with him, I knew that there'd be no changing their minds.

I walked down the road to the house of a kid who had invited me a few times to shoot BB guns with him. We'd shot cans off dirt hills and pretended to play war, and one time, we spent the afternoon in hiding with our faces painted in camouflage while holding Tom Whelp in our sights, but never once squeezing the trigger.

I told the kid it was an emergency, that I needed to borrow two guns, preferably at least one with a magazine, that life and death hung in the balance, but that under no circumstances could he ask me why or what I was going to do with them. In exchange, he could borrow anything of mine, at any time, day or night, and for however long he wanted, for the rest of eternity. Even with that on the table, he took convincing, but I walked away with a pair of guns, a mostly wooden Red Ryder hunting rifle and an all black Airsoft imitation M-16 assault rifle, after giving my Scout's honor that no harm would come to the guns. I didn't tell him I wasn't a Scout.

Thakurjeet said in Punjab every man walked around with a rifle, and one of the first things you learned as a Sikh was how to shoot, so it was easy persuading him to test his prowess against mine. I gave him the Red Ryder and set up cans along an old section of abandoned wall on the far side of the field behind our house. Blam! Blam! Blam! It turned out he was as good as he claimed, and one can after another went flying. I barely hit half the cans he did. After we walked backward to extend the range, his lead grew even larger. He was pleased with himself and slapped me on the back. When I was in Punjab, he promised, I'd learn to be as good a shot as he was!

I suggested a few other tests, like running, dropping onto our bellies like real soldiers, and firing. I was pretty good at that, even beat him one round, which got him steamed, and he threw down his rifle in anger. He looked as if I'd personally insulted him and said there must have been a mistake, that something went wrong with his gun.

In the last test, I said I'd walk over to the edge of the field and hide in a small wash and see how many cans I could hit from there. I told Thakurjeet to stand where he was and wave off anyone who walked by because I didn't want anyone getting hit by accident.

From my hideaway, he looked martial, standing with his gun at the ready and a look of fierce alarm on his face. I took my first shot and missed, as did my second and third, and soon he was bent over laughing at my failure. I shot off some more, all of which missed, or missed the cans at least. "Not one bloody can," he shouted happily, waving his gun in the air. "And not one landing anywhere near! Where are you aiming? The moon?!"

He was right, I wasn't aiming for the cans. As soon as I had dropped into my hole, I turned my gun away completely and pointed the barrel at Tom Whelp's windows, which were a lot closer to me than the cans.

The gun wasn't powerful enough to smash the windows, though it probably dinged a few, and in less than a minute, there was the man himself in ugly gray shorts and a T-shirt roaring out through his yard, hollering at the top of his lungs. Before he got a chance to see Thakurjeet, I shot him once on the shoulder for good measure, which really set him off, then I ducked down and hid. I hadn't thought about what was going to happen when he found my cousin standing there with a rifle in his hands and laughing his head off, except that somehow I'd get out of going to India and my cousin wouldn't replace me in the family.

Thakurjeet was still laughing at my failure and didn't see Tom Whelp until the man was almost on top of him. A lot of shouting happened, mostly along the lines of faggot A-rab cocksucker and other such pleasant sobriquets. My cousin stood there shaking, having no idea what was going on or what Tom Whelp was accusing him of.

I realized too late, or let myself realize, that something terrible was about to happen and that I was the one responsible. However much I hated my cousin, even I knew I couldn't let Tom Whelp loose on him.

I climbed out of my hole and was about to charge across the field to my cousin's defense when Tom Whelp threw out a hand and slammed Thakurjeet's face and shoved him violently to the ground. Thakurjeet flew backward and let out a cry. Tom raised a foot and aimed for his head.

I came running at the two of them, wildly slapping the soles of my sneakers against the dirt, and held the gun high and shot into the air.

Tom stopped and turned, and I shouted, "It's me, it's me, I was the one who was shooting your stupid windows!"

I came to a halt maybe twenty feet from him and dropped the gun on the ground.

"There," I said, "I was the one who shot your windows, not him. Hit me, don't hit him."

My legs were jelly and my heart migrated into my mouth, then jumped out and sat on my head. A few local kids, on hearing the commotion, showed up and stood in a loose row at the edge of the field.

Tom advanced across the field toward me and the gravel crunched under his boots. I wished the earth would open up and swallow me, which unfortunately it didn't, for seconds later, there was his gaunt, unshaven face spitting insults into my eyes.

The kids were right, a tiny swastika was tattooed into his forehead, and it was doing all sorts of gyrations as he screamed into my face while his veins pulsed under his skin.

I closed my eyes and prepared for his fist to take off my head. Tom grew silent, and I felt his face right next to mine. The hot odor of his breath poured over my skin like some foul exhalation. Drops of his spit leaked down my forehead and onto my eyes, and I was sure I was about to puke my guts out. What felt like minutes passed and the sun scored itself into my face and soon warm piss was dribbling down my legs and onto my shoes, and out of nowhere I started to cry.

I couldn't stop myself and felt like a loser and a fake, but the tears just streamed down my cheeks, and I thought, this is it, I'm gonna die pissing my pants and burning a hole in my cheeks. Then I heard his boots again crunching across the gravel and I opened my eyes and there he was, a small man with his back turned to me, shriveled and distorted through my tears, walking away toward the wreck of the home he lived in, having not so much as touched me.

Thakurjeet wasn't badly hurt—a nosebleed and a few rips to his suit when he fell—but he accused me of trying to get him killed. I couldn't deny he had a point, but at least when I'd realized what I'd done I came running to his defense. I thought that deserved credit, but no one at home was willing to see my actions in any particularly charitable light.

Mom was furious, and a lot of phone calls happened between her and her brother in India, which resulted in a lot more shouting. My cousin was booked on a plane back early and announced to everyone how happy he was to get out of "evil America." Dad blamed me for all the expense, the international phone calls, the cost of changing my cousin's ticket, which he was expected to pay for, etc.

After Thakurjeet was put on his flight and sent home, Mom told me she was taking pills again to calm her nerves. The fault lay squarely with me. If I hadn't run away, if I hadn't tried to kill my cousin, she would be sitting at home happy as any other mother in the world. She was right, and I knew it, but I knew there was nothing I could say that would change anything. Each time I tried, she accused me of some new crime, and walked away and said her real son, her proper Punjabi boy, was gone, and now she was stuck with the American one.

We moved away a couple months later. Dad gave no reason, though he never gave a reason any time we moved. A deep, shrouded need, somewhere so far inside him that it had not seen daylight in decades, seemed to cry out to move and move constantly. He would keep his job, which in those days was in a factory, and just lengthen or shorten his commute, sometimes by as much as an hour. Mom usually had to change her job. She didn't drive and Dad refused to allow her to learn.

Of all the towns we lived in, I was saddest to leave that one, home to Tom Whelp, because I'd finally made some friends. The local kids thought me a kind of hero for not backing down from him and I spent my last few afternoons there with them, roaming the local roads and investigating old grain silos and abandoned barns or trailer homes, their windows smashed and graffiti covering the walls, and shot-up, rusting hulks of cars from the fifties, which to us looked like visions of a bygone, more glamorous age.

For years after, I had nightmares of that tiny swastika pulsating against the veins in Tom Whelp's forehead.

ELEVEN

THE NIGHT LILY TOLD ME ABOUT HER MOM SHE WAS SITTING where she'd sat three days earlier, in the booth at the diner where we encountered the Chinese family, and there I was, with her, paging dumbly through the oversized menu. I marveled at how we seemed to circle certain spots: the same row at the dollar theater, the same booth at the diner, the same winding roads through the hills. It was as if we were spinning on an actual orbit and our lives were nothing but an expression of its track through the heavens.

We ordered burgers and Bloody Marys. In those days, outside the big cities, no one carded you unless you were actually crawling out of your mother's womb. By the time the drinks arrived, neither of us was saying much. There were no Chinese families in the joint that night, nor other Indians, just white people and a black family over in the corner. I was glad, because for all my bravado, my mind kept returning to the faces of those two terrified kids in the back of that car and the dad's outraged, horrified face.

Lily pulled the celery out of her drink and laid it on the table. "I don't like celery," she said. The stick lay there, spreading a wet stain across the placemat. She didn't like that either and called over the waitress.

"Can you take this away?" she said.

"Something wrong with the drink, honey?"

"Not the drink," she said, annoyed. "This." She pointed to the stick of celery.

"It goes *in* the drink," the waitress said.

"I know that. I took it out."

"Oh," the waitress said. "You can't just wait?"

Lily shook her head so mournfully she might have been looking at the dead body of her child and asking a doctor to please take him away.

"Fine," the waitress said. She disappeared and returned with a couple bar napkins and used them to grasp the celery stick. "Next time, just ask for it without, okay."

"I couldn't care less one way or the other," Lily said loud enough for the waitress to hear. "But if it's out, I don't want to see it, and I don't see why I should."

The waitress stopped and briefly turned her head, then walked away.

"It was a lousy thing to do," I said.

"The celery?"

"The other night."

"You liked it then. Said you wanted to do it again. What, you don't want to do it again? Gone chicken on me?"

"Not what we did to that family."

Lily lit a cigarette. She didn't offer me one, which she almost always did. I took her pack and tapped one out and lit it myself.

"I liked the other part," I said.

"You can't pick and choose. It's all or nothing. That's the way the world is. No one tell you that."

She reached out a hand and asked for mine. "Palm up," she said.

"What you gonna do? Read my future?"

"Sure."

I held my hand out and she cupped it in hers. "You have strong lines."

"What's that mean?"

"No idea."

"Tell me something," I said, feeling the warmth of her fingers against my hand. "What is it about your mom?"

She grimaced and released my hand, then oddly smiled, as if she'd made some kind of decision deep inside her, that it was finally okay to speak.

"Sure," she said. "Did I tell you we had a view of the cemetery? Lovely place," she sneered, and added with contempt, "Daly City. I slept in the living room, Mom in the bedroom, though I'm not sure you'd call what she did sleeping, least not at night." She crushed her cigarette and lit another. "That cemetery gave me nightmares. Dead people floated through the walls. We had a washing machine but no dryer, so clothes were strung up over my head and I'd wake in the middle of the night, sure they were ghosts."

She took my hand again and turned it palm up and let her fingers play across the lines.

"Of course sometimes they weren't ghosts."

"What do you mean?"

"Guys, I guess, got lost on their way out."

She said it so casually that I didn't understand, and then I did, and then I felt like an asshole for asking. Before I could say anything, her voice turned savage.

"Mom was a whore, average Chink whore, trying to get by, who knows, raise a kid she had by some john. The most common thing in the fucking world. I'd lie there and listen. Just the two of them and she making all these noises like she was enjoying it and saying how big his cock was."

She imitated a fake Chinese accent. "So biggee dickee, so biggee dickee!" I wondered if that was how her mom really talked, but held the question back.

"I left when I met Eddie. She begged me to stay, kept telling me she'd done everything for me, all the men she'd fucked, the abortions, the whatever. Guess whores have it hard. Maybe she *had* done it all for me. That's a lot to do for someone, so don't put it on my shoulders, that's what I thought. She's old now, looks like a used-up dish cloth, still has customers, loyal old timers I guess. Cooks me a big meal each time I show up and I feel like a turd 'cos I hate her food, always did, and I don't know what to say so I pick at it and pretend to eat some. If she's not looking, I throw it in my bag and dump the whole thing on the street, even if it's my favorite bag."

She said nothing for a minute, then blew smoke across the table and took the cigarette in her other hand and held the burning tip over my palm.

"Let's see," she said, her eyes locked on mine. "What're you gonna do?"

I didn't know what was happening until it was too late, and then I felt the heat from the cigarette against my skin grow hotter as she lowered it and I told myself I was going to do nothing. I was sure she'd pull it away at the last second.

"Well?" I said.

"You play you pay." She plunged the burning tip into my palm and I let out a cry and snatched my hand away.

"Hey!"

"What? Think I'd let you go that easy, little boy? Everything has consequences. Ask a question about my mom, ain't no way you're walking away like you're a newborn babe." She grinned and relaxed and lit another cigarette. "Don't worry, you did good." She nudged a glass of ice water in my direction. "Most guys wet their pants."

I nursed my hand with a half-melted cube from the glass and felt secretly proud of myself. The burgers arrived and Lily checked hers to see if the waitress had spat on it. We ate in silence and afterward drove to a lookout off Alhambra Valley where we could see small East Bay towns dotted around us, swimming amid vast oceans of darkness and the odd ribbon of a highway. A shade of tragedy hung over her shoulders that night—maybe it always did. It was the kind of tragedy a person doesn't step back from, not easily, maybe not ever. I wanted to hold her close and push her away and cry in her arms all at the same time.

She had a bottle of gin and we sat on the car's warm hood and passed it between us. The air was cool and filled with the sound of crickets and the pops and creaks of the cooling engine. My hand still hurt where she burned it and the breeze felt good against the skin.

"I know it was a fucked-up thing we did the other night," she said finally. She said it like a confession, and I wondered why she was telling me now. Either way, I was relieved to hear her admit it. I hated to think of her as not understanding what we did. I wondered if talking about her mom had opened up other parts of her. "Like I told you," she continued, "I've done it before and I knew it was a shit thing to do then and I'll probably do it again, and I'll still think it's a shit thing to do. I'm sorry, guess that's who I am."

The faraway lights of the other towns seemed to grow dimmer and more distant and it felt as if we were stranded there, high on a ridge, while all around the world retreated. I told her I was glad she said that and she told me to shut up, she hated it when people said the obvious thing, the boring thing, and before I could say anything else, she wrapped an arm around my shoulders and kissed my neck. I tried to kiss her back, but on the lips, and she pushed my mouth away.

"You can't do that. I have rules," she warned sharply. "I'm married, remember."

"Strange kinda rule."

"Whatever, they're mine. Don't worry, I still like you."

She gave me a mischievous grin and unzipped my fly and pulled my dick out. The night air against the flesh felt like a liberation. All my thoughts of tragedy and pain and the sufferings of abandoned mothers vanished in the first touch of her lips between my legs. This time was nothing like before. It was gentle, sensual, intimate, as if she wanted to prove something to me, that she wasn't the evil daughter in her story, that within her she held multitudes, and that among those multitudes, she too could feel and touch and be hurt. My head fell back against the windshield and I floated on warm currents of pleasure, my eyes rolled back in my head and my heart lost and pounding.

Later, as we descended the hill, the car banked through sharp turns and each time the headlights lost the road everything became dark and I found myself filled with an unexpected sense of beauty and sympathy and love. The world was strange and wide and there were mysteries. That night I had tasted one. I felt for

Lily, and for her mother, and for the nameless john who no doubt was her father. This was the world, it held them in the palm of its hand. It held me too.

TWELVE

THE WEEK I BOUGHT THE BOOK BY SPINOZA AT THE BOOKSTORE run by those women with the goofy smiles and saw the swastika and the words DIE JEW scrawled onto the page, I didn't think of Lily or the Chinese family and what we'd done to them—not at first at least. No, it was Tom Whelp who shouted out from that page at me, like he was right there, screaming at me, and it was Tom Whelp I wanted to crush when I pulled my pen out to scratch out the hate. Once again, I was staring at his forehead, had been staring at it for years, and I was standing again in that abandoned lot, pissing my pants, waiting to die.

It was only later, after I took a drive into the hills and sat looking down on the ribboning Delta below that my thoughts turned back to what Lily and I had done. Maybe the neo-Nazi was no different from me, just a kid doing something ugly, egged on by a girl he loved. And maybe sometimes you have to follow your instincts and do something rotten to learn a little truth about yourself, which I guess is what I did.

Of all the rotten things I'd ever done, I felt worst about what I did to my cousin that day. I could've gotten him killed by that shithead Tom Whelp. But there he was, inside me now, a little Tom Whelp screaming at everyone. I was angry at Mom, at Dad, at Jag, I was angry at the world that had pushed me into that bookstore with only a dollar in my pocket. And now I was as angry at Spinoza and his world and his ideas as I was at the vandal who scrawled his hate into the book.

If I was to believe the dead philosopher, all I had to do was adjust my vision to the world, resign myself, regulate my emotions, and all would be fine.

Was that how a young man was supposed to find a path through this world's disorder? Through simple resignation? And was that what a young man in love was supposed to do? Especially one in love with a married woman? Calmly moderate his passions?

Give me a fucking break.

I knew what Lily would do. She'd act, she'd take Spinoza by the neck and shove his ideas back down his throat. That's what I meant to do. Direct, unerring action. Feel, don't think, *do*. I could almost hear Lily whispering to me, her tongue playing over my earlobe, telling me how right I was.

The following night, it was my turn to pick Mom up at the train station. Mom took the commuter train to work, but bus service was so poor at the station that Dad dropped her off mornings and Jag or me usually picked her up evenings.

Before I left, I pulled a sixteen-ounce can of Budweiser from the fridge. I felt a thrill as I did it, for this was action, I was doing something wrong and just a little bit dangerous.

I carried the can hidden in my jacket to the car and drank it while watching the sun winch itself down through the trees of the neighbor's house. The buzz soon caused the dashboard to undulate.

I finished the beer and dropped the empty can onto the floor of the backseat and started the engine. On the road, cars appeared out of nowhere and disappeared as quickly. Stoplights arrived with the steady ease of a sunset on a summer's day.

Mom couldn't drive herself to the station because she'd never learned. Dad refused to teach her or have her take lessons. He said that if she got a license she'd end up getting into an accident and our insurance would go through the roof, and then none of us could drive because none of us could pay the premiums. But he had me on his insurance along with Jag, and we were young and stupid.

After I got my license, I offered Mom secret lessons. She thought about it for a couple days and sat with me in the car, gingerly teasing the brake and accelerator and admiring herself in the rearview mirror. "How do I look?" she asked. "As a driver?" I could read the longing on her face. A car, freedom, the possibility to drive when and where she wanted.

I told her she looked like a natural and she couldn't be any worse than Dad.

After five minutes, she turned and shook her head and gave me a false smile. "No. We both know it. He'll never say yes."

She was right, of course, no way would Dad agree, but it broke my heart anyway and perversely made me angry at her. She should have tried, she should have fought. But I knew her well enough. She had tried, she had fought, over a thousand things small and large, and she knew Dad better than any of us. I guess she decided to start choosing her battles. I couldn't hold that against her.

It was growing dark by the time I reached the station. I pulled into a space and fluorescent overheads flickered on. A row of spots was reserved for cars waiting for pickups. Seconds later, a soft tap on the glass jolted me.

A red denim jacket and a black silk shirt hovered beyond the glass.

I rolled the window down. "Lily," I said.

"I saw the car," she said. "I thought it was you."

I climbed out and stood my ground awkwardly.

"It was," I said. I didn't know what else to say.

Her head was down, staring at the blacktop, and she stepped from one foot to the other, distracted. When she raised her face to me, her eyes looked swollen and red.

"Did something happen?"

She shook her head, "No," and a moment later changed her mind. "Yeah, guess it did."

"What?"

"It doesn't matter."

A train pulled out on the elevated track and the glare from platform lights bore into my eyes. She unzipped a pouch pocket in her shoulder bag and produced a small flask, which she unscrewed and handed to me.

"Here," she said.

The first sip of whiskey burned my throat. So did the second. And the third.

"Don't hog it," she said.

I took another and handed the flask back and watched her tilt it over her mouth and let it pour. The liquid hiccupped through the spout and into her mouth. Her throat worked as it grabbed every drop.

I stood and watched as cheap, golden whiskey spread through her bloodstream and into every corner of her body. When she was done, she threw out her arm and tipped the flask upside down. The last drops spilled to the ground.

"All gone," she said.

She lit a cigarette and handed me one and we stood there and smoked for a long moment, me admiring her and feeling the ground shift under my feet.

"I just got back," she said. She nodded over her shoulder to the tracks behind her.

"From where?"

"The city."

"Something special?"

"I was seeing Eddie."

"Oh."

"You wanna get a drink?" she said.

"Right now?"

"Sure."

"I can't. I'm waiting."

"Oh."

"What about later?" I suggested.

"I can't later," she said. "I'm having a fight."

"A fight?"

"I'm planning it."

"You plan those things?"

"This one, yeah."

"What do you have to fight about?"

She leaned against the hood of the car and stared over my shoulder into the night.

"Deep?"

"Yeah?"

"Shut up."

A train appeared, deposited its passengers, and started the long journey back into the city. Yellow LED signs announcing the destination flashed on the platforms. Figures in silhouette emerged from the burning lights of the station and disappeared.

Lily turned back to me and said she was sorry for telling me to shut up. She didn't mean it. She'd just found out something, that very day, at least for sure. It was the reason she was coming from the city.

It was about Eddie, she said. "He's cheating on me."

She'd suspected for weeks, maybe months, who knew. It was one of those things, she said, you just know. She watched them together, Eddie and his secretary. They were smooching in one of those little French shitholes near Union Square.

The joke was on him.

"His secretary?" she spat in disgust.

He didn't have the guts to cheat with style.

"The least he could do was pick a teenager. Someone fucking younger. Not that washed-up whore."

Her eyes blazed and I stood mesmerized. She was trembling from rage and hurt, and all I was thinking was how much I wanted her, to kiss her and feel her flesh against mine. The lights seared my eyes, the whiskey burned my throat, and the smell of Lily standing so close intoxicated me.

"I don't get it," I said.

"What?"

"You and me. I mean—"

"That's not cheating. I don't do that. That's just passing the time. Understand." She looked away and repeated, almost wistfully, "Passing the time."

"And Eddie?"

She turned back to me, her eyes ablaze. "He's fucking a shitty little whore."

Right then, I knew: it was time for action. Do what Lily would do, I told myself. I didn't think, I didn't hesitate, I simply spoke what was at the very heart of me.

"I love you," I said.

She snorted in derision. "Ain't no such thing."

"I love you." This time I said it slowly and deliberately and took a step forward.

"We just do shit, Deep, that's what happens, don't read anything into it."

I walked straight forward and pushed her hard against the side of the car and brought my face against hers and pressed my mouth into her mouth. If it was a kiss, it was as awkward a kiss as was ever attempted. My lips struck her lips, my nose jabbed into her cheek, and the bone of her jaw struck my teeth. She released a sharp, violent cry and sent me reeling back with a fierce push.

"Get off me!"

I found my balance and a sudden fury electrified me. Here I was, offering myself, offering her something real and honest and true, the one thing she said she wanted, and all she could do was push me away. I walked straight back, and I was going to kiss her again, just to show her that I meant it, that I wasn't another lying jackass, but her hand flew out and knocked my arm.

It happened in a flash. I brought my other hand up and punched her across the face. She let out a cry and I flew back instantly. I was as shocked as she was by my action. The sting of where I'd hit her rang through my knuckles and I told myself I had acted, I had done what she would do. Almost as quickly, the sudden rage disappeared and I was left hollow and nauseated. Her face was a riddle of shock, and looking up at it, all my excuses vanished and I felt small and miserable and stupid. What had I done?

She grabbed her bag and held it like a shield and spoke in a low, frightened voice. "Stay the fuck away, you maniac."

I felt the door of the car at my back and used the surface to let myself slide down to the blacktop, where I sat, knees to my chest, staring up in sorrow.

"I liked you," she said, leaning over me. "I *liked* you." There were tears in her eyes.

She pursed her lips and spat. She missed my face and struck my shoulder.

A moment later, she was hurrying along the concrete pavement, appearing and disappearing in broad pools of lamplight, the bag flying at her side. I watched her final, anxious steps with a rising horror at myself. They were swallowed by the darkness at the edge of the station, and, as if in a flash, she was gone.

All the combined misery of the world came and crashed right on my head. I closed my eyes and was soon drowning under a wave of humiliation. My hand burned from where I'd struck her, and so did my cheek, as if I'd struck myself. I sat shivering, thinking I would never move again.

A moment later, I heard someone say my name.

I opened my eyes and there stood Mom with a look of terror on her face. I had no idea what she'd seen or how long she'd been standing there. As she stepped toward me, I felt an odd relief, for she was holding out her hand to me and however much I wanted to hide from her, I was also glad to see her and feel her hand grip mine.

"Deep?" she said again, and added, "Is something wrong?" I shook my head. "Everything's fine." My voice trembled. "I was sitting down."

She lifted me to my feet and I buried all the warring emotions inside me. I opened the car door and held it wide for her and said nothing while she stepped into the car.

She hesitated, one foot inside, the other on the ground, and stared at me, opened her mouth, closed it, opened it again, turned away, turned back to me, and finally said, "It's hot this time of year."

"Hot?"

"Except now. In the evening."

I nodded, climbed into the other side, and waited as she dropped her handbag at her feet and buckled her seat belt, folded her arms on her lap, and stared steadfastly forward.

"Hot?" I said again. My limbs were rubber and my heart was beating fast and I was battling a dozen emotions simultaneously.

"Hot," she said. "This time of year."

I slipped the key in, turned the ignition, and dropped the lever into reverse.

I'd backed out a couple feet when a horn exploded behind us. I slammed the brakes and Mom let out a cry. Twisting around, I was met by a truck and, inside, a red-faced guy shouting nonsense.

I missed him by inches.

Mom didn't turn to look at me. She was looking at her feet. The beer can had bounced off the backseat and shot forward. It sat now, light and empty, between the soles of her white athletic shoes.

"Mom?" I said.

One sharp jab of her heel sent the can flying backward. It vanished as fast as it appeared into the oblivion of the backseat, where it produced a tinny rumble of a death throe, never to be heard from again.

"What?" she barked.

I eased off the brake and pulled out. The ten-minute drive lasted years, for I took a detour through certain fiery regions where the damned spent their summers. Mom didn't say a word. Not about Lily, not about the beer can. Lily's outraged face hovered before me, mocking me in the oncoming headlights of other cars and dancing along the street. I tried to tell myself that I had acted, that what mattered was action, but I knew how weak that sounded. My hand burned from striking her and I gripped the steering wheel tighter and tighter, trying to push the memory out of my mind.

We pulled into the driveway and the headlights made an arc across the front lawn and came to a rest as two drunken eyes staring back from the garage door. I turned off the ignition and Mom placed a hand on my forehead.

"You're sick?" she said.

I violently shook her arm away. "No!" I felt like a pathetic insect. It was slowly dawning on me what I'd done. I hit Lily, I hit the woman I loved, and I forced her to run away from me terrified and hurt.

Mom gathered up her bag and opened the door.

"We'll have dinner together tonight," she said.

It was always Mom's idea that we eat together. She had grown up in a big noisy family and missed it. About once a month she rebelled against our solitary habits and insisted we sit together and eat. Ideally, we'd also achieve that state that, in other families, is called talking. In ours this was generally defined as one or the other of us making noises with our mouths. The noises soon became shouts.

Mom's dream was that we'd do this every night, sitting, scowling, shouting. One day we'd get it right.

I tried to picture it, the four of us gathered around the kitchen table, scowling and grunting into our plates. That night, the idea nauseated me. All I wanted was to be left alone to bathe in my own humiliation. But I didn't have the courage or strength left in me to say no.

Perhaps she was right, that all we lacked was practice.

THIRTEEN

THE TABLE WAS DRAPED IN A FLORAL-PRINT VINYL COVER, and over this a thick clear plastic sheet was wrapped tightly. Under the plastic Mom had secured photos of family and sentimental pictures cut from magazines of animals and laughing children. I sat opposite Dad and next to Jag. Mom was at the head of the table, bustling back and forth between her seat and the stove.

Dad's back was to the television and the news was on, which forced him to turn between his plate and the set while fiddling with the volume on the remote.

Mom stood at the stove, preparing fresh rotis, and announced in a loud, clear voice, one that could be heard over the din of the television, "Mr Walia called me at work today."

Mr Walia owned the local Indian grocery. It was the only place this side of Berkeley that rented Indian movies.

"Mr Walia?" Dad said.

"He owns the store on Contra Costa."

"I know who he is." Dad made a face. "What does he want?"

Mom turned to me, frowned, and considered me for several seconds. She returned her attention to the stove. "Some videos came in."

"'Some videos came in,'" Dad mocked. He raised his hands in the air and made a violent sound. "He called you at work to tell you that?"

The question was rhetorical. Dad enjoyed these movies as

much as Mom did, but he never failed to make a production about actually paying to rent them.

"How much is he charging now?" he said.

"The same," Mom said, refusing to take the bait.

Dad asked what right Mr Walia had calling her at work.

"What business is it of yours?" Mom said. "I told him to call me at work. Where else is he going to call me? I'm not home all day."

Dad turned the volume on the television up.

"What—?" he said.

Mom started shouting. "And he had a question for me. About our son!"

Another time I might've asked: Me or Jag? Not tonight. The scene kept replaying in my head. I walk forward, I try to kiss her, she pushes me away, I walk back, I try again and strike her instead. I felt sick and played with my food and pretended to eat and hoped no one noticed. All the Mr Walias in the world could have crowded into that room with their questions that night and I would not have cared.

Mom slapped a freshly rolled roti onto the pan and walked over to Dad and snatched the remote away and turned the volume down. Dad crossed his arms and made a face.

"He had a question about our son," she said again.

"What is that man doing asking questions?" Dad said. "He has no right."

"He can ask questions, anyone can ask questions. You don't have to pay to ask questions."

"He has to pay. I don't want him asking questions. Next time he asks a question, tell him you want ten dollars first!"

Dad stood and stalked to the television and turned the volume back up. He crouched, his face inches from the screen, flipping channels manually. He stopped at a news report. A politician was standing at a podium making a speech.

"Look at these bastards," he said, tapping the glass with his knuckles. "They think they run this country. I'll tell you who runs this country. The fat man runs this country."

"What's he talking about?" Mom asked me.

"The fat man," I said.

She stared at Dad, crouched in front of the television, and turned and walked back to the stove. In Dad's universe, everyone gave to the fat man—rich, poor, in between—and the fat man dealt with all equally. He simply took and took. And never gave anything back.

"The fat man with the deep pockets," Dad continued. "That's the bastard that runs this show. Don't let anyone tell you different."

"You and your fat man," Mom said.

Dad returned to his food and started eating.

"Next time I see that bastard Walia," he said, "I'll make him pay if he wants to ask a question. You tell him that."

"Tell him yourself."

"Ten dollars. Not a penny less. Ten dollars for one question. Twenty for two, twenty-five for three. I'll give him a discount for three." Dad turned to me. "Look at this one," he said, gesturing vaguely. "Even he knows, this useless boy, even he has some sense." He pressed a finger onto the table. "How much for four, eh?" he demanded. "Twenty-five for three, how much for four?"

"Let him eat," Mom said.

"Can't he do math while he eats? Isn't the boy going to college?"

Dad grimaced and returned his attention to his plate, having lost interest in the game.

His thoughts were soon back on Mr Walia. "What's he do with all his money, eh?"

"Buys something good for himself," Mom said.

"I'll tell you what he does. He does the same thing this one does." He gestured toward me. "Wastes it. That Walia eats out once a week. In a restaurant. I've seen him. Is that what you want? McDonald's and—what's that other place, the place this one here goes to?"

"Denny's," I said.

"Denny's," Mom repeated with triumph. She flipped the roti and rubbed the hot surface with butter.

Dad let out a derisive laugh.

"I ate a sandwich there," he said. "Three dollars for a sandwich!"

"Is that what the fat man pays?" Mom said.

"The fat man pays nothing. Everyone gives to the fat man. I give to the fat man, you give to the fat man. Even this idiot boy gives to the fat man."

Dad brought his hand down hard on the table across from Jag.

"What about you? Do you give to the fat man?"

Jag didn't so much as blink or raise his head. The magazine was out, the one I saw him reading earlier, and his eyes stuck fiercely to the page.

"The fat man cut his tongue out?" Dad said, and turned to me. "At least he has some sense—he knows how to keep his mouth shut."

Mom slammed a pan down on the stove.

"Do you want to eat or do you want to talk more rubbish?" she said.

"I'll do what I want."

"Then do it," Mom said. "But shut up about it."

Dad shifted his shoulders, appearing for a moment chastened, made a sullen face in the direction of Mom and, holding his plate up, turned back to the television.

"Look at that bastard," he said, nodding at the weatherman. "What does he know? They get it wrong every time. I watch, I make notes. Tomorrow it's going to snow, tomorrow it's going to rain, the sun will be out, all day long. They take your money, that's all they do."

Mom struck the counter with the rolling pin definitively, sending a cloud of flour into the air and Dad finally fell silent. Jag paged through the magazine spread out before him. An added dose of ferocity sharpened his motions and every now and again I could feel him looking over at me.

Dad finished his meal and banged a spoon against the sink. Jag stood and abandoned his plate and retrieved the remote and started flipping channels.

Mom turned to me.

"We'll have to send this one to India. He needs a wife."

"He doesn't need a wife, he needs a servant," Dad said. "Cook, clean, iron his shirts. You want that?"

I said nothing.

"Of course he wants to get married," Mom said. "Everyone wants to get married. Live like us—happy, healthy, free."

She made a face and pulled my hair.

"Say it, say you want to get married," she pestered, though I could tell by the sound of her voice she was being playful.

"Good food," Dad chimed in. "Every night, home cooking. None of this restaurant garbage."

"Tell him," Mom said. "Tell your father."

I pulled my head away and continued eating.

"We send him to India," Dad said. "This year."

"Not yet," Mom said. "He's sixteen. Wait a year."

"He takes a look," Dad said, "he doesn't have to buy. He makes a down payment. Five years from now and he'll be ready to settle up, move in."

Mom nodded. "Listen to your father."

Dad turned to me directly.

"You go there, you take a look, you say no, not this one, no, not that one, no, no, no, then one comes along, you take a look, you say yes, this one, I'll take her. You don't have to talk to her, you just point. That's it, everything settled. We do the rest. This is the modern way."

"Fresh made rotis every night."

"One day he'll say yes."

"Clean shirts, someone to talk to," Mom said. "You need a time pass, everyone needs a time pass. We all get bored."

"Bored?" Dad said sharply. "Who gets bored? If you get bored, maybe you shouldn't be so lazy!"

I knew right then what was coming. The argument. I could hear it in their voices, the undercurrent of frustration and anger and mutual loathing rising to the surface. It happened once a week. Mom said the wrong thing. Dad banged his fist on the table. And so it began. Just like that. This time I welcomed it, anything to push me out of myself, to hide my own actions from my soul.

Mom was the laziest woman who ever lived, Dad shouted. Ignorant, stupid, know-nothing! How could she possibly find a wife for her sons? Mom shot back. Every day the same garbage poured out of his mouth, the same rubbishy nonsense. Year after year, never a change! The reason no one wanted one of her sons was because everyone knew what a bastard the father was! Oh, how she hated him!

I walked out. I wanted a drink. I knew where Dad stashed his whiskey, and I'd stolen drinks a few times. This time I took a long slug and refilled the bottle again with water from the bathroom tap.

The entire time, I heard them shouting.

They were cut short by the doorbell. I knew who it was and felt thankful for my one fucked-up and unhappy friend, Chuck.

I walked back into the kitchen.

Mom turned to me, tears in her eyes, grinning with surprise, "You're going *out*?"

"Chuck," I said.

"He wants something to eat? Tell him come in. He can't go hungry. Tell him he's welcome. We'll have a party."

Dad chimed in. "Where's this one going?"

"Coffee," I said.

"Coffee," Mom said, pulling up a corner of her dress to wipe her face.

"Coffee?" Dad scoffed. "Who drinks coffee?"

I was already out the door, while behind me the shouting exploded in earnest.

Mom slammed a pan against the stove. "Everyone drinks coffee!" she cried.

Dad's voice sang out fiercely in response. He once drank a cup of coffee! It made him sick!

FOURTEEN

CHUCK DROVE A 4X4 PICKUP WITH A HIGH SUSPENSION
that towered over most other vehicles. The seats elevated us into
small-time gods hovering above the people trapped inside the
sedans and compacts passing below us. He slipped a tape into
the deck. It was steel string guitar, hard-fisted and fast. I still
owed Chuck five minutes in a booth at Bill's all by himself, and
tonight was the night. We were on the main road heading west.
All there was to look at were the drive-thru liquor stores and
pizza joints and shuttered nail salons.

"How many?" Chuck said.

"How many what?"

"Guitarists. Playing."

I wasn't even pretending to listen. "Three, maybe four."

Chuck rapped the dashboard with his knuckles in triumph.
"That's one guy," he said. "One guitar, one take. This guy blows
my mind."

I nodded, "Uh huh," and tapped the dash with my knuckles.
"Does he get paid four times?" I said.

Chuck ignored me and took a left where we should have tak-
en a right. Apparently we weren't going to Bill's anymore. Plans
had changed, he explained. He had a better idea.

This was the Buena Vista Hot Tubs, one of Chuck's new
enthusiasms.

"You lie there," he said. "The water is warm and you watch
the stars and you have your own private room with a redwood
deck and everything."

He'd gone several times, always by himself. He'd tried to persuade me to join. I didn't mind the idea of two guys in a hot tub. What made me anxious was the idea of the hot tub itself. I was opposed to the very idea of relaxation. I looked on it with the same suspicion I reserved for any potentially criminal enterprise, for that is what it seemed, a theft of a part of a person's own being, their natural born discomfort with the ugly state of the world. But that night was different. Too many rules had been broken. I was no longer sure who I was and assented to Chuck's idea without comment.

I said, "I punched a woman tonight."

"Clever boy. That requires some real hand-eye coordination."

"I said I punched a woman. In the face."

"Your so-called Married Pussy?"

"Don't call her that."

"Hey, I'm not the one who punched her."

"She's still got a name."

"No she don't, and the sooner you learn that the better."

I folded my arms and said nothing.

He fished in the door pocket and produced a joint. He lit it while waiting at a red, took a toke, held his breath, and coughed.

The smell of pot filled the air. I wanted some. Chuck refused.

"Too young," he said. He extinguished the tip between his fingers.

I found a cigarette instead, rolled down the window and leaned an elbow out. A pair of sunglasses sat in the glove compartment. I put these on and the dark world became darker. Chuck flinched beside me. He hated it when I touched his things.

"You gonna put those back?" he said.

"You gonna make me?"

I felt the tug of the road as the car accelerated. We were driving on the boulevard, with most of the stores closed for the night and few cars around this late. He sped through one red light, then another. The frame shuddered as the speed increased. We were coming up fast to a T-junction. If he kept going straight, we'd drive into a parking lot, and if he kept going straight after that, we'd do sixty into the plate glass windows of an office park. Nothing frightened me. The world unrolled, inked in browns and blacks. The lights were amber dark.

Chuck came to a stop somewhere in the parking lot and cut the engine. He sat breathing softly in the car, refusing to look at me. I waited a minute before I took the glasses off and replaced them in the glove compartment.

"Fucking hothead," he said.

He pulled the joint out of the pocket, lit it, and offered it to me.

The attendant at the counter at the Buena Vista Hot Tubs sported a goatee and dirty blond hair. He said nothing when we walked up. Chuck slapped the counter with his palm and the attendant raised his head, a dazed look on his face. He wore a green and red jersey with BUENA VISTA in a rainbow of colors written over the chest. His eyes were bloodshot, no doubt from the chlorine in the tubs.

"One?" he said.

"One," Chuck said.

He wrote something in a book and Chuck gave him a bill. He looked at the bill for an extended moment and opened a drawer under the desk and the bill disappeared.

"Towels?" he said.

"Yeah," Chuck said.

This forced him to look into another book for an extended moment, after which he wrote something down and walked away. When he was back, he held out two folded white towels. They smelled faintly laundered.

"Number twelve," he said. He added, "Behave yourselves, understand. I've had trouble tonight."

Chuck and I both shrugged.

"We're here for the water," Chuck said.

The attendant pointed us toward a gravel path, and after a short walk we found a squat wooden door that led onto a redwood deck. Everything Chuck promised was there. A hot tub, a deck, the stars overhead. A wooden bench curved along one wall while above the sky was open except for a tree, whose branches were illuminated by lights from the nearby freeway.

Chuck stripped his clothes off.

"How you like it?" he said.

He reached down and turned the jets on full blast. The water gurgled and small whirlpools formed.

I shrugged. "Looks fine."

"Fine? Wait till you get in."

Chuck was naked and in the water before I had my sneakers unlaced. Voices rose from nearby decks. A woman was laughing somewhere.

We were not alone.

I was in no hurry to join my friend. I dug around for a cigarette and lit it and stood in the cool air in my underwear, watching Chuck splash and play with the controls. The boards were wet underfoot and the rumble of the freeway staggered through the air, rising and falling with the late-night shifts in traffic volume.

FIFTEEN

A LOUD THUD INTERRUPTED MY SMOKE. IT CAME FROM THE neighboring deck and was followed by a grunt and a curse. A woman's voice called out, "Anyone over there?"

"Here?" I called back. "You okay?"

"Why wouldn't I be?"

"Sounded like you fell."

"I did. Hold on, lemme take a look at you. Do you mind?"

"Go ahead." I was still in my underwear.

A woman's face materialized over the high wooden wall. Her blond hair was wet and stuck greedily to her head. An ear-to-ear grin filled her face and, guessing from her bare shoulders, she was naked behind the wall.

"I slipped," she said. She looked me up and down. "You wearing those?"

"I haven't got in yet."

"It's nice out, ain't it?"

"Yeah."

"You got anything to drink?" she said. "We're clean out over here."

I shook my head. "Sorry."

"Pity. I would've invited you over." She let out a laugh. "Only kidding."

"Wanna smoke?" I said.

"Sure."

I walked over and handed her a cigarette. She put it in her mouth. "Light it," she said. "My hands are all wet."

She exhaled through her nose and said thanks. The smoke hung lazily in the air between us.

A man's voice from the other side called out. "Who is that? That Ted over there?"

"Ted? Ted who?" the blonde said. "This is some guy."

"Ask him they got anything to drink."

She turned away from me. "I asked. They don't." She lowered her voice. "You don't have something else?"

"He does," I said, indicating Chuck.

His head was tilted back, eyes shut. He might as well as have plugged his ears. He was practicing full ignorance of the presence of the blonde. "What's his name?"

"Chuck."

"Chuck?" she called. "Hey, you there. Chuck." She turned back to me. "Is he okay? Shake him. Make sure he's not dead."

I walked over and gave him a nudge with my foot just to make sure he was still with us. He grunted his annoyance but refused to turn.

"He's fine," I said, and walked back.

"There's health warnings about these places. You can't stay in the water too long, especially if you have a bad heart. Maybe your friend has a bad heart."

"What's your name?" I said.

"Laxmi."

"That's Indian."

"My folks were hippies. That's Mike. Say hello, Mike."

I heard water splashing in the darkness, then footsteps, and finally Mike's head appeared next to Laxmi's. It was large and misshapen, with short, curly red hair and a gray beard ending in a point that sprouted from his chin. He reached a plump hand over to shake mine, revealing an arm covered in a blanket of hair.

"You don't have anything to drink?" he said.

"We did that already," Laxmi said.

"Oh."

She asked my name and laughed when I told her. She had

no idea I was Indian. She reached a hand over the wall and took mine in hers.

"From one Indian to another," she said, letting her fingers play along the inside of my wrist.

"Mike," she said, and turned away from me, "this guy's a bona fide Indian."

Mike watched as her hand played with my wrist.

"His skin is so soft," she said. "I never felt skin this soft."

Mike grinned. "You like it, baby?"

"Feel it."

Mike reached out his hand again. This time he rested it on my shoulder.

"It is," he said.

He ran his fingers lightly over my collarbone while Laxmi started to rub my back. I let them do what they wanted. The pot was having its effect and I felt a dizzy disengagement from my own body, like I was one more spectator on that crowded deck. Laxmi said she was a psychic and a reader of Tarot cards. If I ever visited her, she'd read my cards. Her teacher was famous, from the Uck.

"The Uck?" I said.

"England, but no one calls it that, they call it the Uck, even the Queen."

She couldn't stop herself from giggling when she said that. "The Uck!" I couldn't tell if she was joking. I decided it was better not to expose her ignorance.

Mike pulled his hand away from me and slapped her hard on the ass. She kissed him on the ear. Her face hovered inches from mine. The scene was beginning to turn surreal. As her tongue slipped down Mike's neck, her fingers played with the hair on the back of my neck.

"I love you, baby," she said to Mike.

Here was a genuine seer, Mike boasted, slapping her hard once more. His breath smelled thickly of onions and alcohol.

"Look at that," she said. "He loves me."

Mike made a sort of growling noise.

"Do you know what she predicted," Mike said. "It's amazing. Go on, tell him."

"I predicted the Rubik's Cube."

"She did."

"And the Pac-Man."

Mike let out a low howl.

"Honey, we're in company," she said.

She started kneading one of my shoulders.

"What's your friend doing?" Mike said, looking over at Chuck. Chuck didn't move.

"His name's Charlie," Laxmi said. "Or Buck or something."

"Hey, Charlie!" Mike called. "What you doing over there?" Mike turned back to me. "Is he meditating?"

"Leave the guy alone," she said. "It is clear he is having a private moment, and are we not allowed that?"

She found my nipples and brushed a finger absently back and forth across them.

"You're not having a private moment, are you?" she said.

She pinched one and I let out a cry and she giggled.

"You smell nice." She looked down at my underwear. They were ballooned and my dick was pressed against the wooden wall. "Look at that," she whispered. "I think you like me."

I took a step back and Laxmi turned and started kissing Mike on his Adam's apple. He groaned loudly. Chuck remained immobile in the hot tub. I was amazed, but he was steadfast, eyes shut, body rigid, the water pouring in jets around him. I found Chuck's pack and dug inside and pulled out the joint. I took a hit and returned and tapped Laxmi on the shoulder and offered it.

Her tongue was in Mike's ear.

"Baby," she said, full of admiration when she saw the joint. I lit it for her and she took a drag and handed it to Mike.

"Thanks," she said. Suddenly she wrapped a hand around my neck and pulled me to her and kissed me. Her lips felt full and wet and soft. Out of the corner of my eye, I could see Mike. He was just standing there, taking a toke on the joint. Laxmi slipped her tongue into my mouth and between my teeth, then fell back giggling.

"That was good," she said. She turned to Mike. "He's good. You should try." She looked at me. "You wanna? With Mike?"

Mike smiled. "It's alright, friend. Laxmi likes to share, but I don't feel the need for man parts tonight."

"Really?" Laxmi said to Mike, not bothering to hide her disappointment.

"Really," Mike said.

I was relieved Mike wasn't interested in man parts and took a step back, concerned he might change his mind. Laxmi turned to me with imploring eyes. "Baby," she said. "Come back."

"Give the young man space," Mike said, coming to my defense. "He hasn't even gotten into the tub yet."

"I guess," Laxmi said, pouting. Her face brightened and her voice became childlike. "Hey, let's show him."

"Show him?" he said.

"The dance."

A year ago, she'd been visited by a spirit guide, a genuine Indian dancer from the court of a long-dead raja, and he'd chosen her to pass along his ancient secrets. These were dances that no one had performed in over a thousand years, she said breathlessly. It was her sacred responsibility to bring them to the world.

"It's humbling," she whispered. "Without me, these dances will never be seen again. It's taken me a long time, but I feel like I'm beginning to understand my purpose for this incarnation and why I chose this body."

"She's going to bring it to the world," Mike said.

I stood on tiptoes to watch, which is when I discovered that hair covered nearly every inch of Mike's squat, burly figure while the only hair visible on Laxmi's body was the delicious shock of pubic hair between her legs. Her skin was pink from the warm water and her breasts were full and round. They'd been partying for a while. Maybe a dozen empty beer bottles lay on their sides, along with a bottle of tequila. Water was everywhere, as were their clothes.

"Just you stand there and watch," Laxmi said.

She stood with her legs apart and brought her hands together in a drunk namaste and bowed low, keeping her back straight the whole time. Mike clapped out a beat, which sent his belly shuddering and his dick jumping with each clap. Laxmi shot out a leg and pounded the wooden boards as Mike's beat quickened. Her hands made a series of severe gestures in the air while Mike started humming something like a tune—a repetitive and ridiculous moan that, if it resembled anything, it was Indian war chants from bad forties' westerns. Laxmi closed her eyes and tilted her head back, legs wide, knees bent, arms bending at the elbows and shooting into the air. Like this she moved from side to side, throwing her head into every conceivable position. I glanced back at Chuck. He could hear everything, yet he persisted in an almost monk-like lack of interest. Whatever, I thought, this show was all mine.

Mike's voice rose into a hoarse growl while Laxmi's torso undulated in the cold air. With two fists, she grabbed hold of her nipples and violently pulled, and, still gripping them fiercely, began a circumnavigation of the hot tub. Mike dropped to his knees and followed her, waving his hands until the tips of his fingers brushed against her ass. This caused periodic eruptions from Laxmi of confused, shrieking giggles. He came to a stop and threw his head back and let out a violent scream. Laxmi froze in a haywire jigsaw piece of misplaced limbs. Her belly began to shudder, after that her legs, and finally her arms, and she launched into a sort of wild, jerking explosion that made considerably less sense than the rest of the show.

A sudden loud rap of knuckles against the hot tub door brought an end to the performance. It was the attendant.

"I've had enough from you two!" he shouted. "I won't be telling you again!"

I could see his red face rising barely over the top of the wooden fence, staring angrily at Laxmi's naked figure. Mike fell silent.

Laxmi put her finger to her own lips as if to tell herself to be quiet. She glanced at me and grinned. The attendant disappeared once the scene had quieted, but not before shooting me a glare too, no doubt for encouraging the display.

Laxmi turned to me and whispered loudly, "We'll meet again. In this life. Or the next. It's written."

Mike slapped her on the ass. Soon she was on all fours, proceeding on her hands and knees in a circle. This time she didn't make a sound. Mike followed behind, eye-level with her ass. His mouth was moving but no sound was coming out. I turned away and found a cigarette and listened to the sound of knees scraping against the hardwood and breaths coming in short, quick bursts.

Chuck still hadn't moved. He sat where I'd left him, shoulders out of the water, head facing away, jets pummeling him all over, like an unhappy little Buddha meditating on the causes and cures of suffering.

I pulled my underpants off and slid into the tub.

He was right. I hit the water and began to melt. The jets shot at my back and I tilted my head and stared up at the night. There were stars. They seemed to swirl and dance.

"You done playing footsie with those freaks?" Chuck said. "Because if you have, I've been thinking."

"What?"

"So you punched a woman, huh?"

"Yeah."

"And now you think you're a man?"

Truth be told, a part of me did, but I didn't say this to Chuck. Nothing made sense, me least of all. I had struck the woman I loved, and mixed in with the shame and disgust at myself was a murky surprise, a sense of power. The surreal dance of my new friends seemed to be speaking directly to me. I didn't have to be the person I was, the world didn't have to be what it was, things could fall apart and still hold together, and I had done something awful and couldn't yet decide what that made me.

Chuck talked on, about men and women, about things I didn't really understand, and I doubted he did too. I wasn't listening. I felt immensely superior. I had kissed a woman that night, I had struck another earlier, and I had felt her mouth around my cock. Chuck had done none of these things and, worse, he had spent the evening cowering with his back turned to everything that was happening. All I felt for him was scorn.

I let my body slide until my ears dipped below the water-line and his voice dropped to a gurgled whisper. I knew a man should never hit a woman, but if he did, I rationalized, he should know how to make it up to her. It was what men did in movies, after all, which even as I thought it sounded like the cop-out it was. I knew then, as I knew later, that I was looking for any kind of handhold, any reason that might help lessen the vileness of what I'd done. I could still feel the soft flesh of Lily's cheek against my knuckles.

Another thud interrupted Chuck's monologue, as either Laxmi or Mike toppled over. I looked up at the stars and for a brief, blinding moment it was as if I could see them, really *see* them, like I was a kid again living in a no-name Valley town and lying on my back on a dirt levee while a truck rumbled by every ten minutes and I dreamed of hitching a ride.

SIXTEEN

DAD'S SILHOUETTE WAS FRAMED BY THE KITCHEN WINDOW
and I saw it before I opened the front door. My body was rubbery
from the water and the pot and I knew what was coming.

His face was lit by the ceiling lamp and cast half in shadow.
Spread out across the table was a Triple-A map, one of mine,
showing the local streets. He had a ruler out and a lined notepad
at his elbow. Several figures and simple additions were scribbled
across the topmost page.

I would have walked right by and fled to my room if the growl
that escaped his lips hadn't stopped me. I lingered in the hallway, looking in on the kitchen and the table and my father fidget-
ing. He glared, sitting all the way back in his chair, and dropped
a hand onto the table.

"Well?" he said.

"What is it?"

The weed's lingering effect caused everything to lag two defiant steps behind, then catch up with a sudden jolt. I pulled out a
chair and stared down at the broad map with its hazy iconogra-
phy of streets and color sweeping between us.

Our home was marked with an X, as were other spots: college,
the mall, bookstores, Chuck's house, movie houses and coffee
shops I frequented. I had marked them on Dad's instructions.
The rationale he offered was so he'd know where to search in the
event of an emergency.

Now he watched, foot tapping nervously against the floor.

"Where did you go?" he said after a pause.

"Coffee," I said. "With Chuck." I knew that wasn't what he was asking.

"No, during the day. Where did you go today?"

"Oh," I said, feigning surprise. "Today?"

"Yes."

"College."

"Where else?"

"I don't remember."

"That can't be possible. You didn't just go to college."

I knew it was a trick the day he asked me to mark up that map. What I didn't know was what kind of trick. It didn't take long before I learned its real purpose. He'd check the odometer on my car, pull the map out, and take the ruler and measure where I said I'd gone the previous night, and if he tallied a difference of more than a mile or two, he'd demand an explanation. Whatever explanation I offered, he refused to believe. If I took a detour to a bookstore in Berkeley he'd give me a look as if I'd just taken the car on a tour of the ruins around Mexico City.

"Where did you go?" he said again.

"I drove around."

"Around?"

"I went to a bookstore, and after I drove around before I went to college."

"You just drive around without going anywhere?"

The interrogation continued for a while. It always did, and I answered with all the flat-lined enthusiasm of a stoned teenager wondering why the fuck I had been dropped down here, into this house, with these parents, and forced to confront such a situation. Eventually, Dad closed his eyes, brought a hand to his forehead and made a fist. He lowered it soundlessly until it rested on the table as a challenge and opened his eyes and stared coldly at me.

"I talk, you listen," he said. This was how such lectures always ended. "I say, you do. That's it, nothing more."

With that, it was over and I breathed a sigh of relief.

Pressing his hands against the map, he took hold of it by its corners and made a hash of the folds by squeezing down hard to force the shape into something approximately rectangular. He slapped the misshapen map against the table and stood. I watched as he checked the locks on the garage door and the sliding glass door leading to the back patio. Returning to the kitchen, he strode past without so much as a grunt in my direction, checking the front door lock and switching off the porch light. Passing the kitchen on his way to the bedroom, he clicked the only remaining light off, plunging me into darkness.

I listened for the bedroom door to shut before I stood and turned the light back on. The sound of crickets filled the room, along with a stiff, lazy nighttime heat. A car passed on the street outside, sending its lights arcing across the ceiling. As I watched, the bedroom door clicked open again and the soft step of Mom's feet approached along the carpet.

"Deep?"

She walked to the stove and picked up a pan.

"You want tea?"

She often made herself a cup of milky tea late at night if she couldn't sleep.

"Sure," I said.

Her nightshirt fell to below her knees and the collar was embroidered with spring flowers which was at odds with her face, puffy and red from crying. They must have been fighting all night.

She lit the stove and dropped cardamom pods into the water.

This was how they carried India with them all those years. It wasn't the clothes—Mom seldom wore saris or kameezes— or the furniture or knickknacks or other objects. Except for the framed print of the Golden Temple hanging in the living room, everything we owned, from the hand-me-down sofas to the discount store plastic chairs, none of it hinted for a second at even the most fragile roots in anything but this American soil. Looking at that house, we might as well have hailed from Akron or Mount Pleasant or Bakersfield. No, they carried India in their bodies. They'd left suitcases and trunks behind, and with all of India, their India, drawn up into a syringe, they'd injected themselves until the country pulsed in their marrow.

I'd never traveled there myself. To me it was little more than an endless succession of Thakurjeets in their ridiculous green three-piece suits and blurry scenes from Bollywood movies on endlessly copied VHS tapes. Neither Mom nor Dad had gone back since they left, two decades already. When Mom's father died, Dad vetoed our traveling for the funeral. His reason was we didn't have the money. This was his response to anything he didn't want to do. Someone who watched a couple of documentaries probably knew as much about India as I did.

What I knew, what I could trust, was how my mother moved from one end of the kitchen to the other. This was my India, circumscribed into the unmarked maze of her footsteps, felt in the brush of air from how she raised a hand to sprinkle cardamom into tea. She turned to me, leaning against the stove, yawning. "Tomorrow," she said, "you'll tell him you're sorry."

"For what?"

"Does it matter? Just tell him. He's mad at you about something."

She carried the mugs over and placed them on the table and sat where Dad had sat a few minutes earlier. Beyond, the living room lay in darkness while I watched two thin ribbons of steam rising from the tea.

I raised my cup and blew across the surface. Mom grimaced, studied me closely.

"Your hair's wet."

"Chuck took me to a hot tub," I confided. I liked these rare moments with Mom, telling her things I wouldn't dream of telling Dad. They were intimate and therefore also dangerous, for either one of us might be set off, say the wrong thing, press a little too hard, as we both found ourselves doing that night.

"Now?" she said.

"Yes, when we went for coffee."

"It was a Jacuzzi?"

"With water jets and everything."

"You'll get sick from those places. Anyone can go to those places. All strangers. Did you take your towel?"

"They're safe. Chuck goes all the time."

"Don't tell your father. He'll get mad, and you know what happens when he gets mad." Mom took a sip and made a face. "I put too much sugar in."

"It's fine."

She pushed the mug across the table toward me. "Finish mine if you want."

I shrugged.

She tapped a finger against the table. "Who is the girl?"

"What girl?"

"Don't be clever. You know what girl."

"Lily," I said matter-of-factly.

"She's your girlfriend?"

"No," I said. And then, without much thought to it: "She's married."

Her hand flew out fast and hard and struck me across the face and almost knocked me from my chair. I instantly felt a flash of hatred and sat back in my chair, close-mouthed and angry. She withdrew her hand and held the gesture, frozen in midair. Tears welled in her eyes and she called me one name after another. I always did this, she said, I had no respect for anyone, I lied about everything, I was rotten. How much she hated it and how it made her sick!

She turned away, wiped her face with her sleeve, and looked back at me. Did she hit me? she asked. It was only a tap, not even that. Why did I make up these stories, she said, rising with obvious strain to her feet. It would get me into trouble one day, she was sure of it. But just as suddenly her face changed and she looked at me earnestly. It was as if she was telegraphing that she too knew that her outburst had been nothing but theater on her part, and all designed for a purpose.

"We love you, you do know that. Even he loves you." It was obvious from her tone she meant Dad. "One of these days, you're going to have to start taking your life seriously. You can't be a child all your life."

She stood and straightened her dress, pressed out the creases with her palms, and walked back to the bedroom. All my life, I had wanted nothing more than to be part of the family, a family that vaguely worked—that somehow we might acknowledge we did in fact need one another and were not just prisoners linked in a chain gang, that maybe we might even learn the plainspoken art of not being cruel. But as she disappeared, that feeling vanished with her. I don't know why it happened then, when she talked of love, maybe I just couldn't bring myself to believe her, or maybe the whiplash of her anger was just one too many.

I remembered an evening years ago. I was a child and it was a wedding in the desert at night. Multi-colored lights were strung along poles inside what to my child's imagination was an endless tent. A group of bhangra musicians from San Francisco played. A cook made fresh naan in a converted oil drum and men and women stood or sat in red-backed chairs while others danced or laughed.

I was eight or nine and I had never seen anything like it.

The world was newly born that night, and I walked wild-eyed among the adults, taking in every face and gesture as if this were the first time I had ever used my eyes. An old drunk handed me a dollar and laughed and I felt princely, clutching it in my hands as I moved among the bodies. Suddenly I came upon Mom. She was dancing in a group of women. I had never seen her dance. She was dressed in a gold and orange sari and every inch of her glittered. Her arms moved in the stylized gestures of a practiced bhangra dancer and I was surprised how good she was, how graceful. I watched transfixed and, as lights and faces swirled, I caught a glimpse of a world I had never known existed and of the woman who might have been my mother.

As Mom left, that old vision returned. How many times had I longed to see that woman dancing in the tent again? It never happened, and as I sat there alone, I realized I'd lost the will to care.

Later, after everyone was asleep, I padded softly into the living room and picked up the phone. Everything I did was deliberate, and as I did it, I watched myself, astonished at my own audacity. I was cutting the past away, making a claim on the future me, or so I told myself.

The green backlit keypad added its glow to the light from the kitchen. I dialed carefully, my heart thumping in my chest, and waited. One ring, two, three.

On the fifth, someone picked up.

There was a sleepy, muffled "Hello... ?" or something close to it, a shine of late-night belligerence buffing up the edges.

"Lily?" I said. "Is Lily there?"

The edge of belligerence sharpened. "Who is this?" It was a man's voice.

"That you, Eddie?" I said.

I didn't wait for confirmation. I launched into what I'd planned to say.

"Listen to me, Eddie. I'm going to marry your wife. I'm going to marry Lily. I love her and she loves me and she's going to be mine. Do you understand?"

Rough breathing was followed by the sounds of someone moving amid a pile of bedclothes. The voice returned, awake and angry.

"Say that again?"

"Lily," I said. "I love Lily. She's going to be mine."

"Who is this?"

"I love her," I repeated. "I'm going to marry her."

Before he could say another word, I returned the phone to the cradle. I sat there for a long while, feeling exultant and disturbed at the same time, not at all sure I had done the right thing. An hour passed and the room became crowded with dense, indignant shadows and a car sent its headlights spilling across the ceiling.

SEVENTEEN

ON MONDAY MORNING, JAG APPEARED AT BREAKFAST AS usual, where he ate an egg and glared violently across the table at me. Without saying a word, he left for work after banging the front door behind him. I'd gone past caring what the source of his anger against me was. I watched him as I'd watch a ghost, with shock, surprise, and no small measure of disbelief. But it had gone on for so long, his haunting the hallway, the living room, the kitchen, that I'd almost forgotten he was there. And with thoughts of Lily to distract me, I had all the more reason to pretend he no longer existed.

That evening, the night aged without any sign of his return. Mom shuffled between the kitchen, the bedroom, and the living room, her eyes constantly returning to the door or the phone. Dad remained oblivious. When she raised the subject, he didn't move. I almost expected him to turn and say, "What son? We only have this idiot one." Instead, he kept silent, his eyes fixed on the television.

The next morning, Mom asked me to stay home from work to call his boss. She was too shy to call herself and remained home so she could wait and listen. When I called, no one knew where Jag was. He hadn't been there the day before either. Jag's boss wouldn't be in until noon. He might have answers.

Mom bustled in and out of the kitchen and the house filled with the clang of wooden spoons battering pots. I checked the lock on Jag's door and walked around to the side of the house to find the curtains shut. No one but Jag had entered that room in over a year. The door had become invisible, and when Jag disappeared beyond it, he walked through a wall and into another universe. At least twice, over the past year, I had caught Mom struggling with a bent hairpin inserted into the lock. She'd seen someone do this on television, she explained, giggling like a girl.

"He needs to clean in there," she added. "You know he never cleans."

We pooled our break-in artist resources but remained unequal to the lock's mechanism. After the first attempt, Mom returned to the kitchen and made a pot of tea and insisted I sit with her. That whole afternoon, she refused to say a word and sulked, staring down at her mug. Each minute felt like an hour. The sun began to shoot horizontally through the kitchen windows and I finally stood and walked softly out of the room. An hour later, I found Mom still sitting there, the tea untouched at her elbow.

The second time, she struck her fists against Jag's door. How much she hated him! Tears welled in her eyes. She hated both of us! She raised her hand against me, but after a moment let it drop. We could both go to hell!

She walked away and slammed a door. I could hear her yelling for half an hour.

The next night she was smiling. I should forget everything that happened yesterday, she told me. She was sorry, she didn't mean it. Jag had invited her into his room. The two had sat up talking, just like a mother and son should. She was relieved to see he kept it tidy, and he was busy at work on an important project. Books and magazines everywhere, and one day soon, he had told her, he planned to get married. Maybe she'd help pick out a wife for him. That was up to him, of course. She was an American mother, after all, she wasn't going to push her choice on either one of us.

I listened with growing impatience. She was lying, and we both knew it, and I was tired of feeding her lies. I had been with her all night, I reminded her, and Jag had not returned home until late, and when he did, we both watched him walk into his bedroom and bolt the door from the inside. There was no way she could have talked to him.

"You think you're clever? You think you know what's going on? Then why don't you tell me? Eh?" She clapped her hands and sneered. "You know nothing," she said, and her lip began to tremble. "I did see your brother last night," she insisted. "We talked. He told me about his plans. Not like you, he says something." She fell back in her chair. "Everything is going to be alright. At least I have one son I can rely on."

"Jag?" I said.

"Who else? He knows how to talk to his mother."

I knew that underneath Mom's denial was a blistering hurt, that all she was doing was trying to protect herself. She was powerless here. Dad made all the decisions, her eldest son ignored her, and whenever I tried to bring any of this up, she turned on me instantly and cruelly, calling me the cause of all her problems. It was as if we were all locked in a static fight with our hands around each other's necks and none of us knew how to release our grip. I doubt there was anything else she could have done. She didn't have a language that described her own powerlessness, and for me, as time went on, anger was easier than trying to punch through the lies we told ourselves in that family.

One night around this time, Mom and I sat up late playing gin rummy. I'd decided to keep my high scoring cards to the end and let Mom win, so maybe she'd feel better for an hour or so. She had played the game as a kid in India. It put a smile on her face, until she realized I was deliberately losing. She used to do the same with her father, she said. He died ten years ago and all I knew of him was a single portrait hanging on the wall. It showed a stern old man with a long white beard and sympathetic eyes and wearing a beautifully wound turban.

She pulled the photograph from the wall.

"That's Jag," she said. "When I look at his face, I see your brother. I see the future."

She was right. The old man was his spitting image. I thought of her playing cards with him during hot summer nights. The only light was from oil lamps. It would have been easy for her to let him win.

I asked what kind of man he was.

"The best," she said. "He'd hate me now. He'd take his belt to me. That's the kind of man he was. A good man."

She returned the framed photograph to the wall and looked down at the cards scattered across the kitchen table.

"You cheat," she said definitively. "He'd take his belt to you too. And he'd be right."

That was the week Mom's prescriptions began to change. I knew this because she usually handed them to me to pick up on my way home from school, as the pharmacy was near where I changed buses. I was still learning to drive then. As Jag's silence deepened, Mom's prescriptions grew in number and the bag of pills I brought home grew larger, with longer and stranger names, odder shapes, and brighter colors.

I tried a couple and spent the day sailing through a gauzy haze. Everything felt soft and pastel colored. I wondered if this was how Mom now saw the world. It felt like being continually pummeled with a fist made of cotton wool.

I got through to Jag's boss in the early afternoon, and when I talked about Jag, I felt as if I was talking about someone I hardly knew, at best a mere acquaintance. Jag's boss's name was Irwin and he was from Florida and in 1964 he took a Jeep all the way from Alaska to Peru by road. He told me this in the first thirty seconds I had him on the phone.

"You can't do that no more," he said. "The roads are shit today, if there is a road. You take your life in your hands. Communists, kidnappers, banditos, starving campesinos. They cut your balls off soon as look at you. Regular Wild West."

It was only after repeated prodding that he told me that Jag was on vacation. The whole week, had been scheduled months ago. Mom was listening on the extension. She cut in to say that she knew, that Jag had told her last week and she'd forgotten all about it.

I hung up the phone and walked into her bedroom. She was sitting on the bed, talking to Irwin. They were chatting about Jag. After a couple minutes, she said good-bye.

"He said he talks about his magazines," she said.

"Did you really know?"

"I forgot." She clicked her tongue. "People can forget." She slapped her forehead dramatically. "I forget everything. Well, everyone needs a vacation."

EIGHTEEN

ON TUESDAY AFTERNOON, I LEFT MOM TO HER KNITTING and her pills and stories of conversations with her eldest son. She had the television on and was watching a game show about married couples and how little they knew about each other. As I walked out, she called after me. I ignored her. I had stolen a couple more of her pills and popped them before I left. The world quickly became soft-shouldered and my feet walked on balls of lamb's wool.

The streets were luminous in the hot gray afternoon. Oddly for the season, a brief tumult of green had livened up the town earlier in the month. Grass sprouting from pavement edges, the surrounding hills an always unexpected jolt of color. It seemed as if things were alive, not merely on the fringes, but everywhere, soaked through with a year's worth of rain and now bursting out of cracks.

My eyes were unaccustomed to the colors, and it took the Valley heat a week to claw everything back to a universal tan. The dust finished the job, coating what remained in gray. The return to normality was a relief. So much vibrancy in this town was pure hypocrisy.

I pulled into a drive-thru liquor store and rolled down the window and asked for a six-pack.

The guy behind the glass shook his head and said, "ID, kid."

I looked at him for a long minute, squinting, and repeated my request. His tune didn't change: produce ID or get lost.

He was skinny, unshaven, with thin strands of white hair clinging to his head, and looked to be maybe in his fifties. I'd seen him before—we both shopped at the Purple Heart Thrift. The store sent its profits to vets, most of them from Vietnam. Each time I bought a shirt I thought about some guy in tattoos and a POW/MIA baseball cap getting a dollar in the mail and it left me pleased, like I was doing something good in the world.

But recognizing a fellow philanthropist had little impact, for what were we but lowly consumers, hardly men of action, so instead I kept staring. The soft edges of the world suddenly hardened and I pressed my palm onto the horn and let it sit there.

The horn emitted a long, continuous blast. The guy shook his head, leaned forward, and shouted that if I didn't get the hell out of there, he was calling the cops.

It was a nice scene while it lasted. I sat there a good minute longer, and only when I saw him dialing did I ease off the brake and allow the car to roll gently forward, the horn blasting the whole time. The town blossomed after this encounter. The stoplights greeted me in cheery reds. Inside the spectrum of universal gray, I noted whole dramas of color jostling one another and knocking shoulders. I turned the volume on the radio up. The speakers strained, a tinny howl emerged. The car steered itself in the direction of the mall. The mall where Lily worked.

All weekend I had thought of no one but her. I called Eddie again on Saturday night. He hung up the moment he heard my voice. I tried a second time, but he left the phone off the hook. It didn't matter. I loved Lily, I was going to make her see that. Together we would get away—me from my family, she from Eddie and the shitheads. We would be a pair of outlaws of the heart, true rebels, because we would love each other the way two people were supposed to, with passion burned into every word we said and everything we did.

I made the final left into the driveway to the parking lot and it all seemed so obvious and easy and clear. I couldn't imagine how anything might go wrong. Inside the covered parking garage, the air mixed car fumes, noise from engines and industrial air conditioners, while underfoot, concrete vibrated to the funereal groan of tires screeching through tight turns and echoing on all sides.

Nothing looked real.

I leaned against the pillar and smoked a cigarette. A couple walking toward me hoisting bags took a sudden turn and offered me a wide berth. I felt cool and adult and threatening.

A sudden cold hit me the moment I stepped through the sliding glass doors, and immediately on its heels the noise, that hushed drowning bustle peculiar to indoor malls. On one side stood a cutlery store, on the other a year-round Christmas store with 60% OFF! signs in the window and etherized reindeer hanging from the ceiling. The display was dominated by a gold-painted tree with angels and bulbs hanging from branches, drooping sickly under fake snow. That same tree had been standing there for years.

Stale air mingled perfume, hot dogs, pizza—all chilled. Someone was trying to keep the smell on ice for the benefit of future generations.

At the far end, the stores disappeared and a glacial stillness set in. The Muzak barely penetrated. Turning a corner led to a pulsing red tunnel that looked like an artery leading to a giant heart—the mall entrance to the diner. The name of the diner had the word RED in it, thus the tunnel. The smell of roasted coffee greeted me as I ventured forward.

One free seat remained at the counter. Some sort of cream pie sat covered on a glass cake dish and a puddle of coffee lay spilled from whoever had occupied this seat before. On one side of me sat a couple saying nothing to each other over tuna salad. The salad was saying nothing back. On the other, a guy smoked as he paged the paper and sipped coffee. Lily was holding coffee pots aloft and dancing between customers, refilling a line of mugs. The moment I saw her, my courage vanished and I forgot everything I came here to say. My hand began to sting at the thought of what I'd done.

Using the tip of a finger, I brushed Lily's name into the coffee spill and wished at the same time that I hadn't sat down. A sense of unreality had been trailing me all weekend. I didn't feel like I was there at all, or anywhere, in the diner, at home. I wanted to blame the pills, but I'd only just taken them and I'd been feeling like this for days. Everything felt wrong, a stupid mistake. I'd practiced apologies in the bathroom mirror all weekend, but every word rang hollow. My voice broke or the words weren't right or I couldn't find the feeling behind what I was saying.

Lily waited a few minutes before walking over. She threw a rag onto the counter without looking at what I'd written and wiped it down and shook her head.

"You've got a fucking nerve," she said.

"Why?" I bit my tongue and struggled to make eye contact.

"Coming here."

"It's a public place."

"Eddie's out to lynch you."

"Let him."

"So am I. Now he thinks I'm the one having the affair. Makes life fucking rosy at home. Why, Deep? I mean why the fuck you little fuck?"

"I'm sorry," I said, sounding false and idiotic. "I don't know what happened. I just..."

"Yeah?"

"It happened. I don't know why. I *am* sorry."

"You *hit* me."

"I know. I wish I could take it back."

"You can't."

"I love you," I said, but it came out wrong, hurried and hurt and weak.

She shook her head. "Deep?"

"I want to marry you," I said pathetically. "I want to take you away from Eddie. He's the real asshole here."

She dropped her head down and leaned in close and whispered angrily. "Do you know what you did to me out there? I trusted you, I thought you'd get it, that maybe I just need someone to talk to, to tell all this to." She shook her head. "You're worse than every last shithead who's walked in here. It *hurt*, Deep, it really fucking hurt. And I don't mean the bruise."

She walked away and I slammed the counter with my palm. "Hey, I mean it. I'm not lying. I love you!"

She kept her back turned as half the diner stared at me and the other half snickered. Everything had gone wrong. My hands shook and I lit a cigarette and I closed my eyes. My face burned and I felt the seat sinking below me. When I opened them, there she was again. She placed a coffee cup in front of me and along with it a check for fifty cents. Her eyes were as angry as I'd ever seen them. It didn't matter. I retained a spark of hope, for she was looking at me, right at me, with those beautiful eyes, and I thought, Yes, she will say yes now, she had time to think, and she will say yes, yes, I knew it, yes.

She leaned forward.

"You think you can come in here, do whatever you want, say whatever you want. I'm not yours, Deep, I'm not anyone's. Got that? What you're doing ain't fucking funny, you fucking creep. So drink your fucking coffee and don't come back. Okay?"

She walked away and I pulled several wadded-up dollar bills from my pocket, unfolded and straightened each one, and laid them down as if I were resting on the counter objects of priceless value, one after the other, in a small pile. Lily stood and watched from afar. The money added up to twelve dollars in singles. It was all the money I had.

"Here," I said. "Keep the change."

She shook her head and turned to help another customer. I turned the check over and produced a pen and wrote across the back, in large block capitals, the exact same way the vandal had written in my copy of Spinoza.

CHINK.

I wrote the word again, and again, and soon I had filled up

the whole check, front and back. I raised the coffee cup, dropped the money into the saucer, and tipped the cup over until the coffee spilled. The coffee overflowed the rim of the plate. It started pouring over the edge of the counter.

The couple sitting next to me let out a cry.

I ignored them, stood, and walked out through the parking lot entrance without looking back. The sun blasted my eyes and I felt a great sense of relief. The rage was gone, but I knew what I'd done was idiotic. For a moment I thought maybe she'd see through the anger to the passion below, recognize what I was *really* trying to say. But in the drab gray of the parking lot, my rationalizations fell away and I wondered why I'd done that, why once again I'd been so blind.

NINETEEN

WHEN I GOT HOME, THERE WAS MOM, WATCHING A SOAP AND knitting at the same time and sitting where Jag usually sat, looking shrunken in the dark living room. I didn't say hello. I walked to my room and dropped onto the bed. I told myself to push my fear out of my head. I had acted, I had *done* something, that was what was important.

Mom opened my door and stared at me. She looked distressed.

"That uncle of yours is coming," she said. She was talking about Uncle Gur.

I asked why and she said just to put his nose in, make a fuss and noise and pretend he was doing something.

"Help search?" I said.

She made a motion to spit. "Jag's on vacation. How many times do I have to tell you?"

Later, I heard Dad come home and lock himself in his room. I stole five dollars from Mom's purse and walked out without telling anyone.

Come sunset, I was back at the mall with a bottle of schnapps I'd bought at a friendly liquor store. Each time I took a sip I thought of Lily. The sun disappeared behind the covered garage and the orange sky darkened and the lights came on all together, and I wondered why it was we modern humans who had nothing to fear were so afraid of the dark.

A few tables struggled on, punk kids laughing loudly and throwing sugar packets at each other over endless cups of coffee and a few aimless drunks settled with their heads down over the tables. A guy was standing behind the counter with the name Pete stitched into his uniform. I asked if Lily was there.

He shook his head. "You and Lily, huh?"

"It's none of your business," I said.

"You got that right."

"Well?"

He was emptying one cream jug into another. It looked like edifying work. "Do you see her, buddy?" he said. He was a brawny-looking guy with a blond crew cut and a gap that showed when he grinned.

"I'm not your buddy," I said.

"And she ain't yours."

I spotted her standing in the kitchen smoking a cigarette and not looking at me. She was talking to some old guy, maybe the cook.

"Give me a coffee," I said.

"Closed."

"You let me in."

"And I'm gonna let you right out."

As soon as Lily spotted me, she stopped talking and turned in my direction.

"That's her right there," I said. "Just get her. This is important."

The guy shook his head.

"You're drunk, kid."

"Who isn't these days."

Lily was following all this with a cigarette in her mouth and looking straight at me. Slowly, she raised a single finger, higher and higher, then turned away and spat.

The guy behind the counter watched along with me as if it were the midnight show and nothing else was on. She finished it off by blowing a puff of smoke in my direction and walked away and disappeared. The guy turned back to me.

"Got the message?" he said.

"Give me a check," I said.

"You don't learn, do you?"

"Give me a fucking check," I snapped.

He shook his head and tore one off and pushed it across the counter.

"Your funeral," he said.

I pulled a pen out of my pocket and drew a circle on the back of the check. Inside I wrote Lily's name. Around the circle I drew a heart.

I added, in bold letters, "MARRY ME."

"Give this to her," I said.

He looked at it and smirked. "This?"

"What's wrong with it?"

"Nothing. Wait here."

He was gone after that. A moment later, I heard a bright burst of laughter. It was Lily's laugh, sharp and cruel and deadly. The laughter didn't stop. The guy returned, grinning ear to ear.

He handed the note back. It wasn't screwed up or burned. Lily had added to it. Across my message, she'd written her own in bold letters.

One word: PAKI.

That one word gave me hope.

The guy sneered at the check, but I took it and folded it and pushed it into my pocket and climbed off the stool and started walking out.

"Hey," he called, laughing. "Come back sometime. You liven things up."

I leaned against the stucco wall next to a pay phone outside the mall and lit a cigarette and watched a group of kids through the thickening air. They were pulling soda cans from the dumpster and crushing them by jumping. The loud stomp of their boots echoed among the buildings.

I picked up the handset, dropped a dime, and dialed. Eddie answered.

"Yeah?" he said.

"Eddie," I said. "Remember me?"

There was a pause. "Who is this?"

"I love your wife, Eddie. I'll tell you something more. She loves me back. She told me herself. Do you understand? I'm taking her away from you. You don't deserve her. She's gonna marry me."

I don't know what I expected him to do. Shout, swear, call me a liar, maybe agree that I was right, that he'd abandoned Lily, no longer loved her, that she was free to love whomever she wanted to. I would have welcomed any of those. That's not what happened. All I heard was silence. Long and drawn-out silence, so long that finally I had to ask if he was still there.

"Eddie?" And then again, "Eddie?"

I knew he was there. I could hear him breathing. The silence lengthened, and oddly, in that silence, all the bravado, the certainty, my own love even, began to choke. My heart dropped like a stone below the surface of a muddy lake. In desperation, I shouted into the phone, "Eddie! I don't know what you're doing but you can fuck off, okay, just go fuck yourself! I love Lily! I love her!"

The kids turned to look at me.

Eddie said nothing, and then I heard the beeps that told me the line was dead, had been dead for a while. I felt suddenly cold. I returned the handset to the hook.

Of course he had been there, I told myself, I could hear him breathing.

That feeling of cold spread through my body and transformed into a kind of terror. What was it I couldn't see? The kids had set a fire in one of the dumpsters. Flames shot up, lighting the side of the building red and glowing brightly through the fog. I loved Lily, and together we would get out, I knew it—she loved me too, she must know it too. I pushed the terror back with these thoughts.

The kids jumped on their skateboards and were gone. The sound of their wheels rattling on the blacktop lingered before that died too, and I was left listening to the crackling fire, too far from it to feel any of its warmth.

TWENTY

A BOTTLE OF WHISKEY WAS OUT AND OPEN ON THE COFFEE table and Uncle Gur was holding court. He'd been driving all day and now sat, red-eyed and exhausted, in a chair opposite Dad. On the turntable, an old Hindi movie sound track from the sixties was playing. They were singing along and stopped when I walked in, swaying slightly and trying to hide how drunk I was. Uncle turned to me and grabbed my wrist and pulled me toward him. I almost toppled over, but steadied myself against the wall.

"Eh—? What do you say? We call the police?"

I worried for a second they'd realize I'd driven home like this, but Gur and Dad were too far gone themselves to notice.

"Sure," I said. "What else are we gonna do?"

Both men burst into peals of laughter.

"Call the police?" Uncle Gur shouted and thumped the sofa with the palm of his hand. "Did you hear the boy?"

The laughter continued unabated and I stood, swaying on my feet, too drunk to do or say anything coherent. Uncle Gur's visits loosened Dad's tongue, and it was on such nights I heard tales of Dad's boyhood and, a few times, of their voyage to America. The stories often contradicted one another. I never minded that. It made them seem closer to life, the way it was actually lived and remembered and not cut into stone. In one version, it was their father who ordered them to leave India; in another they took it upon themselves to escape a life of village small-mindedness. "I wanted the open road, the skies, the way

I'd heard that people lived in the West," Uncle Gur said. "Your dad wanted the whiskey!"

They had worked side by side first in a bread factory and later on a farm and after that for a trucking company hauling apples from the Valley to corrupt wholesalers in San Francisco.

"Those were good days," Uncle Gur reminisced. "We got into some fights, really learned how to knock a few heads together." He turned to Dad. "Do you remember the German brothers? What were their names?"

"Wolf something?"

Uncle Gur clapped his hands. "Wolfgang! Wolfgang and Kurt!"

"Kurt?" Dad mocked. "What kind of name is that?"

"That's what you said! That same night! Then you laughed your head off and they got angrier and angrier." He turned to me. "You could see the steam coming out of their ears!"

"What happened?" I said.

"Kurt is not a real name," Dad said. "A man should have a real name."

"We were at those dockside bars, near the water. A lot of bad characters. Your father was still wearing a turban then. This Kurt fellow made a remark about your father's turban."

"I showed him what kind of man I was," Dad said.

"We showed them both. One ended up in the water and the other ran for his mommy!"

When they left India, they had traveled together here by boat. This was Dad's favorite story, and the one he liked to tell the most. One of the officers aboard the vessel had poured continual abuse on all the Indians, calling them niggers and coolies and wetbacks. It was Dad who stood up to him.

"One day I got him by the collar," he said, demonstrating by holding a phantom figure in his fist. "I shook that bastard so hard he never said another word the whole trip. He made our lives hell, and I told him he was nothing—*nothing!*—that he had no right. It's what Sikhs do. They stand up to people doing wrong."

That ship occupied my daydreams as it cut across the Pacific, the sway of the hull, the sky kissing the horizon on all sides.

When I'd get angry with Dad, sometimes I'd think of him standing up to the racist officer as they sailed from one continent to another and I'd watch as the anger disappeared. The story conjured images of packing crates covered in stickers from exotic ports, of intrigue and violence, of spies, love, shipboard entanglements, and hinted at a different Dad. If he had lived once, maybe he could live again.

Then, one day, Jag showed me a copy of Dad's old Indian passport. He'd found it in a shoe box high on a shelf in the garage and handed it to me without fanfare. The little book, with its worn green boards tied together with string, was wrapped in a length of rough cotton cloth that smelled richly of sandalwood. I paged through it, looking for port stamps, for any clue to his mythical stories, but the customs stamps were unmistakable. He had never boarded a ship in his life. He flew to San Francisco, with several stops, each lasting no longer than a couple days. Jag looked at me coldly. "No one's who they are," he said. "Don't ever forget that." He walked away, leaving me doubly stunned, for he had never spent a single night with us while Dad and Uncle spun those tales. He must have been secretly listening the whole time. Oddly, the deception only further softened Dad in my eyes. It made him more human, and I liked the story he made up. I told myself that if he had been on that ship, that's exactly what he would have done.

The laughter in the room subsided and I looked from Dad to Uncle Gur. Their eyes were red, their faces swollen, and their hands muddled the air with unfocused gestures. Uncle Gur reached out again and took hold of my arm and pulled me close.

"Well," I said finally. "So he's back?"

"Does he look like he's back?" Uncle Gur said.

"So, are we doing something?"

"What do you think, eh? Go on TV, like one of those women crying her eyes out and telling the world to feel sorry for her?"

He made a mock show of blubbering and I tried to pull away.

"Don't worry," he said, tightening his grip. "I'm not making fun of you. I want to tell you something. Something you need to know."

He pulled me closer and I could see the veins on his nose like the map of a delta.

"This is family. We never talk about family to anyone. Understand. No matter what happens. The family takes care of it. In private."

He released me and I fell backward and steadied myself against the wall. Their laughter erupted once more as I made my progress down the hall to my bedroom. I waited, because I knew he would be coming, and soon enough he did, holding a glass of whiskey that he offered to me as I sat up in bed.

"Lot of books," he said, looking around. "You read all these?"

He said this every time he walked into my room. It had come to sound as if he were repeating a private password. I had the radio on and turned it down. "Most."

"Drink. It's good for you."

He dropped into a chair and rested his large, bare feet on the edge of my bed and watched me as I sipped—it burned my throat as it went down.

"Don't worry," he said after a minute. "He'll be okay. He's my nephew. That boy knows how to land on his feet."

Suddenly he jumped up and spread his legs out and raised his arms.

"Do you exercise ever?"

I shook my head no.

"Come on, on your feet. Like this."

While I watched, he started performing drunken jumping jacks at the end of my bed. He managed twenty before he collapsed, puffing and wiping his brow.

"Every night, before bed, this is what I do."

Saying that, he walked out, banging the door. Seconds later, he reappeared. He'd forgotten the whiskey.

Uncle Gur never announced his visits. There was no point. He knew we never went anywhere. Two long blasts of his truck's horn and his voice thundering from the rolled-down window heralded his arrival. He'd be standing in the driveway with a duffel bag and a bottle of whiskey. Dad would grin and let Uncle Gur take him in his arms, the only times he ever allowed anyone else to embrace him in public.

Those nights when he and Dad stayed up and shared a single bottle of Johnnie Walker, their voices shook the house. Uncle told one joke after another. Dad fell backward and laughed. They moved easily between English and Punjabi, but when they told a joke, they spoke solely Punjabi so at best I understood a quarter and always missed the punch line.

Now that I was sixteen, Uncle insisted I stay up with the men. He had tried this on Jag, but Jag ignored him as easily as he ignored the rest of us. Mom sat with us until she fell asleep. Dad would poke her and she would rise and depart, and I'd be left alone with the men.

When no one was watching, I'd steal a sip of whiskey and fall asleep, bored by all the quarter-heard jokes.

Uncle sold insurance, usually to other Indians, mostly Sikhs, who lived up in the mountains or in small desert communities, owning the only motel or liquor store for a hundred miles around. I stayed with him a few times and tagged along on sales calls. When we came upon one of these lonely outposts it felt like driving up to a fort in the Old West, beleaguered on all sides by combative natives. There was always the smell of onions frying, framed photographs of holy shrines, and whispered foreign tongues, Punjabi, Hindi, Urdu. Uncle Gur would be ushered into a stuffy room with couches covered in plastic and photographs of the children on the walls, the boys always above the girls, and a petrified forest of knickknacks sitting on the shelves.

He started soft. The benefits of insurance, the dangers of the desert life or the mountain life, the roads, the drunks, the fires. This policy versus that policy. Various rates and returns. None of this ever worked.

The man sitting opposite would invariably rub the back of his neck or the tops of his thighs and say that this was all very good, but it was also very expensive. He was a poor man, eking out a living in a new country.

Uncle Gur was always ready with deals and discounts. A Fellow Sikh discount, a Fellow Indian discount, a Friend of a Relative discount, a New Baby Boy in the Family discount, a So Sorry You Have Three Daughters discount, a Fuck Pakistan discount, a Fellow Drunken Shithead discount, a Screw Those Racist American Moneygrubbing Bastards discount.

Name the prejudice, Uncle Gur had a policy ready and waiting.

He'd undertaken a serious study of the American psyche upon arriving in the US and discovered that people here hated one another as much as they did in India. The major difference was that here, they were willing to stake money on their prejudices. This, to him, was the American Way.

When all his pre-packaged discounts failed, he dropped to his knees and begged. This worked once when I was with him. When begging failed, he'd start to curse, and threaten to ruin the man's reputation, and storm out of the house and slam the door on his way out.

"Don't think you're ever going to get one of your blasted daughters married, not if I have a say in it!" he shouted as he raced for the truck.

In the cab, he'd be grinning from ear to ear, rejoicing equally in not selling a policy as when he succeeded.

"Did you see the face on that bastard?"

If by some miracle he caught a sucker on the line, he habitually pulled a bait and switch, raising the premium and reducing or eliminating the benefit. It was his duty as an American, he told me once, to cheat his clients. To his credit, he was fair. He did the same to Sikhs, Hindus, and whites alike. Only Muslims got special treatment. He enjoyed screwing them. "They live in filth," he assured me. "I have to wash myself from head to toe after I go into one of their houses!" But the times we visited a Muslim home to sell a policy, it looked like any other: the same knickknacks, the same plastic on the couches, the same anguished face of a middle-aged man explaining how he was a poor man trying to eke out a living in a new country, and all the while Uncle talked endlessly of how proud he was as a Sikh to know such kind and noble Muslims.

Someone was always suing him when they discovered the bait and switch, but Uncle Gur knew that his reputation was unlikely to be tarnished. "These bastards all hate each other," he told me once. "If I screw them, they're not going to tell anyone. Too embarrassing! They're all ashamed of their own shadows. And they'll know I'm screwing the others too. You know what they're going to do. They're going to sing my bloody praises to the bloody heavens! And then they're going to sit back and laugh!"

One time, he was sentenced to five years in the state penitentiary for wire and mail fraud and just about every other kind of fraud on the books. He accused the black DA of racism and consequently the term was reduced to six months' probation and the fine wiped out.

TWENTY-ONE

THE NEXT MORNING, UNCLE GUR WAS ONCE MORE STANDING at the end of my bed and clapping his hands and shouting for me to get on my feet. He was dressed in a white kurta pajama cinched at his waist and his long black hair riddled over his shoulders in tortured strands.

"You can't lie there all day. We've got your brother to find. Do you think he's going to find himself?"

He started a session of jumping jacks and insisted I join. The strange excitement of the day before lingered and along with it a memory of that terror I'd felt when I called Eddie. I watched Uncle Gur with amusement and told myself that I would build a new country with Lily and no one would have to jump like this ever again.

Our antics shook the house and Mom shouted at us from the kitchen to stop. She'd decided to spend the whole week at home. It wasn't out of concern for her eldest son's absence, she insisted. She had talked to him and knew all about his vacation.

Every boy needed time off, she said.

She had decided to follow Jag's example, take a few days to herself, things were slow at work, why not take the week. There was so much to do at home after all.

She fretted between the kitchen and the living room and the bedroom, starting one project, putting it down, starting another, forgetting which one she was working on. She announced she was off to the stores, but the moment she found herself standing at the threshold, dressed now for a long afternoon wandering through the mall, in comfortable shoes and a simple jacket, she stopped and changed her mind. There was nothing she needed, and she would waste money. No, no, she ought to stay, she sighed, and shut the door and turned and stared at the telephone and asked if anyone had called.

Of course no one had. She'd been home to listen.

After the morning calisthenics, Uncle Gur enlisted my help in tying his turban. It was inconceivable to him that I didn't know how.

A Sikh who can't tie a turban! He'd make it his solemn duty to teach me.

I stood at one end of the hall while he took up residence at the other, and we folded gauzy yellow fabric between our fingers until it formed a loose rope. After gathering this, I watched as he wound it around his head. When it came to teaching me how to tie my own, Uncle Gur decided he was hungry.

"Eat first, then work!" he announced. He shouted for my mother, "Well, I'm not going to look for your son on an empty stomach!"

Soon he was sitting at the dinner table, tapping his knuckles against the plastic cover. One, two, three, four butter-soaked parathas later, he stood, brushed the food from his mustache and beard, and plopped onto the couch, groaning with enthusiasm about my mother's cooking. His own wife was useless. How lucky my father was!

Any idea of instructing me on how to tie a turban was forgotten. Further, it was soon clear Uncle's method of searching for his lost nephew consisted of picking up the telephone and yelling at someone about one of his insurance policies, after which he'd return to the couch and complain of a headache while he massaged his unwieldy feet.

If the phone rang and it was for him, he waved his arms furiously.

"No, no! I'm not here!"

The moment he said that, he raced to the phone and shouted that the man calling was a goddam bastard and how dare

he call here—*here!*—where he was on important family business searching for his nephew.

"Don't you know he's gone missing? I'll have your balls
for dinner!"

Saying that, he slammed the phone down and turned to me.

"Why do you let these good-for-nothing Paki niggers call?
Don't pick up the phone next time, okay!"

Next time the phone rang, I stood idly by. Uncle roared
from his perch at my mother. "Where's that bastard son of
yours? Does no one answer the phone in this house?"

I picked it up, only to be confronted by a voice screaming
on the other end. Holding the handset at arm's length, I could
still hear the incensed squawk.

The ballet repeated itself, with Uncle eventually returning
to the couch laughing about how much he loved doing business in America.

"This story of Jigu is gold. I call these rotten liars up and
tell them I can't say a word, not one word, because here I am,
searching for my nephew. Can I sell them anything? Bloody
no! Not one thing! What kind of man do they think I am? This
is family emergency, they ask me to work during family emergency?! Next week, when that bastard boy returns, I'll have
these monkeys by the balls, they'll be bending over and whip-
ping themselves to buy something from me. I promise you,
next week I'll be selling hurricane coverage in the mountains!"

Later, Uncle Gur finally stirred himself and found me and
said we should do it, we should go hunt for my lost brother.

"We'll find your son," he promised Mom.

She didn't see the point. The boy was on vacation, he was
having a good time, Uncle Gur was making a fuss over nothing as he always did.

We took the road east, through Valley towns no one ever stopped
in and no one ever left with their dusty general stores and flac-
cid levees. These were the kind of towns that raised me. I knew
down to my bones the lazy-eyed routine of days here. As a kid,

I'd watched trucks shoot by on the highway, or lay on my back and watched crop dusters arc through the ozone blue of the hazy skies. Uncle Gur said little, and without having to tell me, I knew this journey had nothing to do with actually finding Jag. What it was about, I wasn't sure. Maybe reassuring Mom, maybe reassuring me, or maybe Uncle just had nothing better to do with himself. I didn't mind. I was glad to get out of the house.

In this blank landscape, alternating between the harsh green of irrigated fields and dust blowing along the arid roads, I remembered how Dad's suspicions of those around us only grew and usually extended to our new neighbors. He'd greet a friendly knock on the door with a hello, a brief conversation about the weather or the day's news, and then immediately retreat. With the door shut, he'd pour abuse on the man or woman who had dared to say hello, for no doubt they were after something. If the man was black or Mexican, he was sure his sole purpose was to case the house for a future burglary. We moved every couple of years, usually when Mom or Jag or myself started to make friends. No reason was given and often no notice. Dad had found a new house in a new town. That was all. Jag and I were packed up like luggage and carried along.

One year he promised things were about to change and we drove as a family to Fresno for the weekend, where he was going to apply to be a franchise owner for a mini-mart. An extraordinary thing happened. We stayed in an actual motel, which I'd never done before, and in the morning, Dad dressed himself in a suit and tie. He'd bought the tie especially for the interview.

"These things make money hand over fist," he said to Mom. "And there's no work. You could do it and sit at home all day. You hire a couple stupid fellows and make sure they don't steal and a couple times a day you drive over and take the money."

Mom warned him he shouldn't talk like that in the interview and he got immediately angry.

"No one's going to tell me how to talk! I've seen these fellows, they're so fat they can't even get out of their chairs, and what do they do? Nothing! Not one bloody thing except make money hand over fist!"

Two hours later he returned, the tie missing and the shirt unbuttoned at the top, his face a clenched study in fury. The long drive back he said nothing. The windows were open and the wind whipped through the car. It was only when we reached the outskirts of our town that he spoke.

"He was one of those fat bastards," he said, and added with an extended sneer, "Mister Arvind bastard Sharma. Couldn't get out of his bloody chair." He let out a mocking laugh and the subject of owning a mini-mart was never raised again.

Sometimes he kept the impending move a secret even from Mom, causing one of their week-long arguments. It didn't change anything. When it was time to leave, she'd throw her clothes into black garbage bags and pull them out to the truck while Dad bickered with the driver over the route or the price. If the truck was too small, rather than hiring a larger one, he'd pull mine and Jag's bags off and toss them onto the curb, where they'd sit forlorn, diminishing in the rearview mirror as the truck pulled away.

This was how, one day, Jag lost his drawings and all the plans for his wild inventions, even the ones for the fantastical movie camera. There was room on the truck that day, I was sure of it. But Dad was in a sour mood because the rental company jacked the price up at the last minute and he didn't have an alternative. He pulled out Jag's drawings and unfolded them and stared. The hot sun blasted against the bright white paper.

"What is this?" He turned to me. "This is your homework?"

I only then realized he'd never seen them before.

"They're Jag's," I said, and felt like a traitor.

He called Jag's name and my brother appeared, but he refused to explain what the drawings were and what they were supposed to show. He stood there with arms folded over his chest, watching Dad's hands as he creased the paper each time he looked at a new page. There was no room on the truck, Dad said definitively, these had to stay. He folded them into fours and dropped them on the sidewalk. Jag didn't look down. He walked around to the front of the truck and climbed into the cab, where he remained until we started on our way.

I usually got my handful of prized belongings, which were mostly comic books, onto the truck early and buried them at the back where it was hard for him to search. Mom and I competed over who could get their belongings on first to make sure they wouldn't be thrown out. Jag refused to participate. He watched with blank detachment as, in town after town, the few things he owned were tossed unceremoniously into the trash.

Uncle Gur pulled into the parking lot of an outlet liquor store off Highway 4. He offered no explanation. The whiskey was on sale and he bought a case. I wandered the aisles, admiring the selection, amazed at all the different kinds, and finally asked if I could have a small bottle for myself.

"If you were one of my sons, I'd whip you from here to Mexico." He pulled a fifth from the shelf and slipped it into the cart. "Don't tell your mother. This is between us. Hide it when you get home."

On the drive there and back, neither of us spoke of Jag. I'd thought little of his disappearance, and even now, with Uncle Gur's dramatic arrival, it seemed to take on nothing more than the shape of a bruise, signifying something else, an unseen impact that I was happy to ignore. I thought of the day when he told me to die. I looked back on it as only a sound, a dead limb twitching. I couldn't think about such distractions any longer. I faced larger questions. The more I thought of it, the more I became convinced. Lily and I would found our own nation, hidden in the heart of this world, fight for it and die if necessary.

If I squinted I could almost see it, a shadowland in all this light, beyond the highways and the flattened towns, high up in the mountains, or near the ocean, not even a dot on a map, but somewhere placeless, out of tune with the world around it, where even orphans might find a foothold.

The dry, flat landscape slipped by and Uncle Gur, made voluble perhaps by the happy prospect of all that whiskey, waved his arms, tapped the glass, and said this was what Punjab looked like. He sheltered a dream of returning there. He wanted to move back and start a little honey farm.

"Bees," he said. "What do you think? A life with bees? No more of this bloody bother, just buzz buzz buzz. All the honey you can ask for, fresh air, outside, work with your hands, there you are, master of insects."

One town became another, and propane tanks and idle tractors and the whirr of crop dusters filled the narrow isthmus that was existence here, the world being limited to the width of the horizon. Uncle started talking about the civil war. Or whatever people were calling it. The war for independence, the trouble, the insurrection. He'd been sending money regularly. Many Sikhs abroad had. That's how the rebels bought their guns and bombs. These were real warriors, every one would fight to the death, and before they died, they'd take a dozen of those Indian bastards with them.

He thumped the steering wheel. Soon Khalistan would be free! He could smell it. The coming months would decide it, he said: Would the Sikhs be crushed or would they win a homeland? With victory, he'd have his little honey farm.

"You fly out there," Uncle suddenly offered, squeezing my thigh. "They give you a gun, bombs, whatever you want, you kill those bastards. I'll buy your ticket. No worries. Lot of fun for a young man. You'll be a freedom fighter, like George Washington? They'll give you fresh rotis every day, like home. All you do is shoot. And you blow up trains. Like Rambo. Big bloody explosions." He paused and turned his face to me, "Well, what do you think?"

So this was why he took me out for such an aimless drive, to recruit me for the war in Punjab. The speech sang to all my fantasies. To fight and die for something real. For a homeland, whatever that meant. For a fabled, future Khalistan. I could hardly call myself a Sikh, couldn't speak Punjabi, didn't wear a turban or know how to tie one, and stayed as far away from services at the gurdwara as possible, but instantly I saw myself holding a gun, wearing a bandolier, battling alongside comrades-in-arms, all for a foolhardy country I didn't even believe in. I might have done it too, just to get away, to do something in the world, to act and not to sit at home languishing. Except I knew Dad would say no. Not even Uncle Gur would have been able to persuade Dad to change his mind. Dad was the older brother, his say was final. I said all this, hoping Uncle Gur might have a plan, but he nodded thoughtfully and agreed. "You're right," he mused. "Your father will never say yes."

Not to worry, he assured, because maybe in only a few short months the Sikhs would have their country. As he talked of a Sikh homeland, I thought of mine taking shape, a nation of the heart. With Lily as its Queen.

Mom was sitting by the phone when we returned. Uncle Gur said nothing of our so-called search. I could see she had been crying. I told her we'd find Jag, and that either way he'd come home, there was nothing to worry about.

"I know where he is," she said, flashing me a look of anger. "You think I don't know where my son is?"

She stood and grabbed my shoulder. "No muscles." I pulled away, but she took hold of me again and turned to Uncle Gur. "This one'll never find a wife like this. What do you think?"

Uncle Gur groaned. He had been trying to make an escape, but now stopped and considered me as he pulled at his mustache.

"He's young still," he said finally. "But that doesn't mean we can't start thinking. Let him stay with us, he spends a week, a month, we'll find someone. What do you like? These girls today, they have diplomas, they go to school. Just like you."

I pulled away, feeling hotly superior. "Get off me. I'm not marrying any of those women."

Mom made a face at Uncle Gur. "Look at him, he thinks he's a man now, he can do what he wants."

Uncle Gur grinned. "Don't worry, the boy will get desperate. I've seen it happen. He'll come around."

There *were* girls out there, Mom said, her mood lighter, she'd had offers. "That girl, remember? The one with the magazines? I meet her on the bus sometimes. All she talks about is you, the other one. She said you two had a conversation. Is my boy ready? What's taking him so long? But she's a real low class type." She clicked her tongue in disapproval. "And I know you," she sighed, all the anger gone from her voice, "you don't want one of these gum-chewing monkeys. I always make up some story to tell her."

I thought back to that afternoon while the strange woman had paged through one magazine after another, and I had said not one word to her. Then I remembered. I'd asked her who her favorite movie star was. Was that what she called a conversation? I was glad Mom knew me well enough to keep her at arm's length.

The phone rang. It was for Uncle Gur. My future wife would have to wait for another day. Uncle was soon pouring obscenities into the phone. Mom returned to the kitchen and brought the cleaver down with a thwack onto the chopping block.

I smuggled the fifth Uncle bought me in my jacket and carried it to my car.

I knew where I was going, what I had to do to get there. First I needed Lily's forgiveness. I'd outlined a plan on the drive home with Uncle Gur, a baby step toward winning her back. A love letter, telling her how sorry I was, how much I needed her, my heart spilled onto the page, skewered to the paper itself—just the two of us, the country, against the Eddies of this world. I'd leave it for her before her shift started, so she could read it on her own and in peace.

TWENTY-TWO

A GRAVEL PATH CUT THOUGH THE FRONT LAWN OUTSIDE Chuck's house, or his parents' house, which was where he still lived, snaking for twenty feet and adding useless steps to the distance from the pavement. I kicked at the gravel and let it fly against the window. When I got to the door I ignored the bell and gave the thick oak a kick and shouted Chuck's name. A minute later, there he stood, fat Chuck, stupid Chuck, insensitive Chuck, boring Chuck, delusional Chuck, half-mad Chuck, who-the-hell-did-he-think-he-was-calling-himself-my-friend Chuck.

Before he could say a word, I pounced on him and started punching him in the face.

An hour earlier, I'd been sitting at the counter at the diner where Lily worked, composing that letter of apology in my head. The plainspoken note I'd finally written, those simple words, "I'm sorry," repeated over and over, said all I was able to, however inarticulately. The old poets, the dead ones I would come to read, wrote that tragedy is born from a defect in character, that our fates are twinned with the deepest impulses of our souls. I would learn something different. The birth of tragedy is silence, and the birth of silence is a failure to see. There was so much I was blind to that day and so much I remained silent about. Even as I walked out of that diner, the thick-armed waitress' fury ringing in my ears, I couldn't see the mirror that was being held up to my own actions; and if I couldn't see that, how much else did I miss?

Weeks later, as I wandered lost, an outcast on the desolate northern coast, little more than an orphan, I'd think back to that afternoon as I retreated out of the diner and ask myself if it was my rage that day, and in days to come, that left me blind. I walked to my car and started the engine, feeling the thrum of hatred inside me, so that all I saw was a world painted within the frame of my own impotent rage and longing. I'd soon be a murderer, or that's what I was called and would call myself, and wondered if the birth of that particular tragedy was born then, when I took the car east, still intent on getting Lily back, along those same blank boulevards that had led me here, eyeless in a rising storm.

Chuck grabbed my wrists, twisted me around, and threw me face-first onto the gravel and dug a knee into my back.

"What the fuck! What the goddam fuck!"

My face hit the ground hard and I let out a cry and swore at him, and he twisted my arm further. I was surprised how fast and strong he was. His leaned forward and brought his mouth to my ear.

"You kick my goddam door, you punch me in the face, I mean what the goddam fuck!"

My arm was beginning to hurt and I did my best to cry uncle, but Chuck wasn't mollified.

"What the goddam fuck is going on with you?"

Finally I said, "Lily, it's that woman Lily," and I felt the pressure ease.

"Lily, huh?" he said.

"Yeah."

After a few seconds, he released his grip and helped me to my feet. My back and face stung and I brushed the gravel from my shirt. He looked me up and down and shook his head in disgust.

"Come inside," he said.

"Have any beers?" I asked, walking past him into the kitchen.

He did, he said, but he didn't see how I was going to get one. I ignored him and opened the refrigerator and pulled out a can. This did not please Chuck.

"What the fuck is going on?"

I mocked him. *"'What the fuck is going on?'"*

He grabbed a can of beer for himself and told me to take my goddam can and get out, not come back until I was sober.

I mocked him again, and just as he was about to start shouting, I threw the can on the floor and flew at him, using my head as a battering ram. I hit him square in the belly and he flopped back and crashed to the ground. I was on top of him in an instant and started pummeling his face. This time I had the advantage. I called him all sorts of names as I hit him. It felt good. People always say violence feels good, but I never believed them, but here I was, hitting my best friend in the face and enjoying it mightily.

After I'd got in three or four good punches, Chuck kneed me hard in the stomach and threw me off him. My head banged against the floor and in a second he was standing over me. He landed one mighty kick in my gut and my whole body exploded in pain. A second one curled me into a whimpering ball.

He aimed a third kick but held it suspended in midair.

"Are you done?"

I nodded weakly.

He shook his head and dropped the leg.

"Get the fuck up, asshole."

His nose was bleeding and his cheek looked cut. I felt proud of that, but also surprised. The anger that had launched my body against his was nowhere to be found, and I felt a strange slackness in my spirit, as if something had been pulled out of it. The room looked gray and dull, like the set for a sit-com shot in the Soviet Union.

Beer was spilled all over the kitchen floor, and after wiping his own face, Chuck started mopping it up. I offered to help but he told me to stay the fuck away.

I sat down at the table. My belly was singing in agony.

"Well?" Chuck said finally. He leaned the mop against the wall and pulled two beers out of the fridge. His own had gone flying when I attacked him.

I opened my can and took a drink. I didn't know what to say. As far as I was concerned, my world was over. Lily hated me, her co-workers hated me, and I hated home and my family and everyone I knew.

"I should throw you out," Chuck said. "Tell you never to come anywhere near me again."

"Why dontcha?"

"Because I'm a friend."

"Yeah?"

"Is that what you want?"

"I don't care. Do whatever you want."

I finished half the beer and stood to leave.

"Shit," he said, looking at me and shaking his head. "C'mon, I've gotta walk the dog." I must've looked a sight for Chuck not to happily get rid of me right then. After what I'd done, I was amazed I was still in that house.

I shrugged. "Whatever."

The sun was low and the cul-de-sac was stirring into its evening ritual, a slow drowning in gray tones spilling from the hills. I leaned against the hood of his Toyota and watched him disappear around the side of the house. A minute later, Fred let out a sharp bark. This was Chuck's dog, a mostly black mutt who lived in the backyard.

Chuck underarmed a tennis ball down the road. Fred barked and bolted after it. The ball bounced and rolled down the slope and was lost beyond the corner. The road swam in the warm tones of my drunkenness and I no longer cared why I was bothering to stand out here with Chuck.

"There's something I gotta tell you," Chuck said.

"What?"

"I'm gonna be in movies."

I rolled my eyes. "Oh yeah, Steven Spielberg finally got you on the blower?"

"Not those kinda movies, I'm talking the movies people really watch."

"Huh?"

"Porn. I'm gonna be a porn star."

I looked at him, fat, heavy-breathing Chuck. He was already sweating from throwing the ball. "You?"

"It's a different industry, everything's changing, it's not all six-pack abs and a dinosaur-sized schlong. People wanna see themselves, and there's a whole lotta guys out there like me, fat asses. Erika thinks I have potential."

"Erica?"

Obviously he read my mind, because he corrected my imaginary spelling. "With a K. She's German. Erika von Something-or-other. She's got her own production company, started out in Berlin, now just moving here. She likes the sunshine. And she likes making movies about people who just look average, says there's a market for fat-ass porn, a lotta people get off on watching fat guys getting fucked."

"Don't you mean fucking?"

"That too. I did a screen test." He added, "You want me to tell you about it?"

"Sure," I said, wondering how long Chuck could keep up either the delusion or the charade.

It all happened in one room. They gave him a joint and handed him a bottle of oil. It was just Chuck and the camera and Erika von Whatever telling him what to do. Look seductive, unbutton your shirt, massage your balls through your pants. Finally, he had his dick out and I wondered when the woman was supposed to show up. He lay there stroking himself, dripping oil onto his dick. The guy with the camera kept zooming in for close-ups and the German woman kept telling him how big his dick was.

The door opened and another guy walked in. He was naked and already oiled up.

"A guy?" I said, still not getting it.

Chuck said nothing and Fred ran back up the road toward us. "So?" I said.

"I kissed him," Chuck said. He got off the couch and kissed the guy on the lips. It went on for quite a while. They did other things too, a lot of other things, just about anything a person could possibly imagine one man doing with another man.

"Oh," I said.

"Are you going to say something?"

"Like what?"

"Like call me a name?"

I didn't say anything for a minute, and finally I said, "No."

"Good."

"So?"

"They want me back. I have potential. Do you want to see the tape?"

I shook my head. I *really* did not want to see the tape. Chuck gay, Chuck an aspiring porn star? It shook everything I knew about him and it gave me a sick feeling. Maybe nothing I knew about anyone was true.

"How long you known?" I said.

"About what?"

"About uh, you know—being gay."

He shrugged. "It matters?"

That was classic Chuck. Drop a bombshell and then pretend it's nothing. I wanted to punch him again, but told myself I couldn't just because he was gay. The whole thing was disturbing me greatly. It wasn't just Chuck being a porn star, if the story was true. It was Chuck being sexual, actually having sex, and talking about it like it was normal and natural and happened to people like Chuck. I hated him for being so easy about it, but that seemed too petty a kind of hate to really get behind. If I was going to punch him for a third time tonight, I needed something bigger.

"You've done this before? I mean with guys."

"A few times," he said.

"But when we go to Bill's."

"Those booths are private, man, you have no idea what I'm looking at."

"Why you telling me this now?"

"Looked like you shook the fight out of you."

He was mostly right, but I knew if he kept on giving me non-answers things would change, and change quickly.

"So how did you find out?"

He shook his head in dismay. "How did you find out you were straight?"

"So you've been lying to me the whole time?"

"Sure I have," he said, like there wasn't even a question about it. "And? That got some point to it, 'cos if it has, you're a long way from getting it across."

"I'm just trying to figure this out."

He looked at me and shook his head in that way only Chuck could, a gesture that held pretty much a whole world's withering disdain inside it. I knew it then, it was either punch or figure something else out. My best bet would be just to walk away, but I couldn't. I had too many questions.

"Okay, so you wanna know something," he said finally, throwing the words at me, as if he was being forced to make a confession. "Couple years ago, I started going to bars, that sorta thing. Gay bars out on Polk in the city and a new one out here, on Camino Diablo, place called Just Rewards. Heard of it?" I hadn't, and he continued, "But the thing is, I've always known, man, just never knew what to do with it. I mean it's not something you just start yakking about. Shit has consequences. Next thing you're probably gonna ask is if I've secretly wanted to bone you this whole time." He was right again, which pissed me off. Before I could deny it, he added, "The answer is none of your business. Do you ask all the women you know if they wanna bone you?"

Fred barked from down the road and came running back at us.

"C'mon," he said. "Let's go for a walk."

He pushed through a break in the backyard fence and reluctantly I followed him out onto the lower slopes of a hill.

We were both carrying our beers. I felt supremely unhappy climbing that hill, for I had lost the sexually clueless and insecure Chuck I had always known and found in his place someone who seemed to know more about himself and the world than I possibly ever could. It was unfair, and I felt small for thinking that. For the first time since I'd known him I was actually jealous of Chuck. The grass was knee-high and already a crisp yellow. We ascended in silence along a deer track with Fred running ahead. The evening drone of insects sifted through the air while clouds of flies appeared dark against the failing light.

The dog ran back and forth, twisting his head and panting.

The crest afforded a view of a wedge of town life with lights snapping on while the dying sun crowded out the day to leave long shadows drowning the valleys. I lit a cigarette and finished the beer and crushed the can in my hand and dropped it onto the ground.

"That's littering," Chuck said.

I had to stop myself from leaping on him, I was so wound up. Chuck bent down and retrieved the can, and all I wanted was to kick him. Just as suddenly I felt close to bursting into tears. I had lost Lily and nothing would bring her back. I would not speak to her, I would not touch her, I would not kiss her, and we would never run away and build our secret country in the hills. I looked at Chuck—fat, ridiculous Chuck who might soon be well-adjusted gay Chuck. He stuffed the can into his pocket and I closed my eyes and tried to tell myself that I was not here, I could not be, that this was not my world.

"Do something for me," I said. It was all I could think of to say to stop me from trying to knock his head off one more time.

"What?"

"Close your eyes."

"Why?"

"Just do it. Please. Chuck. Just do it." A tone of desperation rose in my voice. The idea came in a flash. What it meant, what I was trying to do, I couldn't possibly articulate. What I knew was this: that I could not live in a world with the thought that I would never touch Lily again.

"What you gonna do? Hit me?"

"No," I said.

What I wanted was simple. Chuck would say he was Lily, and I would kiss him. Nothing more. All I wanted was that he close his eyes and tell me he was the woman I loved and let me kiss him.

He looked at me angrily. "This some gay-baiting shit?"

I promised it wasn't, it had nothing to do with that. It took Chuck a minute to consider, but finally he agreed, telling me he thought it was the stupidest idea I'd ever had, and I'd had some dumb ones.

He closed his eyes. "I am Lily," he said mechanically.

"Say it like you mean it."

"Like what?"

I showed him how, trying my best to re-create Lily's voice.

He said it several times, with me coaching, telling him to soften his voice, to find the right tone. I stood rooted and listening, my eyes shut, asking him to say it again.

And again. And again.

Then I heard her. I heard Lily. It was Chuck's voice, sure, but he said it with tenderness, with a surprising beauty, that for a moment I was convinced, or told myself I was.

She was standing feet from me. All I had to do was take a step forward. I took Chuck's face in my hands and pressed my lips to his dry, flat mouth. He tensed, pulled back, and allowed himself finally to be kissed. His lips were rough. They felt like cardboard. It was a shock, because I had *believed*—I somehow actually expected to taste Lily's lips.

I wrapped my arms around his body and grabbed hold and kissed as hard as I could, telling myself that this was Lily, Lily my love, and kept on kissing him and pushed my tongue between his lips. I had never kissed anyone, not properly, not like this, and I wondered if it was that much different between a woman and a man. I felt miserable as I pulled away, and I was amazed at myself for thinking it might have worked. Seeing Chuck's face and not hers, I knew I had to get out of there, and quickly. It made me want to punch him again.

"Well?" he said.

I didn't know what to say except that I'd been wrong about a lot of things. "Maybe everything."

Chuck nodded. "That ain't news. By the way, I didn't feel anything," he added.

"Really?" That annoyed me. He should've felt something, especially if he was the gay one here.

"Nope," he said. "You're a friend. I think I like it when I don't know who the guy is, not even his name or nothing. That's what turns me on."

Without saying a word, I turned and started walking. Chuck was the real man here, not me, and that made me even madder at him. Fred barked and ran beside me and I could hear Chuck laboring down the hill after me. His breathing came in bursts and as he followed he shouted for me to wait. I ignored him and quickened my pace. Fred's teeth glinted in the moonlight and the first stars showed themselves beyond the blank horizon of darkened suburban homes.

When I reached the street, I didn't turn to see where Chuck was. I climbed into the car and started the engine, and as the headlights arced in a semi-circle through the cul-de-sac, they caught one last image of Chuck struggling heavily through the break in the fence, waving an arm wildly, calling on me to stop.

It was an image of my own humiliation, and I turned the car as quickly as I could and drove away fast.

TWENTY
THREE

DAD KNOCKED ON MY BEDROOM DOOR AND WALKED INSIDE.
The knock was uncharacteristically soft, as was his demeanor
when he entered. I was sitting up in bed, reading, and he took the
wooden chair next to the desk and casually opened and closed
one of my textbooks. The air quickly became tense with the smell
of his aftershave.

"Dad?" I said.

He said nothing for a minute, and I struggled to remember the
last time, any time actually, that he had just walked into my room
and sat down. Sitting there, squeezed into the chair, he looked
like a seasoned boxer who'd been forced, against his will, to read
stories to a kindergarten class.

It was Saturday and we hadn't heard a word from Jag all
week. Three days had passed since my encounter with Chuck
and the disastrous afternoon at the diner. I still felt the sting of
that day in my bones and continued to wonder what I had been
looking for. Perhaps I just wanted to see where I would take all
of it, how far I would push my anger and sense of dislocation.
I really didn't know. All I knew for certain was that I could feel
my world falling apart, and the one thing I didn't want to do was
look for a way to stop the collapse.

Dad, who had yet to acknowledge me sitting there in bed,
opened a notebook, shut it, turned it upside down, examined the

spiral binding, then pushed it brusquely away as if it had failed some fundamental test.

Finally, he said, "This bloody brother of yours. Do you know where he is?"

"No idea."

He shook his head and scratched the back of his hand. "Then you tell me, where do you think he spends his time? Where does he go when he's not at home?"

I had little idea about that either, but I could make a few educated guesses. There were a couple of bars, a bowling alley I remember he'd talked about, and of course there were local hotels and places in San Francisco. He might be at any of those.

"Hotels?" Dad said. The idea seemed novel to him.

"He has to sleep somewhere," I said.

"Does he have friends?"

"I don't think so. Not anywhere. At least I've never met them."

He stood and walked to the window and made a show of looking out and up at the sky.

"Bloody hot day."

"Probably," I said.

Still looking up at the sky, he said, "Today, this afternoon, you and me, we go for a drive. We go to these places, we'll look for him. Think about where to go."

"Sure."

"Don't tell your mother. Tell her you're helping with the shopping. She worries too much." He tapped the glass. "Look at that, all those bloody weeds. Bloody water wasters." He was pointing at Mom's herb garden, where she grew Indian herbs and spices she couldn't easily find in the stores. He added, "When we go out, you will do the talking, you understand?"

"To who?"

"To anyone, these people, at bars, at hotels. You talk to them. I don't know how. I'm not good at talking to people."

The surprising admission, the most personal he'd ever made about himself, filled me with a rare warmth.

"And if we don't find him?" I ventured.

"Then on Monday we call the police. And you do that, not me. I don't want to talk to those bastards."

He walked out, leaving only the lingering scent of his aftershave spreading through the air, and me wondering at all the other hidden admissions, the cloaked vulnerabilities, that must be lurking under the bully's mantle.

Later that morning, the front door opened and Jag walked in. Just like that, as if he really had been on vacation. The sun was no longer slanting through the windows and a tedious gloom had settled over the house. He looked like an apparition, with a fine coating of dust on his face. A week's growth of beard wrapped his chin and his shoelaces were untied. It was obvious he'd slept in his clothes. Mom and I watched, in breathless silence, as he kicked his shoes off and sent them flying through the air. They were caked in dried mud and landed in the middle of the living room and exploded in a plume of dirt. He hadn't washed either. An unmistakable stench of something rotting followed him from room to room.

"See!" Mom said, turning to me. "My boy's back!" She clapped her hands in tense excitement.

Jag walked into the living room, dropped onto the red velvet couch, and picked up the remote control and tuned the channel to MTV.

"I told you he'd be home, and now he is." Beaming, she started making everyone a cup of tea.

Dad walked in from the garden, hands filthy and face streaked in dirt. He'd spent the morning weeding in the backyard. A track of muddy footprints followed him across the carpet. He looked little different from Jag.

"This one's back," he said. His eyes betrayed a momentary relief as they glided across the room and found Mom. "What're you doing? Look at him. He needs food, not tea."

He crouched in front of Jag and rapped his knuckles against the coffee table and started talking rapidly.

"Have a good trip? Little vacation? Seen the world? Took a tour of the sights? Now you're back, time for work again? Did you see the fat man? Say hello to him? I bet he was asking about me. Where's my money? Is that what he said? Next time you see him, tell him to come right here. I'll tell him to his face. I'll throw my dollars at him, the bastard."

Dad continued like this, craning forward across the table and sending soil from the garden scattering in all directions. All the buried concern he'd shown in my bedroom that morning was gone. As Dad talked, Jag pressed the volume button on the remote control and the sound coming from the television gradually rose. It reached a piercing screech and Dad started shouting over it.

Without warning, Dad slammed his palm against the table. I jumped halfway out of my chair. Jag didn't so much as flinch. It was as if he were totally deaf.

"Listen to me, you little bastard!" Dad thundered. "Next time you do something like that, don't come back! I'll cut your balls off if I see you again!"

Jag remained sitting. His hand clutched the remote control and his eyes were fixed on the television. Dad straightened and turned back to Mom.

"Well! This boy's not getting any fatter. Look at him, he's hungry."

Saying that, he returned to the garden. A minute later, we heard his loud grunt as he struck soil with a shovel. Jag remained sitting. I walked over and sat down beside him.

Mom shouted from the kitchen, "That's right, talk to him."

The stench rising off him was overpowering. He smelled like garbage and days-old food and things dead by the side of the road. I poked him in the shoulder with a finger and leaned in close.

"Bastard," I whispered viciously. "You should've stayed out there and never come home. Now everyone'll pretend nothing is wrong, that it's all fine, that we're one goddam happy family here."

He turned his head and studied me with his bloodshot eyes. He raised an arm and took hold of my hand and brought my palm up to his face. With a single quick motion, he spat into the middle of it.

I pulled away and stood, and a sudden, surging hatred blasted through me. It had been him, all these years, around whom we had all circled, the great silence around which our own petty silences were built. I saw it with sudden clarity. He was the source of our problems—all that we couldn't speak about—his madness, his endless stream of bizarre notions and theories. The rot of never being able to say a word against him had seeped into every thought and conversation until we were mute and lost and compassless.

I leaned over and rubbed my hand on his shirt. It left a streak of mud.

"Go fuck yourself and die," I whispered.

Mom called as I passed back through the kitchen. "Did he tell you about his vacation?"

Early that evening, Mom lit a stick of incense and carried it from room to room, waving it in a circle over her head wherever she walked. She planted it near Jag in the living room.

"For good luck," she said, and told me she was looking forward to having a long talk with her son and hearing all about his adventures. But that night, Jag locked himself away. When it came time for dinner, first I was asked to knock, and on returning defeated, Mom rapped her knuckles against the door and forcefully tried the handle.

"Food," she shouted. "You need to eat."

She too was pitched back, having elicited no response.

"The boy is tired," she concluded. "He must be sleeping."

Dad sat moodily at the card table, manipulating the remote control, raising and lowering the volume, changing channels, until banging it down and declaring that tomorrow he would throw that goddam useless television out onto the bastard street where it belonged with all the other trash.

Jag finally emerged the following afternoon, still unwashed, carrying armloads of magazines. He walked abruptly into the kitchen and stalked through the living room and out to the garage and the trash cans. Mom and I watched as he repeated this journey several times, depositing armload after armload of his precious magazines into the trash.

We could smell him too. Mom held her nose and complained of the stench from the trash.

"It's not the trash, Mom. It's Jag."

She turned sharply on me. "Why do you say things like that? You have no respect, do you? Not for anyone. This is your brother you're talking about."

The smell of Jag spread like a corruption through the house. I could smell it in my own clothes and on my skin.

More than just magazines disappeared. Records, books, clothes all joined the exodus. Jag was emptying out his entire room. Dad took no notice of the commotion, and Mom seized the opportunity to light one stick of incense after another. She placed these throughout the house and announced Jag had the right idea. "Throw out the old," she said. "Get ready for the new." Mom certainly had the right idea. The incense soon overpowered the reek coming from Jag's body.

"Tomorrow, he will go back to work," Mom said when Jag finally joined us for dinner. "Everything will be like it was."

Thankfully, he had decided to shower before he took his usual seat in front of the television. Dad occupied the card table and I sat at the dinner table.

"This is my family," Mom said, handing Jag a plate. "Just like I always wanted it."

I could hear the strain in her voice.

Jag said nothing and turned the volume on the television up.

That night, Mom sat up and we shared cups of tea. She wanted to talk, she said, she'd had a chat with Jag. Cleared the air, learned about where his recent travels took him, everything.

"He talked, huh?" I evaluated sarcastically.

"Of course he talked. He talks to me."

He told her about his vacation, the places he visited, where he stayed, that no one should be worried about him, he was quite okay. He had a good time, felt healthy. And now he was rested. That's what was important. Whatever might have been bothering him was gone. She snapped her fingers to emphasize the point. He was a changed man, and we would see it in the days to come. "That boy will do great things," she promised. "He will outshine all of us."

If I said anything to contradict her, she would have told me I was lying, that I was jealous, that this was what I always did, so I sat there with my fury intact and my fists clenched under the table.

Mom carried the mugs to the sink and started humming a tune. It was one of the songs she used to sing when I was a child and I remembered falling asleep to it in her arms. She looked happier than I had seen in a long time and I wanted nothing more at that moment than to grab hold of that happiness and strangle it, because to me it was built on nothing but lies, lies that had for years been slowly killing all of us. What I didn't know, and what I would only come to understand long after it was too late, was that it was precisely those lies that had kept her alive, kept all of us alive in some sense. It was all she had, her only defense and perhaps her sole power. I suspect she understood better than any of us that admitting to the larger lies that ruled our days would have destroyed us much faster than admitting to the lies she peddled.

TWENTY
FOUR

A RARE MOOD OF CELEBRATION UNSETTLED THE HOUSE
the following week. Mom readied a freshly prepared meal
every night. All of Jag's favorites—old favorites, of course,
from childhood, from the time when he still held such prefer-
ences—one directly on the heels of the other. Surprisingly, the
warm feelings extended even to Dad.

"He's had his fun," he said, energetically finishing off his
dinner on Sunday night. He sounded enormously relieved. It
was not only that Jag was back but that the house was now
returned to its previous order. Any headache of going out to
look for his son was gone. "Now the boy's a man," he added
in conclusion.

That was it, Dad's years-long ordeal at fatherhood success-
fully concluded. It was as if he'd awarded himself a diploma
with a blue ribbon dangling from it announcing him Dad of
the Year. He bought a bottle of Johnnie Walker to celebrate
and sat in pajamas in a plastic lawn chair, while the evening
light sauntered into darkness beyond surrounding trees.

He called me over and offered a sip. "First time, eh?" he
said. "Not bad?"

He spoke drunkenly of the gurus and their wisdom and the
battles they had fought to keep their religion alive. Many had
been martyred, including their children, with some tortured

and beheaded. This warmed him up and he launched into the story of my namesake, who continued to fight an army of Mughal warriors even after his own head was severed from his body. Despite having lost his head, Deep remained undaunted. On he walked, for fifty miles, while reducing countless thousands of his foes to little more than butchered meat before collapsing himself.

Oh, and those British bastards, Dad spat, stealing everything! And Nehru and his wretched clan. Look at what they did to India. Trashed it! Raped it! Nothing good was left after that gang of hoodlums got their hands on it.

Later, hoisting the remote control over his head while sitting behind his dinnertime perch, Dad raised the possibility of allowing Mom to hold an Akhand Path.

Mom stared in disbelief. This was a puja, or ceremony, and required a full reading of the Guru Granth, the holy book. It celebrated special events—births, marriages, new homes—and lasted two whole days and nights and bestowed God's blessing on the family and household.

We'd never held one before, Dad tirelessly vetoed it. It cost a lot of money. Hiring readers was required, and also musicians, and a room had to be set aside, while family and friends were invited and everyone fed three times a day, including strangers off the street.

Mom walked from the kitchen to where Dad sat eating and snatched the remote control from his hand. She turned the television off and blocked his path to prevent him switching it back on at the set. All her suspicions were aroused.

"You never wanted it before," she said. Her hands were covered in flour and sent a cloud into the air. "Every time you say no. Why should I believe you this time?"

It was her most cherished dream. A properly performed Akhand Path would bring order to the house, right the wrongs, forge us into a real family. She had pleaded with Dad for years, and for years he refused her. Too expensive, too much mumbo jumbo, all the leaches would crawl out of the woodwork demanding to be fed, etc. This time, Dad grunted in dismay. With the television off, he found himself forced to turn and face Mom.

He shrugged noncommittally.

"Why not? We have to do it sometime. If not now, then when these idiot boys get married. Look at that one." He tossed a finger vaguely in my direction. "He's not getting younger. He'll say yes someday. Big wedding, all that expense." Dad scowled. "These things have to be done. Puja, why not?"

Mom said nothing and handed back the remote control and retreated to the kitchen, where she finished making the last of the rotis for dinner. If she heard anything of what Dad said, she refused to show it, pretending no discussion of a puja had ever taken place.

Only as the evening progressed did cracks appear in her facade. I spotted her bustling back and forth from the bedroom, carrying a crumbling green address book into which years of phone numbers had been painstakingly copied, waiting patiently for such an event. Included here was our entire family, inscribed with the hope that one day they would need to be telephoned. The only such occasions when this might happen would be a marriage, a birth, a death, or the decision to hold an Akhand Path.

She held the phone book tightly in her fist and tapped it against her knee and stared at my father, weighing the possibility of betrayal. By night's end, all circumspection fled. She was on the telephone, discussing dates, soliciting recommendations for granthis, the holy men who would read the book, inviting farflung family and friends. Any doubts she might have that Dad did not positively agree to hold a puja were buried, and Dad, sitting in his pajamas in front of the television, ignored the rising commotion with the equanimity of a stone god.

In the days that followed, the phone never saw so much activity, not even during Uncle Gur's frantic visits. The moment Mom arrived home, she dropped her purse onto the sofa, made herself a cup of tea, and stationed herself next to it, paging through the small green address book and dialing numbers on the rotary phone.

A date was set for the weekend after next, granthis were agreed upon and hired, and an army of distant relatives and friends were harassed with invitations. I had never seen Mom so excited. It was a full practice run for the day Jag or I would get married. All night long, I heard her proud voice on the phone.

"Yes, we're holding an Akhand Path. That's right, in two weeks. No reason, do you need a reason? You know, the boys are getting older—I think it will be nice for them, and soon I'll be thinking about wives and then where will all the time have gone? We must do these things while we are still young, that's my philosophy!"

Sweets had to be ordered. It was my job to drive her into Berkeley. We made a heady tour of the Indian stores that rubbed shoulders along University Avenue, and together sampled an almost unmanageable variety of gulab jamun, jalebi, burfee, and luddoo.

Tray upon tray was decided on and paid for.

At every store we visited, Mom, spouting giddily like a girl, launched into a passionate description of the coming puja and all the good it would do for our family. On the drive home, she sat satisfied in the passenger seat, arms folded across her belly.

"Your father is a good man," she reflected.

The headlights of oncoming cars sliced through the cabin and lit her face in a shifting chiaroscuro of gray tones.

"I always told you he was, and now I know." Her hand reached out and tapped my thigh. "I hope one day you will be like him," she suggested happily.

It was a contrast to stumble against Jag that night. I was walking to my bedroom when he appeared at his door, a towel folded under one arm. He bumped my shoulder as we passed in the narrow hallway. The night was warm and the air remained thick, and he stood with his back to the light and his features were dark. As he turned, I caught a glimpse of his face. It was that of a vicious and cornered animal. His teeth glinted in the light. I had never seen the expression before, nothing even close to it, and he seemed to me the very opposite of the image Mom conjured of him whenever she spoke his name.

He pushed past me and disappeared into his bedroom. The lock clicked on the inside and I walked on, telling myself that this man, this creature, whoever or whatever he was, with the face of something frightened and untamed, could not be my brother.

Jag didn't return to work that week. He spent it at home, locked most of the day in the airless confines of his bedroom. He emerged for breakfast or dinner, and on finishing his food, he retreated immediately, leaving behind a faint trace of that odor of corruption he had filled the house with on first returning from what Mom still insisted was his vacation. He took baths late at night, when most of the rest of us were asleep. I heard him, if I was home, banging from his room to the bathroom and back. Twice he left the water running.

Lying on my bed, I listened as it gushed for half an hour before I walked out to investigate. The bathroom was deserted, no light escaped from under Jag's door, and there were the taps, working full blast. Steam gushed into the air and filled it, in my imagination, with the shifting forms of ghosts, each appearing for a second with a mocking expression before dissipating into the ever-rising clouds of water vapor.

"He is thinking of bigger things," Mom said when it became apparent that Jag was not returning to work. "Who needs such a silly job? What does he do? He was just some assistant man, no? Taking orders. Not my boy. He will tell people what to do, he will set the rules—that's what he's looking for."

Not only did he not return to work and lock himself in his room for much of the day, but when he did appear, he usually sat by the telephone, whispering in the manner of his old habit. I decided to find out who his earnest friend on the other end was and picked up the extension in Mom and Dad's bedroom. Jag must've suspected. By the time I raised the phone, the line was dead and all I heard was the dial tone. I walked back into the living room expecting to find him staring furiously at me, but I was met by a surprise. For there was Jag, sitting just as he had been, maintaining his urgent whisper into the handset.

It was only then that I noticed that one of his fingers rested firmly on the switch. All this time as he talked, the phone had remained on the hook. He continued his soliloquy as I stood and watched, pausing once to listen to an imaginary response before launching again into his inarticulate babble.

This continued for two nights running. Each night, I first raised the extension and listened, then returned to the living room and spotted his finger holding down the button. On the third night, when I walked into the bedroom, I was met by another surprise. Mom was sitting on the edge of the bed. She held the phone to her ear with a hand shielding the mouthpiece and gave a start when she spotted me. Without a sound, she returned the phone to its cradle and looked at me, the scared grin of a child etched on her face.

"Don't tell your brother." Her voice trembled. "I wanted to listen." She broke off and after a moment continued. "But the line is so bad, there's nothing to hear." She attempted a stronger smile. "And whatever's wrong with your brother, trust me, it doesn't matter. He'll be like his old self soon." A high note of enthusiasm entered her voice. "After the puja, everything will go right. Your brother will be talking all the time, your father will stop shouting, and you..." She paused and rose stiffly. "You're the one I worry about."

The soft pad of her step continued down the hall and ended when her feet met the kitchen's linoleum, where she stopped and called back.

"With this puja," she shouted, "I am sure something good will even come of you."

TWENTY
FIVE

SURE. AND MAYBE I'D FIND THE PERFECT PUNJABI GIRL ON MY
own, a happy little cook-and-clean wife shipped third class direct from the village who'd sit through the evenings watching
television with Mom and Dad and chew gum and stick it under
the table and pin me down with her wrestler's arms as we fucked
the whole night long. I wasn't holding my breath.

Or maybe I'd just get drunk and think of Lily. Which is what I
did, at least when I could find the money to buy alcohol.

I no longer entered the diner. There was no point. I sat and
waited in the car and watched as she left at the end of her shift.
The wait could last hours. I sipped from a bottle of schnapps,
the cheapest liquor around, and stared into the curling heat of
the parking lot, my attention focused on the door to the diner
or her car where she parked it. Sooner or later, she would appear, walking rapidly with a cigarette between her fingers and a
purse hanging from her shoulder. I'd roll my window down so I
could hear the sharp click of her heels. As much as I wanted her,
I wanted more to stop needing her. As the strength of my desire
began to slip away, I forced myself nightly to return, as if I were
a monk of old, wearing a hair shirt and scouring his back with a
whip made of tree bark. I wanted nothing of her left alive in me.

Lily always stood for a moment at her car and cast a wide
glance around while she dug for keys. The interior light re-

mained on after she climbed in as she left the door ajar to check her makeup in the rearview mirror. She'd shut the door, start the engine, and every night I tried silently to say good-bye and every night I failed.

Later, when I'd sit lost in that forgotten town far to the north, friendless and without family, I'd think back to those vigils. It wasn't just an exorcism or some kind of ritual punishment I was attempting to perform. Who was she, I kept asking myself, and who had I become, reflected in the mirror that was Lily? I didn't see much to like, but that wasn't the point, I thought—I doubted I'd ever find much to like in myself. My illusions were mostly gone. Lily didn't love me, never would. I began to doubt everything she told me—about her mom, about Eddie, even about the bruise she got that one time. Had Eddie really hit her? Was he even real? Or was it someone else, another fella like me, strung along and desperate and angry? A constellation of paranoias circled my head, and night after night, as the desire ebbed but the compulsion strengthened, I watched her from a distance, unable to release myself yet certain I'd never get any closer to her than I was at that moment.

Then one night, I did something that surprised me. As her car pulled out of its spot, I turned the key in the ignition and followed her all the way home, which was hidden among meandering lanes snaking through a complex of single-family homes and condos. I parked around the corner, at the top of her street, at an angle from which I could watch. She got out and went inside and a light came on. She lived in a low-slung condo surrounded by bushes, and I too got out of my car and approached quietly, like any local pedestrian might. When I reached her home, I took a few steps to the right and dove into the bushes.

I crawled on hands and knees up to the side of the condo and found the window and peered inside. With every step and gesture, I could feel the ugliness of my actions, but I'd gone too far, felt like an outcast at home and in the world, and knew I had to carry this compulsion to its end, whatever that was. I likened it to exorcizing a demon. What I didn't know, and what I didn't want to ask myself, was whether I had been the demon all along.

The curtains were open and she was standing in the bedroom, talking on the phone. She had a drink in her hand and was laughing. Jealousy shot through me. Who the hell was she talking to? I sat there, crouched, nearly a whole hour, listening to cars pass on the road and watched as Lily turned the television on and flipped channels for ten minutes without landing on anything, then switched it off again.

I had never seen inside her house and was fascinated. The bedroom was large, with a framed print from some art show on the wall. I knew the painting was famous but didn't know who the artist was. Clothes were thrown over the back of a chair, Eddie's along with hers, and a door stood open leading into a walk-in closet, where a row of men's jackets hung while a pile of odds and ends lay jumbled in the back. A few knickknacks littered the single shelf and other surfaces but no photographs. There was little of anything personal. A couple dumbbells sat on the floor and next to them, from a hook in the wall, hung a jump rope.

The room expressed a kind of austere self-knowledge, I told myself. She knew who she was, knew what she wanted; she felt secure in herself.

She poured herself another drink and sat on the edge of the bed and looked forlorn and tired, then stood and walked over and pulled the curtains shut. I dipped my head down, and when I raised it, she had disappeared completely, and it felt as if I had been abandoned there in the cool night. I waited an hour, trembling, my back to the window and looking up at the sky where there were no stars and only a faint grayness where clouds drifted slowly overhead.

The following night as I took up the same position next to the bedroom window I realized any idea of flushing her out of my system hadn't worked, and I felt a renewed compulsion. I *was* in love with her, I told myself. I just had to find the right way back to her heart. But this time I found Eddie stripped to his waist raising and lowering the weights with powerful thrusts, jumping with them held horizontally from his shoulders, and then running in place with the weights high above his head. He was shorter than I expected, shorter than Lily even, and he was already balding though he couldn't have been much older than thirty. Every time he jumped, the wall and window shook and I felt them shiver against my body.

The television was tuned to some show about home repair, and I wondered why he'd watch a show like that.

I heard the distinctive rattle of Lily's car pull into the driveway and crept along the bushes to see her get out and walk to the front door. I could still see the top of Eddie's head from where I was crouched, and as soon as the door opened, he stopped his exercises and stood there, waiting. I crawled back to the window to see him toweling off and Lily standing in the doorway, not moving. He walked past her toward the bathroom, and I felt a secret pleasure when neither said a word to the other.

Without thinking or knowing what I was going to do, I stood and took a couple steps to the left so that I was now in full view through the window. Lily had walked over to the bed and was flipping channels again. I tapped the glass and she turned and gave a start, then stopped, dropped the remote control on the sheets, and shook her head. She mouthed the words "fuck you" several times with slow deliberation.

I don't know why I did what I did next—it just happened. Sometimes that's all the reason there is or ever will be, however deep you tunnel into a fella's psyche. Perhaps I was looking for a way to get back at her, perhaps I was still trying to punish myself. The fact is, even as I did it, I was appalled, and thrilled, and wished immediately I could take it back and keep on doing it all at the same time. But there it was, it was done, etched into time and history.

I unzipped my pants and pulled my dick out and started to masturbate. I pressed my body against the glass so there would be no doubt what was happening. Lily stared, not moving at first, then she stood, walked to the window, and crouched so she was eye-level with my groin. She just stared, like it was the most interesting thing in the world.

Eddie walked back into the room with a towel wrapped around his waist just as I was wiping myself on the glass. We locked eyes, and I felt that I was something vile but also larger and stronger than him. Lily fell back against the side of the bed and started laughing, pointing at him, making him look ridiculous, and Eddie tore his towel off and grabbed a pair of sweatpants and went racing out of the bedroom. Her laugh felt like a triumph. The whole scene happened in a strange, wordless pantomime, as if I were watching an old silent movie. I wasn't even sure any of it was real until I saw Eddie running for me.

I watched Lily for a second. She was on the floor, trembling through peals of laughter, and seeing that made me think I had done something right. I heard the front door bang open and I charged out through the bushes and up along the street. I looked back over my shoulder to see Eddie in the driveway, tripping over his sweatpants as he tried to yank them up his thighs and run at the same time, shouting the worst kind of obscenities as his bare feet slapped against the pavement. I had too much of a head start and was soon out of sight. I ducked behind a truck and he just ran on by, and then I plunged once again into the manicured bushes and waited. Eventually Eddie came back, stalking down the middle of the road. After ten minutes spent listening to my racing heart, I walked to my car, which was parked a couple blocks away, got in, and drove home.

Our house looked desolate when I pulled up. No lights were on and a stillness occupied the air that seemed to welcome the fear that had grown inside me as I'd driven home from Lily's—the fear that I'd crossed a line and there was no turning back from it. What was on the other side of that line, I didn't know and I didn't care to find out either, not unless I had to. My hand was shaking as I unlocked the front door, and it struck me as I stepped inside that who I was, everything that had made me up to this point in my life, had been extinguished in a single blow that night.

Mom and Dad were asleep and I could hear Jag in the bathroom. The air in the house was stifling and hot.

I heard the water rushing into the tub and I waited, listening, wondering when Jag would get out. I needed a shower if I was going to get any sleep. A half hour passed before I realized Jag had once again left the water running. I knocked on the door and no one answered.

"Jag?" I said. "If you're in there, I'm coming in."

I opened the door and was about to walk inside when I stopped.

Jag lay curled on the floor, dressed only in his pajama bottoms, and squeezed between the sink and towels hanging from the wall. He was holding a knife over his wrist and pressing it down against his flesh. The roar of the water vanished and he looked up at me with wide, strange eyes, his whole face shaking from some kind of unspoken terror. I had never seen anything like it. I took a step forward, but instantly he raised the knife and pointed it at me. I recognized it. It was Mom's blunt paring knife. He'd have a hard time killing himself with that. His mouth moved into all sorts of shapes, as if he was once again trying to talk.

"Jag?" I said urgently, raising my hands.

He waved the knife and turned his head this way and that.

In his distraught eyes, something of the old Jag was there, the Jag of my childhood. It made me want to rush to him and take hold of him. If I had overturned myself tonight, then maybe I could overturn the years of Jag the Lost Brother and help bring him back.

But each time I took a step forward, he thrust the knife at me and snarled. There was no one I recognized behind that face, at least no one I had grown up with. The snarl was barely animal, it was something else entirely. He rose to his feet, and I glimpsed it again, if only for a second, the boy who once talked animatedly about his inventions, the one who led his fellow students into the desert nights, who stared up at the stars with the wonder they deserved—that long-forgotten Jag. It was like watching the dead awaken.

I held out my hand, and instantly his face again transformed.

He looked at my hand with contempt. Taking a single long stride toward me, he brought the knife to my face and held it there, floating in mid-air, before my eyes. He passed it silently back and forth, and the new feral creature I had seen in the hall only nights before now stared, his limbs taut and ferocious. His body was a wash of steam and every muscle was stretched.

Before I could say anything, he threw his shoulder into my chest and knocked me hard against the hallway wall. I cried out and he brought the knife to my throat. His face pushed against mine and his short, heavy breaths pulsed into my eyes.

The knife pressed up into my chin, raising my face, and pushed in. I stopped breathing, became absolutely still. His fingers squeezed my throat and he looked at me, eyes wild and lost, and I wondered later, remembering those eyes, if I'd ever had a brother, that if all along he'd been this creature who somehow managed to persuade us he was—however difficult and aloof— one of us. As mercilessly as he came at me, he pulled away, releasing my throat and chest. He took two determined steps back into the bathroom and stood there, trembling.

I dropped my hands to my knees and gasped for air. When I looked up, he was standing far back, the knife held high, as if signaling. The water from the tap roared again into my ears. Voices rose from my parents' bedroom and the door clicked open. Mom charged out in her nightgown, and Dad mumbled an angry complaint from the dark interior behind her.

"What're you doing? What's going on? You know how late it is?"

"Look," I said. My eyes turned back to Jag. He had retreated deep into the bathroom, and stood, holding the knife at his side.

"What?" Mom said.

Dad appeared. "Is this boy up? What is this boy doing up?"

I shouted at them. "Look! Both of you *look*!" I was furious. "Look at your son! Just look at him!"

Mom came and stood next to me and turned to face Jag. There he stood, in the steam, with the knife flagrant and madness written in bold letters across his incensed face. His eyes were wild, his hair at angles, his body twitching, and his mouth working uncontrollably. I could even see the red marks where he'd tried to cut himself. I looked at my parents. Finally, they had to see. Finally, they would know who their son was. That he was mad. That he needed help.

Dad edged forward, but refused to stand where he might actually have a view inside the bathroom.

"He has the knife?" Mom said.

"Yes," I said, triumphant. "He has the knife!"

Mom turned to me with concern. "Is that it? Is that why you made all this noise? Because he found the knife?"

"The boy found the knife?" Dad said. Now he stepped forward. "There it is!"

"What are you talking about?" I said. "He was using the knife."

Mom clicked her tongue. "What do you mean 'using'?" She walked forward and took it from Jag, who surrendered it without protest. "I've been looking all week." She slapped him cautiously on the cheek. "And this naughty boy had it all the time. Why all this fuss? You should have told us in the morning. I'm not going to use it now."

I stared at her with wide-eyed horror. Could she not see? Was she that blind?

"He was trying to kill himself," I said coldly.

Mom turned slowly and brought her face up to mine.

"What did you say?"

"Look at his wrists!"

Dad grunted and turned. "The boy is crazy." He walked back into his bedroom and cursed loudly.

"Look at his *wrists*!" I insisted a second time.

"Don't you ever talk about your brother like that," Mom whispered into my face. "I am looking right at him. He's a fine boy, not like you. I don't know why you make up these stories. Maybe your father is right, maybe you are crazy in the head."

As she talked, Jag sneered at me over her shoulder.

Finally she stepped back, looked at Jag admiringly, and closed the bathroom door herself.

I caught one last glimpse of him. His eyes offered a look of triumph.

"Let him have his bath at least and go to sleep!" Mom said.

Saying that, she followed Dad and her door slammed and locked behind her. I remained alone, standing in that hot hallway in the dark, trembling with fury. The air was thick from moisture from the bathroom. That last look in his eyes haunted me. He had become one of them, he was telling me, with Mom and Dad, and happily so. He had chosen his side, the side of madness. I dropped onto my bed and lay awake, awash in sweat and anger, and wished for one thing and one thing only.

That he *do* it, that he get it over with and spare us all the misery of his presence and finally kill himself.

TWENTY SIX

THE NEXT MORNING JAG SAT AT HIS USUAL SPOT, SPOONING cereal into his useless mouth. It felt like a betrayal seeing him there. What a coward and a failure! I hoped that if one last spark of the old Jag struggled on, the Jag of wild invention, he might have the courage to finish the job and die. That would have earned him some respect in my eyes.

But there he sat, alive and worse than dead at the same time, not the boy he was, not the man he could have been, but a living, breathing absence. My zombie brother. It made me sick to look at him. I hated him that morning with a violence I had never felt before. I had to fight the urge to leap across the table and strangle him right then.

He paged absently through a newspaper, refusing to look at me. One wrist was openly scarred, and when I walked in he rotated it to offer me a clearer view. It looked as if he was boasting.

I stared at him for a brief moment, then walked out. They could all go to hell. I hated everyone in that house—Mom, Dad, Jag. A seething violence spread through my limbs, and as I glimpsed each of them that morning, the hatred jumped to my eyes and I wanted to push them to the ground and shout at them, the blind, stupid lot of them.

I had nowhere to go. All my escape routes were shut. I grabbed a book and sat in the living room and read it hungrily, pretending no one else existed, just me and this one book, which spoke of far-off places and far-off times with names I'd never heard before. And as I read, the family did exactly what I wished for. They all went straight to hell.

The storm broke early. The sounds of battle sailed from one end of the house to the other, and Mom and Dad screamed and smashed doors and crashed their feet against the floor with a rage I'd never before witnessed in either of them.

It started when Dad walked into the kitchen. Mom was already on the phone. She was talking to the granthi and finalizing details for the following weekend's schedule for the puja. Dad poured himself a cup of tea, sat down at the dinner table, unfolded the newspaper and started reading. I could hear him shuffling the pages from where I sat. Mom got off the phone, and without looking up, Dad said, "What was all that about a puja? I never said yes to anything. I really don't think we can afford it right now."

Never in all my life had I seen Mom look forward with such anticipation and pleasure to anything as she did to this puja, and when Dad said he "really didn't think," what he was actually saying—what Mom knew and I knew and anyone who had more than a passing acquaintance with Dad knew he was saying—was that no way, *absolutely never*, would it happen, not even over his cold, dead body.

A long silence followed. It was as if Dad had launched us all off a high cliff and we were careening silently toward the valley floor and waiting to hit it with a great loud thwack. Mom walked hunched around the kitchen table staring at him open-mouthed, holding a rolling pin. He refused to look up and for a long minute she didn't say a word. Suddenly, she brought the rolling pin down with a tremendous crash onto the tabletop and the battle started.

Mom had spent a week on the phone in front of him, making one arrangement after another, calling relatives as far away as

Canada to invite them! Did he dare to think he could say he'd never agreed in the first place? That he'd never heard the discussions with the granthis and musicians?

He'd heard every word she said! If he had wanted to tell her no, he could have done it any time! Now the sweets were ordered and paid for! Half the family had made plans to descend on us a week later, and he dared to say it was not going to happen!

What business was it of his, Dad cried, all that rubbish she talked about on the phone? Did he listen to one word? No! Why should he? Everything coming out of her mouth was garbage!

If she wanted a puja, she needed to ask straight out. But this? Pretending he'd said yes and making all the arrangements. It was disgusting. What kind of woman was she, except a liar and a cheat? All she wanted was his money! She was worse than the fat man!

The major part of the argument, the active screaming, lasted five days and nights. Brief reprieves arrived with sleep or work. Throughout, they shared the same bed and not once did Mom refuse to cook Dad breakfast or dinner. She'd thump the plate down in front of him, calling him a useless bastard and telling him how he'd ruined her life, and he'd eat, spitting food across the room as he called her the most lazy and sickening woman who had ever been born in all creation.

Uncle Gur arrived in the middle of the storm.

This time, he offered no excuse. Not that anyone would have listened. He walked in, ran a handkerchief over his forehead and complained about the heat, and asked Mom what there was to eat.

Things were getting complicated down south, he said. The word he used was "warm." One more corrupt, racist nigger prosecutor was asking questions about his business practices! The bed of his truck was crowded with legal boxes stuffed with business papers. As Mom started cooking for him, he backed the truck into our garage and began unloading.

I helped carry the boxes and we stacked them along one wall. Dad ducked his head in and watched us silently with a troubled expression. He disappeared and the shouting erupted once more.

Uncle Gur slapped me on the back when we were finished.

"Don't worry," he said, nodding to the door leading to the house. "This is what men and women do. They get angry, they shout, they throw things. You'll do it too one day. Just like them. I promise you. It's the only good thing about getting old."

After he ate, and without offering an explanation, he produced a fifty-foot phone cord out of his bag and unscrewed the kitchen phone from the wall. The new cord allowed him to carry the phone into the garage and shout into it in relative peace. He sat there, balanced on a camp stool pulled from the back of the truck, rifling through boxes of papers. An impromptu desk coalesced across the lid of the washing machine, and every hour, he showed his head to ask Mom for a cup of tea. The argument between her and Dad would freeze in mid-sentence and only resume once the tea was brewed and delivered.

Late into the night, Uncle Gur sat in the garage and made calls and berated unknown others on the far end. Now his excuse was obvious. How dare the caller think he could explain the hidden fees of this or that policy at a time like this.

"Family emergency!" he cried.

He was here to save his brother's marriage. Did the bastard on the phone know what a marriage was? Or did he spend his time screwing whores in his mother's bed? I'd sit and watch him, if only to escape the tension in the house, and he'd fill me in on details of the battles in Punjab.

The situation was going well, the fighters were making advances. Hard news was difficult to come by. The government was restricting reporters. He'd heard some were being forced out, even foreigners. It meant only one thing: victory was close at hand. The Indians would soon be on their knees, he was sure of it, and we would have our nation on the other side of the world.

"This time next week, I feel it in my bones," he crowed. "We will have our country. I can taste it!"

In the morning, I discovered him asleep, hunched over an open box, snoring loudly.

Despite the fact that Uncle Gur took little active notice of the argument, his arrival brought a moderating influence. Mom and Dad could not compete with the commotion erupting from the garage. Each time their voices rose, Uncle Gur thundered violently and kicked the washing machine so hard the whole house shook. If this was his idea of saving a marriage, it was actually working. The argument lost steam. Mom retreated into silence, and Dad sat curled on the sofa, knees pulled up to his chin and sulking like a chastened boy.

More than anything in all the world, the Akhand Path was the one thing Mom had wanted, and he knew it. A grim satisfaction blossomed across his face, as Mom continued to drop the plates with a crash on tables, slam doors from room to room, the air crackling with the electric charge of her rage. The family stammered into a stalemate. As days passed, the only raised voice was Uncle Gur's. Jag remained locked in his room and all I wanted to do was find a way out.

College was almost over for the spring, and I worked at most two days a week. I passed the evenings driving along Valley roads with no destination in mind. One day, bored with flatlands, I took the road north, where the untamed switchbacks were a revelation. They rose above the mist and swept out over the water so it felt as if you were going to be shot out into space, then whipsawed back into the land and the canopy of trees on either side. I'd hit the pedal, spin the wheel with one hand, slam the brake, twist, let the wheel slide out between my fingers, crush the clutch and shift down and punch the accelerator once more, and all the while the wide ocean lay at my feet and I felt like a small-change god or a great eagle soaring over his domain.

I drove for hours, unheedful of time or place or how I'd find my way home. A part of me thought I should stay out there, pitch the flag of my new nation inside my car and keep going, a movable land, unfixed in time or place, whose borders would never stand still for a single day.

I pulled over north of Fort Bragg and parked at the edge of the beach and walked for an hour along the pebble-covered shoreline. Here it was, the ocean of my childhood dreams. A barreling, cold wind cut through my jacket and dark clouds ringed the sky. A thunderstorm was threatening. None of this lessened my joy. I thought back to those two failed treks, and that I was here at last, and this fact alone was something bright and glorious and would have kept me warm through a blizzard.

Night came and I took my clothes off in the darkness and waded into the water. The cold didn't touch me. I was immune to it that night. At the far edge of my vision, lightning struck the water and sent brilliant showers of light ringing the horizon. Thunder rumbled through my body and I found myself in the heart of the storm. Yet all around me the ocean remained calm and the sky above clear as I twisted onto my back and paddled with the stars as my blanket. I'd left the cabin light on in the car to lead me back. Sometimes I lost it, drifting for minutes with little idea in which direction the shore lay and which the far reaches of the ocean. It no longer mattered. I would find land or I would not. I told myself I could die here and be happy.

Finally, the cold began to penetrate my bones and I turned my head and there was the car, near the beach, the faint light painting the inside of the cabin. I gazed up at the night sky and across to the horizon of fire and lightning before curling my body in the water and taking long strokes to return to shore.

Legs quaking, I stood naked on the thin line of sand, looking out as the waves circled my feet and swept back. The icy water combined with the wind should have left me frozen through, but the exhilaration of the swim, and standing there naked, on the boundary of the land itself, filled me with warmth. Pebbles and the fragments of shells crunched underfoot as I walked to where

I'd left my clothes. I struggled as I pulled them on over my wet body, and found the last of a beer I'd been drinking earlier and finished it.

The drive back took several hours in my poorly heated car and I shivered most of the way. I had almost forgotten the atmosphere at home. Even with everyone asleep, the house was submerged in a sickening tension. Whatever brief freedom I'd felt swimming in the ocean vanished instantly.

Here I was. Home. Where apparently I lived. Every muscle in my body ached and the weight of the house only added to it, as if it were crushing me down on my shoulders. I walked heavily to my room, truly wishing I'd remained in the ocean.

A note was sitting on my pillow. It was in Uncle Gur's hand-writing. I had to read it three times before I allowed myself to believe it.

Someone called. Her name was Lily. She left a number.

TWENTY
SEVEN

WHEN I WOKE, IT WAS THE MIDDLE OF THE MORNING AND I was drenched in sweat and shivering. I'd thrown the sheets clear off me and they lay piled on the floor. The fever lasted three days and three nights and left me curled in bed. Uncle Gur regularly woke me by thumping the soles of my feet so he could keep me updated on doings with the war in Punjab. He had the radio tuned to the BBC twenty-four hours a day, hoping for news. Occasionally, Dad allowed his face to darken the crack in the door, where he frowned before he disappeared.

Mom appeared every hour when she was home, pressing a hand against my forehead and staring at me with guilt-ridden concern painted across her face. She worried about me, not just about the fever, but about everything. On the first evening of the fever, she settled onto the end of the bed and let her voice drop. Why did I cause so much trouble all the time? And why all those stories about my brother? She too was worried about him, she explained, but she didn't believe any of what I said, not about him trying to kill himself. That was cruel of me to make up something like that. Only crazy people killed themselves, and no son of hers was crazy. He must have his reasons for the things he did, and if he didn't want to talk about them, that was his business.

Her admission surprised me. She had never come so close to admitting she might be wrong about him. I was too sick to draw her out on it.

"It did happen," I said. "I saw it. He was holding the knife over his wrist."

Her face changed instantly. "There," she said, quietly angry, "more of your lies." She leaned forward. "If he wanted to kill himself, why hasn't he done it. It's easy to do, stupid people do it all the time, and your brother is not stupid."

She pulled back and looked at me with dismay riddling her features. "Maybe you're the one who should see a doctor. One of those types on TV who don't give you pills but just talk to you, a head doctor."

It was because I had never seen India that my mind was all twisted up. I didn't know where I came from. And a person who didn't know where he came from, how could he know where he was? The village life was nothing like here, she added. Mist blanketed the fields in the morning. Water buffalo and goats shuffled in the yards. The irrigation canals snaked beside lanes while water bubbled and steamed. Children played games of jacks on the dusty ground.

Then, surprisingly, she launched into the tale of her marriage. It was one she had told many times, but it had been years since I last heard it. On the day she left India, everyone was crying except her father. He promised everything would be alright. The man he had chosen came from a good family, worked hard, was already on his way to becoming an American citizen. Life would be easy and soon she would be flying back and forth, between India and America, like a film star.

Her voice drifted in and out through a haze of illness and medicine. In those first years, she prayed every night to go home. To this day, she could smell the earth. The memory was in her bones. In letters home, she described her new husband as nothing less than the kindest and most generous man anyone could imagine. He gave her everything she wanted. In America, she wrote, she felt like a lazy girl living in a palace.

"Sometimes it's better not to tell the *whole* truth," she said.

As I drifted back to sleep, I wondered what she meant by not telling the whole truth. Was she talking about herself or the things she said about Jag? I was too tired to think further and watched, vaguely, as she stood and wiped her eyes.

"One day you and Jag will be married," she said. "That day, I'll be happy."

In the middle of the night, I woke to discover Jag standing at the foot of my bed. The sole light falling on him originated from the hall, and he looked as he had after returning from his disappearance, covered in a coating of dust, closer to a ghost than a man. If I strained, I could almost see through him to the wall beyond. I turned my head to check the clock. It was past four in the morning.

"Jag?" I whispered hoarsely.

He stood rooted, still as a statue. His eyes shone and only his mouth was moving, trying to form words and once again managing nothing more than formless grimaces and contortions. I struggled and sat up in bed and stared, grasping for any speck of sympathy. But I had stopped caring long ago and I knew it. My heart mirrored his grimaces and contortions, and they were all directed at him. I wasn't afraid. He seemed too insubstantial to actually hurt me, and in the gauzy vision of my fever, any sense of threat was gone. It wasn't even in his face. Missing was the menace he'd shown me in the bathroom. Instead, he just stood motionless, looking lost. I would never see him alive again, and in the weeks and months that followed I would wonder at the meaning of that night. Was he apologizing? Was he trying to say good-bye? More than anything, I wanted to find some meaning in his actions, but try as I might, I failed, and each time I looked back on that night, all I saw were his lips moving and nothing being said.

He must have stood there for almost an hour, as I fell in and out of dreams, and at times I had no idea who Jag was except the shadow of a shadow standing there. Even in the moments when I recognized him, I thought, he will die one day, and the thought horrified and saddened me because I felt certain that when it happened I would feel nothing, nothing at all. I had found my way out and was planning to use it, and once gone, I would not look back, not at him, not at this house, and not at my family.

The key lay under my pillow, scribbled on a scrap of paper. I kept it through the illness, a talisman of my coming escape, for no matter what, I was leaving and I planned never to return.

On Saturday morning, with the fever fast retreating and strength pouring back into my limbs, Mom bustled into the bedroom with a cup of tea, her eyes puffy and red from a week's worth of tears and arguments.

She'd made a decision.

"From now on," she said, holding herself erect and perched on the edge of my bed, "I am only going to think good thoughts. Your father is your father. If he wants me to do something, I will do it, and if he doesn't, then no, I won't. I am tired of fighting. From now on, I will say yes. I don't care what happened in the past. I never want to talk about it. Only the future. The future and happy things. Health, wealth, happiness!"

She clapped her hands with enthusiasm.

"And you too. You must do it also. I will talk to your brother. We will all think good thoughts and say yes. If your father says something, you say yes. Straightaway! Don't question it, not even in that head of yours. If we all say yes, there will be no more arguments. And then, I know it, we will be a happy family. Just like the ones on television."

She hurried out, filled with a new determination, and I heard her thump on Jag's door to spread the news.

Her head reappeared in my doorway moments later.

"Asleep," she announced, speaking of Jag. "Don't forget. Happy thoughts, happy life, from now on, always say yes!"

She was gone, whistling through the house.

"Just say yes," I repeated to myself. I dug out the scrap of paper with Lily's number and called. When she answered I didn't say hello, I simply asked, "Where are you?"

"A condo," she said. "My own. On Solano by the old pool hall."

She'd left Eddie. It was over. There was nothing left to say about him except he was not the man she had believed he was. That night he'd seen me at the window was what caused the final break.

"How?" I said.

"I thought it was kinda funny, stupid but funny. Eddie didn't see it that way. He thought you were some fucking pervert." She laughed. "Who knows? You probably are. He still wants to smash your head in." She added, "Guess I don't. That good enough for you?"

"Sure," I said. "But what happens with Eddie?"

He could keep the house—as far as she was concerned it was all his, the furniture, everything. It was his money anyhow. She loathed him, never wanted to hear his name again.

"I'm gonna remake my life, start over, figure out something new. Thought maybe we should get a drink."

After I put the phone down, I walked from room to room telling myself I was looking at everything for the last time, saying good-bye, and knowing I would miss none of it. Mom's system of happy thoughts and words did not last long. By the time I'd dressed, a new argument had erupted. Mom banged pans against the stove and Dad stalked from one end of the garden to the other, scowling and kicking dirt with his shoes.

Uncle Gur appeared from the garage every half hour saying there was news from India, something was happening, but no one was sure exactly what. The last of the foreign reporters had been expelled that morning. The phone lines into Punjab had been cut. Gunfire was heard near the Golden Temple. Others heard explosions and talked of fires and plumes of smoke blanketing the city.

"They're breaking out, they're taking the war to the streets!"

I was happy for him. Maybe his country too would be born that night.

No one had seen Jag all day.

TWENTY EIGHT

EIGHT THIRTY AND I SAT IN THE CHEVY, WATCHING CARS RACE each other as they hit the block heading onto the freeway, my poor excuse for wheels shuddering in their wake.

The old soldier stood to the right, his once bright uniform now faded, carrying his gun more like a shopping bag than a weapon of war. He was lit obliquely from a streetlamp at the corner and looked like an old tin soldier with his musette bag and Iron Age rifle with an obscure inscription on his plinth. No doubt the names of the dead were written there.

I remained in the car, some thirty yards distant, which offered a view of the statue and its base.

If Lily arrived early, I'd spot her instantly.

In the adjacent strip mall stood Walia & Son with its opaque green-painted display window. A light shone through the glass door, casting a rectangle onto the sidewalk, and shadows moved in the deep interior. To one side stood a shuttered nail salon and on the other a liquor store where I bought a two-dollar bottle of gin. It tasted foul but I enjoyed it anyhow. All the troubles of home had drained away and now, as I looked out beyond the windshield, I found myself contemplating a new world.

Somehow I would find a home in it.

I took another slug. The liquor store was closing up, the guy standing outside rolling down the shutters. A middle-aged woman in a sari exited Mr Walia's store hoisting a large bag with child in tow. That child was me, years ago. Another town, another Walia & Son grocery store. Gaunt-eyed and suspicious, tugged with frustration by Mom from one store to another—oh, what I would have given for a friendly nod from a local, whatever size, color, or shape. When the kid glanced over, I raised the bottle in salute, to him, to myself as a kid, to all the possibilities that lay between our pasts, presents and futures.

The kid smiled back, bringing the mother's wary attention my way. She yanked the boy's arm and swatted him around the head, just for good measure no doubt, to stop him ever thinking he might find joy in opening his eyes once in a while on a mostly empty street at night to encounter a friendly face. I nodded and raised the bottle higher. I didn't have a chance to take a drink. I was shaken by a sharp tap tap! against the passenger-side window. I thrust the bottle between the seats and turned, anticipating Lily's hair in silhouette and a wry smile on her lips.

That's not what I saw.

Exactly where Lily should have been, I found a round and mostly hairless head jerking from side to side. It pulled back when I retreated in fright. My heart sank on recognizing the face, the outline, the dispiriting features. It was Mr Walia himself. He gestured violently for me to roll the window down.

"Ahh," Mr Walia said, propelling his head toward me. "I recognized the car. Very good choice, very good vehicle." He was perspiring and his glasses were fogged. His eyes darted around the interior, landing on the bottle where it lay conspicuous between the seats.

"Good evening, Mr Walia," I said.

He was a short man with a whiff of hair combed perfectly across his head, and wore a striped short-sleeved shirt. He smelled of freshly applied talcum powder, and with the window open the roar of the freeway poured in.

"Drink?" he said, as if practicing the word.

"Drink," I said.

His hairless head expanded in the car's tight interior like a disfigured balloon. "Hot night?"

"Do you want something, Mr Walia?"

"Your mother?" he said.

"She's not here."

"She is well?"

"Great," I smiled, faking geniality, hoping it might get rid of him more quickly.

"Oh. Good. Wonderful. We're closing right now."

"Yes?"

"She has videos. They arrived yesterday."

"You want me to—?"

"If it's not a problem? I thought that's why...when I saw the car..."

"No, Mr Walia," I said. "That's not why."

"I see. Well, shall I?"

"No need. I'll come in."

"Good, good. That's good." He nodded, squeezed his now mammoth head out through the tiny opening so that it popped like an oversized cork shooting from a bottle, and straightened and returned to the store, holding the door open as I followed behind.

"We are closed," he said, explaining, "You know they come at any hour, they don't let a man go home. I have a family, I have a home. Do you think they know I have a home?"

"People don't care," I said flatly.

"They think everything is open twenty-four hours. When are people supposed to sleep? Answer that, you're an intelligent young man—you go to college. When are people supposed to sleep?" he continued to chant softly as I walked inside.

Beyond the door, I entered a suffocating cloud of disinfectant. It was late and he'd been cleaning. Mr Walia took his place standing crushed behind the counter and searched the wall, running a finger along shelves housing several hundred black plastic VHS tape boxes. A few of the tapes sported white tags with the title transliterated into a vague English equivalent. All were pirated, often fourth- or fifth-generation copies of poorly made originals. Once home, all that remained of this fabled cinematic India was a grisly blur.

I'd grown up in the orbit of such stores, with their colonial phantoms haunting corners, out of place and dazed in their unexpected American home. In addition to Indian groceries, the shelves stocked British goods. Dusty aisles housed jars of Marmite, bottles of Lucozade in their sparkly translucent wrappers, indolent towers of Weetabix. There was room enough for Robinsons Barley Water and ancient-looking boxes of baby rusks. Here a dream of another India, an India still infected with the nostalgia of English failure, had come to die while the Mr Walias of this world daily tended the corpse.

It was the only India I knew, carried across oceans on the shoulders of men like him and my father, and left to us, their children. The shelves were poorly built of cheap, unfinished wood, while against the walls tattered boxes housing vegetables waited. Mom would wander, nosing the eggplants and zucchini, complaining how nothing was fresh. The glass counter and cash register exhibited a slapdash quality, as if discovered in an abandoned shop and carried here.

I imagined Mr Walia as stevedore, hulking this long, wide counter on his back in just the way, bent over double, he'd hauled India here. He would do it—a mile, ten miles, across whole continents—his cheeks puffed and sweating, dreaming one day of giving all this to his children.

"Here it is," he said, and pulled five cassette boxes from the shelf, one after the other, and stacked them neatly on the counter next to the register.

"Five?" I said.

"A serial. Your mother asked for this a long time ago. I have been searching. For your mother, anything." He turned away to find a spiral-bound notebook, saying, "Do people think I actually sleep?"

"I don't know, Mr Walia. No one I know sleeps."

He shook his head. "Yes, the young."

"Is that all?" I added, "Mom'll pay when she returns them." I reached to collect the tapes. Before I could take hold he prevented me by placing one of his nervous hands directly on the pile.

"I wanted to ask you," he said.

"I'm meeting someone."

"Here?"

"Outside."

"Ahh. You are how old?"

"Pardon me?"

"You are young for college, yes?"

"Sixteen. Who knows, maybe seventeen. No one ever tells me anything."

"Your first year?"

"Something like that."

"When I saw you outside, I hoped your mother talked to you."

"My mother?"

"Did she?"

"She talks to me every day."

"About, well, at your age..."

"Pardon?"

"She didn't," he said.

"She did."

"Then?"

"Only this morning."

"So when you said you were waiting for someone?"

"I am."

"For me, no?"

"No, Mr Walia. I'm not waiting for you."

We sniffed at each other, equally confounded at what the other was trying to say.

"I don't understand," he said. "You said she talked to you."

"We talk about a lot of things."

"Yes, you go to college."

"Now, Mr Walia, I have to—"

I had a vision of Lily pacing back and forth before the stone soldier, furious at my absence. I turned in the direction of the door and reached again for the tapes.

"Wait!" he snapped, snatching the tapes away. But immediately his tone softened, "Please. I have, you see, and at her age, considering."

"Her age? Mom's age?"

"No, not her—*her!* Your mother thought it was worth asking."

"Who?"

"Asking you."

"Asking what?"

He clicked his tongue impatiently. "Asking *you.*"

"Yes?"

"Well, what do you think?"

"Me?"

"You don't have to decide this minute. Think about it. Take a week, ten days."

"I will."

"In two years, yes. Your studies, after all. These things take time."

I reached for the tapes, anxious at this point to get back outside. But he brought a hand firmly down on the stack and insisted, desperation ringing in his voice, "We are modern, we are very modern people! I watch that man, Phil Donahue, I know all about life here. For eight years I have kept up my subscriptions to the *National Geographic* magazine and to *Reader's Digest.* I read thoroughly every issue. I sit here, behind this counter, and read every word, even the advertisements, yes, even them! The advertisements tell me a great deal about the tastes of the American people. And tastes change—a businessman must know this, how one taste is not the same as another, and I am a businessman. Above all, I am a businessman!"

He seized hold of my hand and pushed himself forward, climbing halfway onto the counter, his fingers squeezing my knuckles as his breath spilled onto my face.

"And I'm not unintelligent," he insisted—"We all must think of bigger things. This is not the village anymore!"

"Yes," I said, desperate, trying to pull away. I wanted nothing more than to run out of the store. Did he think I'd be impressed? Was he looking for someone to discuss *National Geographic* photo spreads with? To admire together the topless beauties of Togo?!

"I understand, for an intelligent young man like yourself," he continued, ignoring my exasperation, excitedly bringing his eyes right up to mine. "Every day, *she* watches *Jeopardy!* and *Wheel of Fortune*. Every single day. In five years she has not missed one episode. This is commitment! And I promise you, I have saved up funds. She will be a dentist. She will not work in the store. *A dentist!*" he crowed enthusiastically. "It takes an intelligent woman to be a dentist. You see, even I think about these things."

Call me dumb, call me deaf and blind.

It took me that long to figure it out, to get to the heart of what he was asking. I remembered what Mom said at dinner that night weeks ago, how she'd started talking about Mr Walia and just as quickly stopped. I pulled my hand violently back and thrust it at Mr Walia, almost knocking him off his stool and to the floor.

"You—?" I said.

He straightened and made no comment on my violence. "There is the store," he said evenly, gesturing. "If you want it. It gives a good income. You won't need to complete your studies. You sit here, every day, read your books. Exactly like home."

It was, of course, a joke—it could be nothing other than a ghastly joke. I looked at him, for the first time closely, the man who was offering to be my father-in-law: those sleepy eyes, the nervous lips, the taut red skin of his face and head. He gave me the impression of having been boiled and served up half done, like a poorly cooked potato.

"Your daughter?"

"I'll show you a photograph."

I had never met her. The image I conjured was of a pudgy, thick-fingered woman sitting on an over-stuffed sofa, its cushions covered in protective plastic, a shawl wrapping her shoulders, remote in hand, concentrating with all her powers on the answers flashing in the little screens on *Jeopardy!* She would answer every single one, diligently in the form of a question, before the first contestant rang his buzzer. And she would do it without emotion, her lips barely moving. And at the end, smugly content as if she'd pocketed the fifteen thousand dollars herself, she would rise and walk with measured steps to the bathroom, where, trembling with inexpressible excitement from her victory, she would brush and floss her perfect teeth!

Oh, to be a shopkeeper and the husband of a fat dentist! Was this the life Mr Walia dreamed for me, to sit like him behind that counter for what, the next forty years, and masturbate to the fleshy wonders between the covers of an endless stream of *National Geographic*s?

"Mr Walia!" I had to prevent myself from yelling. I could feel the gin I'd drunk in the car spiking through my system. I leapt forward, bridging the short distance of the counter, and thrust my face into his. "Do you really think—?" I said.

"No, no, not now, but—"

"What's my name?"

"Excuse me?"

"What is my name?" I spat at him.

"I...I—" he struggled, and produced, his voice thin and weak: "Mr...Singh?"

"Mr Walia, you don't know my name and you're asking me to marry your daughter!"

"I'm a modern man!" he burst out furiously. "It's the parents that count. You would meet, you would get to know each other. Don't tell me what I know and what I do not know."

I gave up, falling back onto my heels.

"Okay!" I cried. My buzz had throttled any judgment. "Why not? Let's do it. Let's get it over with!"

"You will—?" Mr Walia replied, a trill of excitement dancing at the edge of his lips.

"Of course, Mr Walia! I haven't met her, she hasn't met me, what's to stop us? Bring her over. We'll have a party! We'll make arrangements! Isn't that how it's done?"

He stepped back, looking fearful. "But...you—?"

"Yes, Mr Walia?"

"Tomorrow?"

"Sure!" I cried, equal parts hysteric and sardonic. "The sooner the better! Make it in the morning! I'll be dressed and waiting!"

Saying that, I grabbed the tapes, kicked the door open and walked in a rage to my car, unlocked the passenger door, flung the tapes onto the backseat, and slammed it shut. This time I didn't lock it—anyone who wanted the tin coffin of a junk heap could have it. I stormed across the small parking lot, passing the store on my way.

There sat Mr Walia, enfolded in the dim glow of his shop, more shadow than presence, embraced on all sides by an ocean of darkness. Painted across the window was WALIA & SON. Nothing else—a utilitarian and plainspoken facade. Did he even have one? Had he thought of me for years, watched me, weighed me? Perhaps it was me whose name was painted there, whom he dreamt of when he raised the brush and added to his clan a wretched son.

TWENTY NINE

PACING, HEAD DOWN, I MADE A BEREAVED CIRCLE AT THE base of the last soldier of the Great War. Five minutes past nine and where was Lily. My watch was a Casio digital with a black plastic band, the face scratched, the strap threatening to break. When I purchased it I thought it looked splendid and defiant. Now it looked cheap, the kind of thing a son-in-law of Mr Walia might wear.

The other stores were shut: a flower store, a barbershop, a bait and tackle store. The place was deserted. Mr Walia now stood on the pavement and stared, in a slack-shouldered pose, at my deserted car. Looking at him was like looking at a possible vision of my future. I ducked behind the pedestal and watched.

In silhouette his belly bulged, a slim arc of a waxing moon, drawn as if by gravitation to the unlocked passenger door, yearning to orbit in its final days the robust earth of a son-in-law, to pass along his burden, his dream India, to have a new generation shudder under its weight.

He tested the handle and opened the door, surveyed the backseat where the tapes were scattered, clicked the lock down, and, acting out of paternal fantasy, swung the door shut while holding the handle raised to ensure it locked. He walked around to the back of the car and kneeled before the license plate and studied it and raised himself, shaking his head in a dismay I was able to decipher even at this distance.

I watched in amazement.

He was checking to see if my tags were out of date. They were.

He glanced up and down the street, beyond the statue, and, with a sort of valorous shrug, turned, walked back the few paces to the store, and triple-locked the door. He picked up two over-filled plastic grocery bags resting on the pavement at the entrance and began walking, with a steady unwavering pace, in the direction of a battered green Ford. When I saw that Ford I thought of my watch.

I crossed the street and stood outside the tackle shop, next to a pay phone bolted to the wall, from where I could see not only the statue, but also my car and the freeway entrance. Baroque fishing lures, their brilliant colors muted in the dark, menaced from the window display. The pin-prick eyes of the lures, shining dots in the greater blackness, stared back mockingly.

It was growing late and the pace of cars began to slacken. Soon it would be only the brave drunks, veering among the lanes as they attempted to negotiate the on-ramp and survive. My watch said half past. I'd be here for hours. If need be, I'd wait until morning. Maybe I'd camp out day and night, tormenting Mr Walia with my presence. Because what really pissed me off, what lay at the bottom of my anger, wasn't his thinking I'd enjoy the life he planned for me, it was this: he refused to imagine a different life, a better life, a fuller one. This was his best of all possible worlds, sitting behind that counter, ogling the jiggling breasts of the dancing chicks of Togo, while at home his daughter brushed and flossed her teeth and mouthed questions to an unconcerned Alex Trebek. This very place, this was his India, his dream country realized. Mr Walia's world was perfect.

And then it happened.

I turned and she was there, Lily, standing in the shadow of

the last soldier of the Great War, dressed in a leather skirt and a shimmering red top. As I walked across the street toward her, the top glittered in the light, and for one fleeting moment, my world too was perfect.

She pressed forward and kissed me brusquely on the lips. Her breath smelled of alcohol, and she swayed and planted a hand on my shoulder to steady herself. She brought her face to mine.

"I'm fucked up," she said. "I don't know how I drove here."

I held her steady as best I could. She felt small and fragile in my arms.

"So, you little Paki piece of shit, you fucking got me here. Now what?"

She tipped back, stumbled, and regained her balance.

"I wasn't going to meet you," she continued. "It was a fucking joke. My way of getting back at you. I planned to stand you up." She started laughing and her face turned ugly.

"So what got you here?" I said. Neither of us had said hello and now I didn't want to. I was already regretting meeting her. Was this all some joke for her?

"Boredom," she said. "I got drunk. Shit, I don't know. Here I am."

She took a step back and shook her head.

"I didn't mean that. I meant—shit..." Her voice drifted away. "I'm sorry, that's not what I..."

Whatever she was going to say, she lost her train of thought and dropped her head onto my shoulder. I could smell her freshly shampooed hair.

"Do you love me?" she whispered. Her body pressed into mine and her hand fell over my shoulder and lay there limp like something dead.

"We're going dancing," I said, ignoring her question. I'd heard of a place, one of Chuck's eccentric enthusiasms, some sort of dance hall night at a local hotel, though neither of us had bothered to actually go.

She pushed her mouth against my ear. "I hate dancing," she said. She instantly changed her mind. "I mean I love it." She started laughing again. "I can't seem to get love and hate straight tonight."

"It's in the air," I said, untangling myself and stepping back. Looking at her again, in the deathly half-light of the streetlamps, I found a grim reflection of myself. How much I wanted at that moment to simply want her, to be in love and to run away. But all I could summon was a sudden and growing hatred. Her beauty drained away in a matter of seconds and the woman whose face had left me speechless now left me cold. I stepped forward without thinking and pushed her against the pedestal. I wanted to block her face from my mind.

"Sweetheart?" she said, mixing fear and need and desperation all in that one word. She pulled me close and her voice communicated more to me than all we'd done together since we met. I heard laid bare my own arrogance and stupidity and delusion. She had not come here to run away with me, she did not love me, she never would, and in an instant my dreams deflated and once more died.

I pressed my lips roughly against hers and pushed my tongue between her teeth. The kiss held nothing sweet or sentimental in it. It was violent, uncaring. She wrapped an arm around my waist and her mouth greedily accepted mine. Her tongue pressed against mine and I found myself battling a rising revulsion. The old stone soldier seemed to look down with scorn and pity and I closed my eyes and pushed my dick against her crotch. Even as I kissed her I thought I was striking her again. A part of me enjoyed the thrill of it, as if I was punishing her and in doing that punishing myself.

If worlds were born in an instant, they could also die, and as I pressed myself harder, grinding against her dress, a rush of painful memories returned. Chasing the car with the Chinese family. Striking Lily across the face in the train station parking lot. The phone calls to Eddie. Stalking her at her apartment. And how much else, all of it mad. Of all the odd things to come into my head at that moment, Spinoza's words came back: *The world is perfect, just as it is.* What a sham. Here was his perfect world. I imagined him sitting up in the clouds, looking down, while all his bogus words crashed down around his ears.

My body stiffened and I came in my pants and pressed my face into Lily's neck and bit her hard and gasped and wanted to burst into tears but stopped myself. She knew what had happened and pushed me off and lit a cigarette and half grinned, half sneered in the shifting light of cars speeding toward the freeway entrance.

There were tears in her eyes and her lips were quivering and her hands shook and I thought maybe she did feel something, something real and honest. Maybe I did too.

"You do love me?" she asked again. "You just have to say the words. It doesn't have to mean anything."

I said nothing and turned away. Looking at her was like looking at myself, and I didn't want to look at either one of us. I started walking to the car.

"Hey?" she called.

"What?" I yelled, no longer able to suppress my anger.

"What's going on? You're being a shit."

I stared at her. There she was, weaving on her pins, drunk and lost and scared, and I finally softened and said, my voice lower, "I thought you liked that."

She walked toward me and wrapped an arm around my waist.

"I like you," she said.

Her fingers pressed into me and I remained immobile. She dropped her head onto my shoulder and pressed her lips against my neck. They felt icy. Her face burrowed deeper into my neck. "Come on. Tonight. Don't make me be alone. I'm fucked up. Not the alcohol. I mean fucked up. I *need* someone." She added, desperate, "Fucking please."

The last of the violence drained away, and as I stood there, swaying, her body entwined with mine, I felt a rising and deep-seated sympathy, for I could feel her ribs pressing into mine. They felt like the limbs of a bird. The slightest tap might crack them. I am not Lily, I thought, and Lily is not me, and it seemed for a moment a liberation to think that, with her breath pulsing at my ear and the warmth of her face pressing into me.

For the first time, I began to understand she was another person from me, that she existed independently. I experienced an inner shudder. How long had I thought of her as nothing more than an extension of my own need? I pulled my arms free and helped her to the car and promised not to be a shit, not like the others, not tonight. Climbing inside, she tripped and almost tumbled and grabbed the side of the door, and I held her as she steadied herself.

I started the engine and she reached down and pulled the lever and the seatback collapsed to almost horizontal. The only view from down there was scorched vinyl clinging to the roof. Her skirt revealed her legs, bare and flagrant, and a glimmer of lust returned. A whole world was held in that skin, and all I had to do was reach across to touch it. As the car moved forward, I experienced again the exhausting beauty of her flesh and the tug of pleasure. The world beyond the windshield was alien. Once we were on the road, I recognized nothing, not the streets, not the lights, not even the stars. It was as if we were navigating the avenues of an alien planet.

She lit another cigarette and talked about her new apartment. Smoke clouded the air between us. It was all old people and cokeheads, she said. Everyone there was dying one way or another. A fat guy living on the balcony opposite sat in a folding chair all day in nothing but his boxers with his dick hanging out. She asked if I thought she should tell him and I said he probably knew, that he must get a kick out of it. That's what she thought, she said, but maybe if she said something she could scare him.

"Scare him?" I said.

"That people know, that they know this is what gets him off." I wasn't convinced.

"Someone's gotta teach him a lesson," she said.

She handed me a cigarette and pulled the bottle of gin from between the seats. She took a drink and passed the bottle forward. After that, neither of us spoke. The road unspooled itself like a dark band between pulsing buildings and I felt myself disappear into the night. Whoever I was, whoever I had been, I no longer knew. I could sense Lily's naked thighs, and I was sure if I touched them I would lose myself completely, but how, why, was beyond me.

The left turn into the hotel parking lot led to a speed bump, and the town returned with a thud and I remembered where I was. Beyond the building's outline, the tiny airport sent out a nighttime glow. The control tower looked like a toy, the planes all make-believe.

"The Hilton?" Lily said, sitting up when she heard me shift into park. She lit a cigarette and, without asking, slipped it between my lips. She found another for herself. Once more I felt the shock of her touch. We traded hits from the gin. When Lily raised the bottle, she watched me, head tilted back, while her other hand flicked ash onto the floor of the car.

"I don't know anything about it," I said.

She screwed the cap back onto the bottle and tossed it among the videotapes that littered the backseat, collected her purse, and jumped out and stood in the great wide parking lot. I climbed out after her and remained rooted so I could watch her over the hood.

She'd never been here, she said, staring across at the building.

Lily dropped her cigarette and crushed it with her heel. I did the same and we walked together toward the entrance. Her shoulder brushed against mine and her heels sparked loudly as we jumped the low curb to the concrete entranceway. A lobby sign supported on an easel directed us to the ballroom, a floor down. No one waited at the check-in counter, no one else stood in the lobby. On the stairs we met an elderly couple climbing with difficulty. He was dressed in a tuxedo, she in a gown, and seeing them I began to understand the sense of loss that continued to wrap itself around me as we descended.

This was how a life began. You walked from a car to a hotel in the warm air for the first time only once, and now it was happening to me and would never happen again, not like this, and

I thought, as we took the soft stairs down, that every step was a fraud, that I was playing a part, the part of lover to a woman I neither loved nor even fully hated, and the only person in all the world that night I was cheating was myself. We turned a corner and descended a further set of stairs. History came to an end, and in the brief transit from the parking lot I left the world of childhood and found myself standing in the last night of the world.

THIRTY

MUSIC FILTERED UP, GROWING LOUDER AS WE APPROACHED. We walked through heavy double doors and into the sweeping ballroom. Lily's fingers tightened around my own. The music was loud, with a slow, rumbling song, and I felt its somber beat rising through my hand and into my arm after it had traveled through Lily's body.

She flashed me a look full of conspiracy and hurtled forward, me alongside, into an unruly mass of bodies.

"Look at this place," she cried into my ear. Her excitement entered me like a drug. I couldn't tell if she hated it or loved it. Either way, it no longer mattered. Couples were dancing, dim spotlights scanned the floor, cutting through the cigarette smoke. A reluctant path opened up as we staggered among the dancers.

The shallow stage was decorated with paper flowers and streamers hung from the ceiling. A few balloons bobbed and we found an empty booth and Lily pushed me in, sat down and slid across the vinyl until the warm flesh of her thigh pressed against my side. The waiter came at us with sour eyes and a thin mustache hovering on his lip. He wore a uniform with epaulets, and an old-time engine driver's cap was perched on his head. I ordered a gin and tonic and Lily ordered a Long Island Iced Tea, and I wanted suddenly to be drunk, wildly drunk, to tip my head back and let the world spin off its axis so that I could tell myself this was not happening, I was not here, and that the woman I loved was still called Lily.

The epaulets shrugged and turned away.

Maybe ten couples were on the floor, turning like fans in a breeze, arms glued to waists and shoulders. The band was a five-piece, drums, guitar, bass, a horn player and a female singer. I didn't recognize the tunes—they were oldies, from the forties or fifties. No one exhibited great enthusiasm, and the room vibrated to its own steady hum, a bone-deep and ancient beat that Lily and me, with our youth, were so at odds with it put us on the receiving end of punishing stares.

We were the youngest couple in the room, the youngest by decades. The waiter stood idly at the bar as our drinks were mixed, and Lily said how old people frightened her, with their false teeth and sagging flesh and defeated eyes.

"They should give you a gun the day you're born," she said emphatically. "One bullet with your initials on it, to be used only in the event of disgusting old age."

When I looked up there was the waiter standing sternly, with his old eyes and his old hands, a tray supported at his waist and his thin mustache twitching.

"I served in the war," he said. He said *the war* in such a way it was obvious only one war was being talked about.

"What? The Civil War?" Lily smirked.

"The Second World War," the waiter corrected evenly. "Three years. North Africa, Italy, Germany. All the bullets had my friends' names on them."

He deposited the drinks on the table and turned and walked away. Lily grabbed my neck.

"The bastard," she said. "You saw how he hates us. You know what he's thinking."

I took a long drink from my gin. I wanted to order another immediately, just so I wouldn't have to wait. I had no idea what that waiter was thinking except we were a pair of rude, drunk kids he'd rather see the back of. The remainder of the night unfolded in my mind and I felt tired of it already. I told Lily I didn't care about the old man. He was old, I said sharply, he'd fought, he'd killed, he'd watched friends die. What the hell did she want me to do?

"Challenge him to a duel," she said and started laughing.

I nervously lit a cigarette and blew smoke out across the table and watched it drift in eddies among the dancers.

"Sure," I said. "I'll do it right now."

She rested a hand on mine and tipped back her glass and finished half the drink in one go.

"Hey," she said. "I don't totally hate this place."

I finished my gin in a single toss and raised my hand to call back the waiter. I tried my best not to look at her. Each time I did all I saw was myself. She kissed me on the neck and slipped a hand between my thighs and I felt a wild, combustible arousal mixing with venom.

"You never said," she whispered. "Do you love me?"

A moment later, there stood the waiter, looking down with disgust. I ordered another round and this time made mine a double. Lily turned her head and pressed her cheek against mine and looked up at him. From his vantage, we must have resembled monstrous Siamese twins.

"Don't make mine fucking weak," she said.

"I'll make it how we always make it," he said, and walked away.

"Answer my question," she said, and sharply pinched my forearm.

I stubbed out the cigarette. "No," I said. "Maybe I did before. I don't know anymore."

Her body trembled and her fingers tightened then relaxed, and after a minute she said tersely, "Love is shit."

We sat in silence, watching the dancers, her hand now resting between my thighs, and I felt rotten and low because as she spoke the old memory came surging back of how much I had loved her and how much she had pierced me through. It struck me as absurd and cruel, that one moment you could love a person and the next scorn her with equal force. I wanted that old me back, the one who *could* love, but now all I was able to summon was a rising sickness.

The dancers spun slowly, their steps careful, and the song glided to a close and a new one began. The waiter returned with our drinks. I tipped mine back. I thought with one long drink I might erase those last few minutes, buy back from time something of my heart. Lily pressed her arm against mine and I coughed and yanked her without ceremony to her feet.

"Come on," I said. "Let's dance."

She crushed her cigarette in the ashtray and rose shakily. She took a step and tumbled to the floor and started laughing up at me. Heads turned to stare at us.

"I'm a natural," she giggled as I pulled her upright.

I was undaunted. I needed to move, to slip away from the young man who had sat in the booth with her, to pretend he never existed. She swayed from side to side in my arms and pressed herself up against me, and we waddled into the middle of the room with all eyes on us.

"You can do it," I insisted, battling the room, which even for me had begun to spin.

Her hand flew out and struck a man on the shoulder, and acres of dance floor opened up on all sides. I wrapped my hands around her to keep her steady and we moved jerkily and she giggled with every step.

"I've never gone dancing before," she said. "Not like this."

I hadn't either, but I didn't say that. Instead I tried to move her in a circle. It felt like navigating a heavy ship through a tight channel.

The other couples drifted into a soft-focus wall of bodies. I could feel their lacerating stares. I pretended we were alone. Her hair smelled of old perfume and cigarette smoke, and mercifully, the band played something slow. The lights cut into my eyes and one tune melted into another. Lily's hips crushed against mine as she shifted from side to side and I felt the pulse of her groin like a violation, but I was the violator, the criminal, for I had taken her out here on a lie, and now the lie would not end.

Suddenly, she dropped to her knees and vomited.

The dance floor opened up, and out of the corner of my eye I spotted the waiter striding furiously toward us.

"That's it!" he cried, an arm raised and pointing to the door. "Out!"

His anger came as a relief. I offered money but he refused to take it, so I dropped a twenty onto the floor knowing I'd be unable to reach the table with Lily in my arms. Alone, I pulled her to her feet and struggled with her through the barrage of vicious eyes. At that moment, I felt closer to her than I ever had. In a sense, we *had* become a single being—both of us lost and searching and angry. The eyes arrayed against us made sure of that.

We stumbled through service tunnels and exited into the parking lot behind the hotel. Empty lanes were lit by the glow from windows and the airport beyond. The air was cool and smelled of gasoline. I leaned Lily against a wall and lit a cigarette and slipped it between her lips. Swaying, she wrapped an arm violently around my neck and jerked my head toward her. Her lips struck mine. Her tongue pressed between my teeth and she blew smoke into my mouth. I wondered through my drunken haze if this was what it had felt like when I forced myself on Lily at the train station. She tasted of vomit and I pushed her away and she slid to the ground. There she remained, her back against the wall, staring out into the night.

"I like you," she said flatly, looking up.

I dropped down beside her. Our breaths pooled in the air between us. Her face was a bruise of light swimming beyond my drunken eyes. I took hold of her hand. Her fingers were moist. I held it out of duty—this was what a man did, I thought, held a woman's hand when she was in distress.

"Fuck me," she said. "Fuck me here."

"Okay," I said.

Neither of us moved and we sat like that, our shoulders pressed together, for some time.

The ride to her new home passed in silence. When we arrived at the condominium complex, she could barely stand and tripped over the first set of concrete stairs. It was called Breezy Meadows, and after we passed through the gates, a dog let out a series of barks as we struggled along the laid stone path. A large waterless pool was crowded with flyers and old newspapers, and a clanking ice machine directed me through the maze. I half carried her up the stairs and she clung to the railing when we reached her condo.

She unlocked her door and tried to pull me inside, whispering in my ear that I should spend the night. I held her upright and said yes, but once she'd taken a step into the living room I let go and stood there as she toppled backward into the darkness. Her arms worked at the air for a moment and soon flagged, and I walked inside and looked down. Lily—beautiful, strange, hurt Lily. Her feet blocked the door from closing and I took hold of her by her arms and pulled her into the middle of the room. I found a blanket on the sofa and covered her and took one look back. She looked like a child, no older than me.

I closed the door behind me and walked to the pool, not knowing what to do with myself, thinking maybe the empty pool would tell me something.

A wind kicked up and scraps of trash swirled in eddies. Everything looked small, out of breath, diminished.

I searched the balconies of condos opposite Lily's. One of them must belong to the fat guy who sat there with his dick hanging out. Most had plastic chairs placed outside, so you could sit there in the afternoons and stare out into this wasteland. I was about to turn and walk away when I heard a door click open. I watched in surprise as Lily walked out, dressed as I had left her. Oblivious to my presence, she stumbled down the steps and across the courtyard and climbed back up the steps of the porch opposite. She staggered and fell to her knees twice, but not for a single moment was I tempted to call out her name.

She found a door and stood stiffly, swaying from side to side. She gripped the frame to keep her balance. In the weak lights illuminating the doorway, I could see flying insects circling her head and forming a disorderly halo that flashed on and off as their tiny bodies fluttered. After a moment, she raised a hand and knocked. She didn't have to wait long. A light came on inside, and the door opened to the width of a chain.

In the opening I caught a glimpse of a fat, naked man. The light from the apartment left Lily in shadow and I couldn't tell what was being said. Finally, when he unlatched the chain and opened the door, I saw him, briefly, in the full armor of his nakedness. Lily disappeared inside, and as the door began to shut, he stalled and reached his head out and cast a glance all the way up and down the courtyard. He spotted me and our eyes met.

My hands gripped the cool railing circling the swimming pool. Nothing made sense. Not Lily, not me, none of this or the night or the heavens. At that moment, something changed inside me. Everything I thought I'd ever known, the realizations I'd had, crumbled and fell away, one by one, like heavy slabs of marble falling on their sides and shattering. Spinoza's words returned for a second time that night. I didn't know why, and it made no sense to me, but I suspected that maybe he was right, seeing Lily tonight—even in her degradation, and me in my ridiculous, impotent rage—that this world *was* perfect, because it could be nothing else except exactly what it was.

I stood trembling and feeling alive and sorry and wretched and briefly the world looked beautiful and glowed in strange, bright colors that rose out of everything, even the fat man staring at me as I was standing there. Who was I to judge Lily and what she did? Or my family? Or my brother? I thought of Lily in that room with the fat man and realized how little I knew about her, nothing really, and the towering hurts she must have battled through to bring herself to knock at such a door.

After a minute, the fat man disappeared and the door closed and I sensed, in ways I couldn't yet understand, that Lily had given me a gift, and that I owed her far more than I could possibly pay back.

I turned and walked toward the car. Painted dimly against a wash of city lights, the stars swirled and tumbled in a language all their own. I thought somehow I understood it, or a piece of it, a phrase here and there singing softly on the air of other realms and other hearts. It was as if that night Lily had helped me pierce through the darkness and reach a hand out to the unspoken beyond.

Uncle Gur was awake when I arrived home. He heard my car and met me in the living room. He looked drunk and terrified.

There was news from India. Government troops had stormed the Golden Temple. Something called Operation Blue Star was under way. The fighting was fierce. Sikhs were dying by their hundreds. The temple was in flames. The leaders were being murdered, he was sure of it. It was a massacre. There would be no prisoners.

"We're all Indians now," he spat bitterly.

I told him I was sorry and walked to my room, not knowing what I felt, and thought how his country too had died that night. I dropped onto my bed and summoned, through my drunkenness, a dim prayer for the fallen a world away. I thought of Thakurjeet in his green suit. Was he among the lost? There would be hundreds, maybe thousands, who would fall that night, cousins of mine no doubt among them, joining the ranks of the wordless and unnamed dead of Amritsar.

THIRTY
ONE

UNCLE GUR WOKE ME THE NEXT MORNING, BUT NOT WITH more news from Punjab. His fist thumped on my bedroom door and he appeared, standing unaccountably in a suit and tie, yet unshaven and looking as if he hadn't slept.

"Get up," he said. "I never thought I'd see the day. I'm proud of you."

A moment later, Mom's head appeared. She clicked her tongue in fury.

"What have you done?"

The time was ten in the morning and I stared from Mom to Uncle Gur in numb confusion, my head pounding. When I walked into the living room, dressed in a crumpled shirt and slacks, the events of the previous evening came rushing back to me.

There sat Mr Walia, balancing a plate of bright orange lud-doos under his chin and shielding the red velvet couch from his crumbs. He grinned when he saw me and made an anxious little wave. His daughter sat beside him, shoulders slouched, head teetering forward. She refused to look up when I walked in. She was dressed in a golden sari and weighed down with more jewelry than I had ever seen in one place and looked every inch the unhappiest girl who had ever lived.

Arrayed before Mr Walia, on the coffee table, was one of the large containers of sweets Mom had ordered for the puja. No doubt he thought it was planned for the occasion, this imaginary betrothal.

Mr Walia proudly patted his daughter's thigh.

"This is the one," he said, and pointed at me as if I were nothing more than a new automobile or washing machine.

"Are there others?" I said through my hangover.

Mom hurried to the stove. "Tea, everyone?" she called.

Dad turned the volume on the television up. Mr Walia's daughter made a face and raised a hand silently in the air as if to slap me, then dropped it and shook her head.

"Why do you want this one?" Dad said to Mr Walia. "The other one has a job."

Mr Walia straightened his jacket. "I like this one. He has personality. I like personality." He nudged his daughter. "What do you think, eh?"

She ignored him and dropped her head so her chin pressed into her chest.

Mom carried in the tea while Uncle Gur paced nervously between the kitchen and the living room. He held a small transistor radio to his ear. The sounds of a BBC presenter emerged from it in a distant, tinny screech.

"News?" I said to him.

"Bad," he shook his head. "Very bad. Thousands. It's over."

He talked briefly about the deaths and the burning of the temple and Mr Walia produced some sort of dismal cough in apparent sympathy and went on to say these people should never have started this fighting business in the first place. They had good lives, what did they have to complain about. "What is wrong with being Indian?" he said.

Uncle Gur shot him a violent stare and Mom jumped forward and grabbed Uncle's arm.

"Help me with the tea!"

The daughter mumbled something about the wallpaper and the size of the television set. Mom stepped forward and offered her chutney for the pakoras, but she looked at it and shook her head.

"She's picky," Mr Walia said proudly to Mom. "She knows what she likes."

"It's excellent chutney!" Uncle Gur blasted, coming to Mom's defense. "I eat it all the time!"

"People have their own tastes," Mom said.

"Exactly," Mr Walia said. "She is particular."

Mom turned to me. "Where have you been all night?"

"Out," I murmured, rubbing my head. I wasn't supposed to be here. I wasn't supposed to have come back.

The room stiffened into silence.

"This boy of yours goes out," Mr Walia said, breaking the tension. "When I saw him last night, he was waiting for someone. He has friends. A man who has friends is never alone."

Dad grunted in disgust.

"The only friends are family. If he's at home, he has enough friends. If he's out, he's wasting money."

"True, true," Mr Walia said.

"But a man needs friends to get ahead in business," Uncle Gur countered. "Outside friends. He needs people to watch his back."

"I think this boy has a good head for business," Mr Walia said. "When he was in my store, he acted like he owned it."

"He knows nothing about business," Dad said, and added mockingly, "All this one does is read books."

"It's hot," Mom said, her voice rising to a yet higher note of anxiety.

"Hot?" Mr Walia said.

"This time of year."

"Oh yes. Not so hot as last year, I think. Last year was hotter."

"Maybe," Mom said. "You remember?"

"No," Mr Walia said. "Was it?"

"It's hotter in the south," Uncle Gur said. "Much hotter."

"It's always hotter in the south," Mr Walia said.

"Except when it snows," Uncle Gur said.

"Oh yes," Mr Walia said. "I forgot about the snow."

"She'll be a dentist?" Mom said.

"I told your boy this last night."

"Of course you did."

"She wants an educated man. It's not easy finding an educated man."

The daughter clicked her tongue and turned to her father. "Something smells."

"Thousands are dying!" Uncle Gur blasted. "And you sit there eating luddoos and talking of hotness and coldness! Thousands of *our* people are dying! So tell me, you old bastard, he's a good boy! Do you want him or not?!" He flew back and banged the table. "This is how marriages are made! You say yes or you say no! Not with all this bloody tea!"

The plate in Mr Walia's hand started shaking visibly.

"Eh, daughter?" he said. "Are you listening to this man?"

"He's too too young," Mom said with a note of concern. "We need to wait."

"No one is too young," Dad said. "This is getting to know each other. Details for later."

"That's right," Uncle Gur clapped. "There's plenty of time for all the bastard pretty things."

The daughter stared violently at me and jabbed her elbow hard into Mr Walia's ribs. Her jewelry clinked noisily each time she moved.

"You have another one, yes?" Mr Walia squeaked.

Mom brightened. "Oh, him."

"The other one is older," Dad said. "He needs a wife more."

"Tell me," Mr Walia said, craning forward.

"He works. Proper job."

"He's changing careers," Mom corrected. "He's not ready."

"Oh?" Mr Walia said.

"He works in oil," Dad said.

"Oil?" Mr Walia admired.

"And he's more than ready. A lot of discipline, but he wastes money. He goes on vacation."

"These young people," Mr Walia said. "They need vacations. They're not like us."

Uncle Gur thumped the wall. "There's a good one right here. Why do you have to look anywhere else?"

Mr Walia's daughter looked at her father with worry. "Is he the mad one?" she ventured.

Mom clicked her tongue angrily. "Jigu is sweet. He reads magazines. None of my sons are mad. What garbage have you been telling her, Mr Walia?"

"Nothing, nothing, this and that."

"Dad says he's crazy."

"He's a fine boy," Mom said. She turned to me. "Go on, get him. Show these idiots. They won't find better." She added, turning sharply back to Mr Walia and his daughter and flicking her wrist dismissively, "If he doesn't like you, you can get lost and go home."

Dad sprang forward, almost knocking over the coffee table, and hunched violently over Mr Walia.

"You pay me ten dollars, and then ten dollars more and you get lost. I've had it with your questions. You say yes or you say no, but if you say no, I never want to see your bastard face again."

Mr Walia pressed his palms together in apology. "Don't worry, my daughter will do what's good for her. If I tell her to marry your boy, she will. That's what real love marriage is. We know these things, and we know better than they do who they love and who they don't."

His daughter slumped forcefully back in the sofa and sat there mournfully. To my surprise, I found myself softening toward her. She was as locked in a straitjacket of expectation and rules as I was, probably worse, as much a Paki to her father as we both were to the world outside.

Mr Walia ran a hand through her hair. "Look at her. She cooks, she talks, she comes with a store?"

Dad sat back down and folded his arms across his chest and turned sharply to me. "What are you sitting there for? Bring him here."

As I sat there looking from one to the other, and from my family to Mr Walia and his daughter, something of the feeling of the night before returned, when I had stood at the railing and watched Lily stumble from her apartment to the stranger's across the courtyard. For a moment I understood something I'd never known before: how much, despite my anger and maybe even because of it, I *liked* them all. They were who they were and no one else, and they were as much me as I was them. Maybe it was sentimentality talking through the haze of my hangover, but sitting in that room, I felt a genuine affection spreading out toward them. I even wondered if it wouldn't be so bad to marry Mr Walia's nameless daughter and figure out a way to somehow share a life. She was probably little different from me under all that jewelry and outward scorn, and I wondered if I would have behaved any differently if our positions had been reversed.

"Go on," Mom pressed, "get your brother."

I stood and walked out and reached Jag's door while voices again rose from the living room. Uncle Gur pounded the table. Something would happen now, the Sikhs would finally rise up, he was sure of it. Oh, there'd be blood on the streets of Delhi, of Calcutta, of Bombay—all of India would be swimming in its own blood!

The door was unlocked. Over a year had passed since I'd last found it like that. With the magazines gone, along with the books and records, the room looked deserted, as if it had been looted. The floor was vacuumed, the closet doors swung open. Only a single change of clothes hung suspended from wire hangers. Boxes no longer lined the walls in uneven stacks.

The window was another surprise. It was open and air poured through. In the living room, Mr Walia chimed in pessimistically. The Sikhs were useless, they'd get nothing done, he said, they'd not done one useful thing, not since the days of Ranjit Singh. Uncle Gur roared furiously in response. How dare he say that! He must take it back! The argument continued, but the words ceased to mean anything.

Jag lay on his back, perfectly still, his eyes wide and fixed on the ceiling, as if none of this was happening, and somehow looking through the sky and up to the invisible stars beyond.

I stared at him. It didn't take me long to understand.

One arm was flung back over his head and at the tip of his curled fingers rested an empty bottle of Mom's pills. He was fully clothed and his mouth hung open and he was caught in a look of mild surprise.

"Jag?" I said.

I reached forward and shook him. It felt like a formality. He was cold. He'd been dead for hours.

I took a step back and dropped to the ground and collapsed against the wall.

Uncle Gur shouted that he would go himself and fight, if that was what was needed. He would fly that very night to Punjab and join the brave Sikhs who were dying by the thousands.

I sat there, staring at the outline of my dead brother. The sun cut across his body and he glowed in its soft orange light. I was crying. The tears were involuntary. If anyone had told me that I would cry at Jag's death, I would have answered that they didn't know me, that he'd died to me a hundred times already, but there I was, and it was indisputable, the tears were real.

A sudden, desolate sympathy poured through me, not just for Jag and what he must have gone through these last days, but for Mom, for Dad, for Uncle Gur, for our whole pathetic clan. They would enter here in minutes and their worlds would fall to pieces. I knew it and they didn't, and there was nothing I could do to stop it. I was looking into the future and I wanted to shut my eyes to it, to shut everyone's eyes.

I didn't know it then, and would only understand the depth of the change later, but I was falling in love with my own family, with Mom, with Dad, with Uncle Gur, and most of all with Jag. Whatever anger that remained bubbling inside me fell from my shoulders like so much dead skin and I could think of nothing but the coming look on everyone's face when they would walk into this room and everything they knew would come crashing down. Dad was talking. Where was that boy, his son, he said. Mom clapped her hands. She'd had enough of this talk of death and fighting. This morning was about beginnings.

The light shifted subtly and the sun passed behind a cloud. Jag's face fell into shadow and Mom's voice rose in a shout. "If he likes her and she likes him, then yes, I agree!" She added theatrically, "Like the Americans say, I give my blessing!"

Uncle Gur offered his support. "Okay—no more talk of Khalistan!"

"Our two families will be one," Mr Walia said.

Dad grunted and told Mom to fetch us both.

I knew the sound of her step well. It approached along the hall and as it did I heard something different. She was humming a tune. It was an old Indian film song, one of the classics. Her voice was childlike in its excitement. Gone were the doubts. She had come for her son, to arrange his marriage. Her soft step quickened. Years of crushed dreams were forgotten. By the time she reached Jag's door, she had broken into song.

I watched her feet cross the threshold and listened as her voice rang out one last time with a note of lively expectation.

THIRTY
TWO

AT THE FUNERAL, I STOOD AT THE FRONT, NOT LISTENING TO the words, not even letting them wash over me. A great cavern of silence surrounded me, and when I looked into the other mourners' faces, I couldn't see them, I couldn't even see my own blankness in their eyes.

Dad chose a plain casket, white with silver handles, and when I walked around it to view Jag's body, I found I couldn't look at him but turned away at the last moment. I still remembered his face when I entered his room and the unlikely peace that wrapped his features. I didn't want my last vision of him to be something different or cold.

There was confusion at the ceremony. Some guests got lost on the highway and arrived as it was ending, clattering open the doors and scraping chairs. When Dad and I rose to follow the casket to the incinerator, almost everyone tried to join us. A great jam of people, mostly men in their bright turbans, crowded around the door. They had to be pushed back by one of the funeral home attendants. Who were all these people? Where had they come from? I knew none of them, these relatives of relatives, stretching out in a web of invisible connections. I was grateful for their presence, it allowed me to disappear and stand at the outskirts of the drama, like another onlooker, and guard my own deep hurt.

What was said, who spoke, I remember none of it. Someone had taken the time to enlarge a photograph of Jag and it stood on an easel at the front of the hall, but who did that, and how it happened, I don't know. When Dad and I and Uncle Gur stood in the incinerator room, all I remember is a wall of flame rising up and consuming the casket and turning to look at Dad, who was crying for the first time I'd ever seen. He looked older by a decade when he left the hall.

The sweets we had piled up for the Akhand Path were eaten in the days that followed. The living room was emptied of all furniture and the floor covered in white sheets that spread from wall to wall. One after another, the mourners arrived to show their respects and sat cross-legged on the white sheets, backs against the wall, telling stories of other times and other places, and sometimes telling jokes.

Mom wasn't there, she hadn't attended the funeral either. She was lying in a hospital bed in a psychiatric unit, where she stayed for three weeks, barely able to move.

When I visited, she threw something at me, whatever was closest at hand—a plate of food, a glass of water, a bottle of pills—or just turned her face away from mine. It was always a shock to see her. She looked destroyed. Despite her anger, I forced myself to return. I had never felt more a part of the family and more of an outcast also. I didn't ask myself why she was angry. She had lost her son and her world had collapsed. Out of that, I doubt little would have made sense, and pouring her anger on me and only me made as much sense as anything.

The last time I saw her at the hospital, she shouted at me to get out and called me the killer of her son. Dad sat in the corner, head buried in his hands. The nurse rushed in and medicated her, and she soon slipped back into blank dreams.

After the funeral, Dad spent most days at her bedside, and when the nurses let him, he remained by her side all night long. Each time I saw him, his face was a more deeply etched map of woe. She wanted me gone, he told me one day, before she would let herself return home. She never wanted to see me again. He didn't know why, but she blamed me. In her mind I was the murderer. He said it so matter-of-factly, and in such a defeated voice, that I couldn't be angry with him. He didn't dispute it, just looked at me, head down, staring at me from that tortured angle, as if he wasn't quite sure what he was looking at. I didn't have the strength or inclination to argue and nodded and said okay, I'd move out and find somewhere else.

A large part of me thought Mom was right, that if anyone was, I was Jag's killer. I couldn't count the times I had wanted him dead and actively wished for it. Maybe if I had fought harder, shouted louder, insisted that Jag get help, he would be alive today. None of us was blameless—we all contributed to the silence—but that didn't exonerate me. Banishment, as ancient a punishment as there was, seemed fitting for so ancient a crime as killing your brother.

Books, a few clothes, some photographs—everything I owned fit into the trunk of my car with room to spare, and I spent two weeks living uneasily with Chuck, whose mom let me sleep on the sofa and never once mentioned the door I bust.

Chuck asked me all sorts of questions, mostly about what I felt, and I told him I wasn't interested, that it was none of his business. Eventually he stopped asking, which was fine with me. I walked Fred a few times, taking him up the hill and along the ridge, while day faded into night. One morning I told Chuck I'd found a room on the other side of town, which I hadn't, and spent a month sleeping in my car and driving from town to town, when I could afford the gas money.

The day I turned seventeen, the only person I spoke to was the cop who knocked on the car window at five in the morning to tell me I couldn't park where I was, which was a turnout in the hills west of Mount Tamalpais, and that I had to drive on and find somewhere else. I only learned it was my birthday when he looked at my license and told me.

Gradually I moved north, settling in a coastal town with a wide, empty beach, and found a job in a record store. I rented a room and peopled the one shelf with my books. I told myself that all a person needs is a room, shelter from the world, little else. When people asked if I wanted to meet for a drink or a hike in the hills, I always said I was busy.

Every night I bought a six-pack or a bottle of cheap gin or whiskey at the liquor store and drank it diligently alone, telling myself I was learning how to be a drunk, just like Dylan Thomas. As I drank, I lay on the bed, little more than an old military cot, and smoked cigarette after cigarette and watched the smoke curl and rise listlessly until it reached the water-stained popcorn ceiling, which looked at any moment like it might come tumbling down on top of me, an event I knew I would have greeted happily.

If I woke early, I'd walk along the beach, while the morning mist still stuck to the ground, and sometimes I'd strip my clothes off and go for a swim in the icy waters. I was ashamed by how good it felt to be reminded that I had a body.

Grief fades with time, it dies, or transforms, and becomes a hum at the back of the mind, and even that loses its power, and soon you wonder at the young man you were, who stared back shell-shocked every morning from the bathroom mirror, a ghost's ghost, for whom it was torture to lift a razor to his cheek. I didn't know any of this, but I came to learn it, as I came to learn so much else in those months after Jag died. The first was obvious, yet a shock, and almost offensive: that death has lessons to teach. The second: we all die, and we're all professors after our deaths, teaching the living how to live.

The third lesson—that no one dies once, but that they die again and again, and each time you feel it like it's the first time—arrived one afternoon when I was driving east along twisting mountain roads with no destination in mind. The radio was on, tuned to a classical station. The signal came in and out, whispering or distorted at moments, full-throated at others. The car pressed through a thick bank of mist and reached a high ridge where the air was clear. I stopped and parked because I recognized the music. It was Prokofiev, the Suite from *Lieutenant Kijé*. And I remembered: Jag's room, hearing it for the first time and marveling at its beauty, even as Jag told me that its beauty wasn't the point.

The colors were changing, and the road was wet, and the sun broke through the clouds and shimmered among the leaves, and I was weeping, weeping for the first time since I found his body, and only at that moment did I realize that Jag was truly dead, and that for the rest of my life he would be dead and nothing would ever change that. I sat in the car for an hour, looking out through the windshield, which was wet from water dripping from the leaves.

The Prokofiev suite ended, other music began, and I remembered an afternoon when Jag and I were young. We had walked along the edge of a stream and up through trees. It was summer and the sun was blazing down, and we had forgotten to bring water, forgotten to bring food, and ascended the gentle slope of the hill, heedless, not thinking about the time. Sunlight speared the branches and dappled our bodies, and Jag talked in a way he seldom did, with lively animation and excitement, inventing stories about us.

We were explorers lost in the jungles of Africa, he said, searching for the source of the Nile, and we had found what we believed must be the true stream that fed the lake that fed the river. Somewhere up ahead, he was sure, we'd find the spring itself, from which all the waters of all the seas and oceans of the planet poured out of.

I didn't remember how that day ended, how we got home, or whether we found the spring. All I remembered was the difficult climb along the rocky stream edge and Jag's voice casting a spell, transporting us to the high jungles of Africa on the far side of the world.

The days that followed carried other memories with them,

and Jag's voice, a voice I had hardly heard in years, began to return. And not like a ghost's reedy voice, but full-bodied, as if he were standing there next to me and talking—a hidden door had been unlocked, and memories of a Jag I had forgotten came rushing back, along with a few brief summers, when I was young and Jag and I were friends. How had I forgotten those years? Me, following like an acolyte, ever at his heels, and a different Jag, a brotherly Jag, striding forward, talking of the future and his dreams.

Immediately after the funeral, a lot of people came up to me and said that no one really dies, that they live on inside the ones who loved them. I thought at the time it was another stupid thing people said because they didn't know what else to say and were too uncomfortable to say the truth, that the dead are dead and that's it. I was wrong, and there was Jag, inside me, as if he were alive, and I could feel him every day, a presence in my life who talked and walked at my side. In everything I did, every motion of my hands, every word I spoke, how I entered a room, how I slept and ate, I felt Jag's influence and, to my astonishment, love. That was the fourth, and most surprising, lesson. The dead *don't* die, not while they're inside us.

I stopped drinking most nights, gave up the idea of becoming a drunk, and gradually returned to the world. When people asked me to join them, I said yes, and once or twice a week, I found myself sitting at a long wooden table at a pizza joint or bar, while around me people spoke of lives and days, and I listened as best I could and tried, sometimes, to contribute a word or comment.

That winter, I picked up the book by Spinoza again. The first thing I did was to tear out the page with the neo-Nazi vandal's scrawl and burn it in my sink. I watched the corners curl in flame and, after it was consumed, turned the taps on and flushed the ashen remnants down the drain. I had pushed the book out of my mind because I connected it so closely to

Jag's death and to that surprising feeling I experienced when I stood outside Lily's apartment and watched her journey across the courtyard.

Along with the memory came the insight into what Spinoza meant when he wrote that the world is perfect. He did not mean resignation, he meant something else—a larger, open-hearted engagement with things exactly as they are. I didn't expect such abstract thoughts could bring comfort, but they did and helped me build something like solid ground where I felt I might walk along and not always be afraid of tumbling into an abyss.

It was on one of those forgotten days that seemed to stretch unchanging behind me and ahead that I called Lily. No one answered. I called several times over the following weeks. Each time the line rang and rang and I thought of her phone echoing in that ugly, mostly empty condo. I wanted to tell Lily what happened to Jag, to talk, to maybe see each other. Visiting the diner was out of the question—I never even considered it. Eventually, I got a message that the line had been disconnected, no forwarding number left. As I listened to the recorded voice, a sharp pang of my old love returned. It told me something surprising. I really had loved her and perhaps always would.

I had given the phone number at the record store to Uncle Gur. I didn't have my own phone and used the work number for messages. And it was Uncle Gur who called one day and told me that Mom and Dad had moved south and now lived with him.

It was a big, noisy house, the kind that Mom grew up in, with children everywhere, endless talk of grandchildren, and perched on the edge of a hill overlooking a valley and an orchard. When I thought about Mom walking among those trees, I felt a ray of hope for the world and for our small, unhappy family.

A whole year passed and more, and one day I got a call. It was from Dad.

"Your mother wants to see you," he said. "She doesn't blame you anymore."

It was the first week of April, and east of Bakersfield the road narrowed and climbed through mountains. A rare late snowstorm had covered the hills in white. The snow crowded right up against the pavement. I took pleasure in pulling over and fitting chains to the tires. It had taken me a while, but I learned to find joy in practical matters and getting my hands dirty.

Dad met me at the curb and leaned his head into the car and checked the odometer. He asked what the figure was when I set out. I hadn't recorded it, but I told him I'd call when I got back and tell him the mileage home.

He nodded. "Okay, but no detours. I want the exact miles."

It sounded important to him and I told myself I would do precisely that, drive directly back and call him when I got there with the number. How could I say no? For here we were, tragedians without a stage, staring out, shoulder to shoulder, at the ruin of what might have been, if only...but a thousand if-onlys could've ended that sentence.

While we waited for Mom, Dad opened beers and offered me one, and we drank in the living room, saying few words to each other, finally intimate, after all those years, in our silence. Mom greeted me in a freshly knitted sweater. She looked older and smaller and walked hunched, as if she were carrying a heavy weight. She held another sweater up to my chest and said it was for me. Her knitting had taken off. It did get cold in the mountains, she explained, and she was selling sweaters on consignment at the local dry goods store.

We walked along the road and up the hill. The sky was a deep bright blue. I told her about my life and my few friends, and that I was thinking of applying to Berkeley.

"What will you study?" she said.

"Something practical. Pre-med maybe. I'll be a doctor."

She laughed. "You? Never. I know you, you'll do the wrong thing, some subject no one else knows anything about." She added after a minute, "But I think that's good. You've got to be who you are."

She had dreams of Jag, she said, her voice conjuring his presence out of the air—and in them he talked.

"We have conversations," she said. "Sometimes they last all night long."

Then she told me something truly surprising.

"He did talk," she said, and she said it in such a soft and direct and clear voice that I could not help but believe her. "That time when he was talking to no one, he did talk to me. It was only a few times, late at night, in the kitchen. We sat together and he told me of his plans, of the kind of future he wanted for himself. It was nothing special. A better job, get married, have children." She nodded her head emphatically. "Yes, he said all these things. I know I said he talked to me at other times, and I know he didn't. But those nights, when it was just me and him, we talked."

How much else had I been wrong about, I wondered as I listened, astonished at this other Jag who had been hiding from all of us but Mom in that last year of his life.

I told her that in the summer I'd take her for a drive to the coast. I wanted to show her the ocean. She had still never seen it. I looked forward to the idea of her walking barefoot among the breakers on a stony beach while the sun set and the world took on the many shades of night.

The fighting continued in India, Uncle Gur told me. He was still regularly sending money and said that one day he would go himself. We were standing in the large backyard, which climbed halfway up a low hill. He grinned at me, that mischievous grin of his, and pulled something out of his pocket. He had received it a few months ago. It was a postcard forwarded from the old house and addressed to me.

"From one of your ladies?" he said.

It was from Lily and postmarked San Diego and showed a photo of palm trees and a beach.

I knew it was from Lily because on the reverse all she wrote was this: CHINK LOVE PAKI.

"What does it mean?" Uncle Gur asked. "Why does she write words like that?"

I shook my head, I didn't know, I said—except that I did know, and what it meant was this. She was sending me a message. It was all held there, one last gift, in the words she chose and how she wrote them, and that she used the word *love*, right in the center of the card. The thought of her stretched out on a beach in San Diego while the ocean unwound before her feet lifted my spirits, and I hoped I had been wrong about her too—maybe she didn't have such a long journey to travel before she reached something genuine in herself.

I pushed the postcard into my pocket and Uncle Gur led me up the hill, where he now kept several hives. He was taking bee-keeping classes at the community center. Across one of the hives, in shaky red letters, he'd painted the word KHALISTAN, the name of his independent dream nation of Sikhs. It was chilly, he said, but with a little luck we might coax some bees out of their holes. We suited up with the sun high above us and the air sharp and clear, and Uncle smoked the hives with care and showed me how it was done.

He lifted the lid from a hive and I stared with wonder into the mysterious, golden activity of another universe whose laws I could not guess at. This year, maybe next, he said, the war would end and we'd have a country of our own.

"Just like this one," he added.

Bees buzzed, lazy and drugged, and landed on my out-sized helmet.

I didn't tell him what I knew, the fifth and final lesson. There are no countries, there are no nations, only people, the dead and the living, and to be among the living is to owe a great debt to the dead.

Colombo – Brooklyn – Chania – Hanoi

ACKNOWLEDGMENTS

I owe a debt of gratitude to many friends who bought me drinks, cooked me dinner, and kept me sane over the years. Here are just a few: Sara Clarke, Jakob Holder, Lynne Tillman, Karin Campbell, Paul Takeuchi, Titi Ngyuen, Douglas Ross, Alice Hansmann, Jennie Booth, Izhar Patkin, Robert Marshall, Miriam Metzinger, Danica Stitz, Rainer Mack, Christian Baskous, Sonnie Brown and Madeleine Debure.

A shout out to old friends who never failed to encourage me: Moazzam Sheikh, Anand Adiga, Doug Levin, Nancy Cherry, Vijay Iyer, Maria Strauss and Chhottu Rahman.

And to friends in Crete, especially Anna Fiolitaki and Elizabeth Bishop, without whom that island would not have been so welcoming—ευχαριστώ πολύ φίλοι μου.

Thank you to my agent, Kent Wolf, and to my editor at Unnamed Press, Chris Heiser, who both pushed me to make this book as strong as it could be. And a huge thank you to everyone at Unnamed, especially Olivia Taylor Smith for her tireless promotion, and Scott Arany for the gorgeous cover.

A very personal thank you goes to the visionary publisher and editor VK Karthika, at HarperCollins India, who first saw in this novel what many others were blind to.

Thank you to Edward Albee and the Edward F. Albee Foundation, who have offered enduring support to my work for years. Awards from the Lower Manhattan Cultural Council and the New York Foundation for the Arts helped me carve out space and time to write.

And finally, thank you to my family without whose love and support this book would not have been possible.

ABOUT THE AUTHOR

Ranbir Singh Sidhu is the author of the story collection *Good Indian Girls* and a winner of a Pushcart Prize and a New York Foundation for the Arts Fellowship. *Deep Singh Blue* is his first novel. He divides his time between the US, India, and Greece.